Siren Song

Tale Three of the Beanseller Saga

By Avon Van Hassel

ISBN: 9798645120351

Editor: Breanna Clark

Illustrations: Ana King

Cover photo merman: Wesley John Croft

Photographer: Mike Croft

Dedication

To those brave enough to dive deeper and
see things from the other side

Contents

Map

Viehland
Barry House
Istlevafe Island
Cavendy Drift
The Squalls
Lalarn Islands
Senora Current
Rhythlin Island
Crosachee Island
Decembre Island
Aschum
Vurdia
Jalez
Dimothe

Neat Stuff

Prince Okala flicked his green fins with excitement as he waited in the shallows with his family. On their fifteenth birthday, each of King Clyr's six children were allowed a quick sojourn to the surface, to the world of Man. All merfolk, whether they admitted it or not, yearned for the world above the water, but few loved humans as much as the young prince did.

Okala struggled to keep his face neutral. Surely, his sister would have remembered his interest and brought him a souvenir. It would have pride of place in his collection.

'Here she comes,' King Clyr said, adjusting the collar of scallop shells strung across his chest. The other princesses and Okala shifted their adornments and quickly combed their flowing hair as the water in front of them bubbled and frothed.

Two dainty pink feet appeared in front of them and the wizard, Adeto, lifted a wave to cover the girl to her waist. Her thin legs fused into a light pink tail with pale purple fins. Okala's sister, Kyri, flipped her whole body underwater and swam to join the court. Brown spots bloomed across her chest and tiny bubbles streamed from the slits opening along her neck.

'How was it?' Clyr asked, holding out his powerful arms. Kyri rushed into her father's embrace, her thick brown hair swirling, the dusty scent of dry land permeating the water around her. The shark egg pouch on her belt bounced around her bare waist, bulging with something heavy.

'It was so exciting!' Kyri gushed. 'I was almost seen twice, but I got away in time.'

King Clyr shook his head. 'This is why we only go to the surface once, unless we have to. It's not safe. But aside from that, did you have fun?'

Okala couldn't take his eyes off the purse.

'Oh yes, father! It took a little getting used to at first. My legs tingled and itched so badly, no matter how much I scratched, and they were slick and oily.'

'To keep the skin from drying out,' Adeto's deep voice said. The old merman glided on orange fins, his long grey braids accentuating the heavy lines in his square face. 'It's a side effect of the potion.'

'The sand was rough between my toes. And my hair-- it got so stiff and coarse! Okala, I don't know why you're so fascinated by the surface. It's awful.'

Okala startled. *Why'd she have to single me out? And anyway, she said she enjoyed herself.*

'We watched the sailors and I sat in the sun. It burned more than I thought it would.'

'You've learnt a valuable lesson,' Queen Marya said in her smooth voice.

Though also one of Clyr's daughters, Marya embodied the role of queen, with her deep purple tail and golden fins, long strands of golden pearls and a diadem of yellow spiked coral.

'Oh yes.' Kyri drew a hand under her chin and yawned. 'I am glad to be home. And now I must rest.'

Quiet, yellow-and-black-tailed Neri and outgoing, red-

and-blue Ytaso rallied around their younger sister, and glided away with her.

'Wait, Kyri!' Okala called. 'What's in your purse?'

A snide smirk flicked across Kyri's face. 'I didn't bring you any human rubbish. Your Breaching is coming soon enough. You can pick your own leavings off the beach when you go.'

She allowed herself to be pulled away, sagging in her sisters' arms as they put their heads together. One of them whispered the name they called him in private when they thought he couldn't hear.

Okala's ears burned, making the water around him shimmer. Vila, his second-eldest sister swam closer to him and beat the water with her peachy tail.

'It's true, you know. Soon enough, you can go up there yourself and bring back all the little treasures you can carry. But only little ones.' She pinched his cheek. 'You're running out of room in that cave of yours.'

Okala pulled away. He resented being treated like a funny child or like an outsider in his own family. Kyri had hated being on the surface, yet she told the story like she'd had the time of her life, just to make him jealous. And now his father and Marya watched him like he'd done something disappointing again. He followed Vila back to the colony.

He detoured before he reached the palace, and darted through the seaweed along a path he'd made long ago. Over this rock, under that rotting shipwreck, and around a chunk of coral. The walls of his not-so-secret cave glowed blue and green with the bodies of thousands of tiny creatures who lived there.

The 'cave' was more like a cave complex with half a dozen rooms branching off from the first chamber. The rising and dropping of ancient sea levels formed shelf-like bars in the sandstone, and burrowing creatures made little niches. For years, Okala had been collecting things and hiding them here, safe for him to visit when he needed to be alone. He would hover along the shelves, running his webbed fingers over the corroding surfaces and strange shapes. Occasionally, something would disintegrate and he'd have to dispose of it in a small artefact 'graveyard' to keep them safe, respectful of the significance they once had to him.

But today, everything was perfect. Strings of clear polished rocks winked at him in the cyan glow and carved faces stared down from their perches.

He sang to himself, a song with no set lyrics, just words that came to him, and combed his fingers through his blue hair. He sang about his feelings about his toys, his jealousy about his sister's Breaching, and all the human words he would remember.

The day would come soon when he would take the potion from Adeto and feel his tail separate, his fins split into feet and toes. He'd dig into the sand and embrace the wind and lay in the sun until his skin bubbled and peeled. Just one day to breathe the air through his nose, feel the dry world, the heat of the sun, and not just cold water.

I wonder if there's a way to get more than one day out of it...

Chapter One
The Call

Meltythia swayed, sending a bottle sliding across the table in the officers' salon. Sulat caught it before it fell, poured a long stream of claret into a glass goblet, and drank deeply. The fruity-yet-dry wine wasn't to her liking, but it was all they'd found on the last Vurdence ship they'd taken, and she wasn't about to let it go to waste.

She leaned back, kicked her heels up onto the table and settled into the rolled leather chair. Life was finally good. Her ship, her rules, a whole crew of men under her command. She hadn't taken sleeping powder in months.

Freedom, at last.

Well, as free as I can get.

A stained and creased sheet of parchment tacked to the dark wood-panelled wall of the salon read:

By order of His Royal Majesty King Bertold of Viehland and Cavendy, Sulat (Captain) of Meltythia (Ildecoke Courser) is hereby Licensed to Trade goods and services for those monies and chattels deemed Appropriate by Value, and to Defend herself, her Ship and

Crew, and her Kingdom against aggressors of Foreign origin.

The Letter of Marque and Reprisal was a license to attack and take ships and their cargo. As long as she had her papers, any action she took was legal. To be caught without papers would mean being arrested and possibly hanged as a pirate.

Her heart soared and plummeted. She was free...to do the bidding of the king. She could travel far and wide, but she had a business to run and heavy taxes and fees to pay. And she could wage war on the sea, so long as she only attacked foreign merchants.

And there's Foth.

Sulat scowled at the door of her salon and the hazy shapes moving about on the other side of the frosted glass.

Viehland was a country proving itself in almost every arena of culture, which made it a target for pirates, merchants, and navies. Sulat had only been a part of that for a little over three months, but due to her unique position as both a privateer and importer of fine goods, she represented an intrinsic and irreplaceable cog in the wheel of international relations.

'Irreplaceable,' she whispered, running a slender dark brown thumb over the tin tag, stamped 'Captain,' hanging from the neck of the wine bottle.

Muffled voices shouted back and forth at each other as the ship nestled itself into its berth at the Port of Ildecoke. Making berth at the Viehlish capital was always a gamble, but they had to do it. Repairs had to be made and cargo had to be unloaded and sold. Legitimacy was a strange twist in Sulat's unconventional life.

She and her previous partner, Alois, had spent three years travelling the countryside, employed to steal items with mysterious properties. It was dangerous and illegal work, but it paid, and neither of them fit well into society. The last job they worked together culminated in delivering the kidnapped princess to the capital, thereby saving the Crown an unimaginable scandal, but at the same time exposing their own crimes to the highest law of the land. A bargain was struck: each of them received their dearest wish, with the caveat that they occasionally resume their lives of crime to carry out missions for the king, and generally behave themselves the rest of the time.

Sulat's gift, the ship, had recently been a member of the Viehlish navy's reserve fleet of decommissioned ships. Light and fast, what she lacked in space she more than made up for in agility. She'd been given a fresh coat of paint and a new name, *Meltythia*. Ancient sailors had given the four winds names and personalities, and Meltythia was the name of the east wind, the wind of luck.

Meltythia was often depicted as a bad-tempered woman brandishing a sword and coin purse, symbolising the mercurial nature of business and the sea. Sulat found it a fitting name, given that her captaincy itself was subject to shifting circumstances. Plus, she liked swords and money. Her new figurehead had appropriately Ebian characteristics as well, to match her captain's--wide, round features, and a puff of thick curly hair, carved in dark wood.

Alois had spent the last year enjoying the comfortable life of the country squire, with his highborn wife and the child who was secretly his.

Sulat retrieved another bottle from the cabinet behind her seat under the skylight.

He's getting fat. And bored.

The ship rose and fell with the waves, ropes creaking and wood groaning in time. It felt sometimes to Sulat like it was breathing, a living thing, and not just wood, iron, and canvas. This was the closest Sulat had ever felt to maternal affection for anything. Each detail was perfection, and every splinter, frayed thread, and burr was hers.

Someone knocked at the door, pulling her from the loving examination of her quarters.

'Messenger from the Palace, Captain,' a reedy voice called. Sulat opened the door and Second Mate Wese put a knuckle to his dark, weatherbeaten brow. 'Looks official.'

Souls, I knew there'd be something.

'Where's Foth?'

Elmor Foth was the king's representative on board to watch Sulat and make sure she ran her ship according to the laws of the kingdom. 'Why didn't he tell me?'

'Scarpered, ma'am.' Wese pronounced the last word like *mem*. 'He went ashore as soon as we lowered the gangplank. The messenger just arrived.'

I should tell them to pull up the plank after I leave. Leave the weasel here. 'I'll go now and see what Renir wants.' Sulat swept past Wese, pulling her tricorne over the scarf wrapped tightly over her thick hair.

'I'd ask nicer'n that, ma'am,' Wese said, shuffling along behind her. 'Should I go with you?'

'Want to see the Palace, Wese?'

'Ahh, no, ma'am, not I. The wife would've, long past. But these legs ain't walked a-land in too long. I wouldn't know how to keep me balance. I just thought I'd offer. For reassurance, like.' He attempted a comforting smile, but the small eyes squinting in leathery skin above missing teeth gave him a lost and confused appearance.

'He's a messenger, not a bailiff. I'll be fine.'

'Ahh, y'have a point there, cap'n.' Wese knuckled his brow and bobbed away as Sulat stepped onto the gangplank.

A carriage waited at the dock, and Sulat climbed inside. The young messenger in his blue coat and powdered wig offered no more information than Wese had as they rode to Roddlemere Palace, at the tip of the spiralling city that capped Ildecoke Island. When they reached the entrance, he leapt out and bowed, holding out a gloved hand.

'In the Map Room, is he?' Sulat shot over her shoulder, stepping past him.

'Yes, Captain,' the boy said. He must have decided that she

knew the way because he didn't follow. He'd have been right; only one person ever summoned her.

Lord Chaput Renir was the Minister of Shadows, in charge of secrets and silence in the Kingdom of Viehland. He, like Alois, had been a commoner who rose to power through good deeds done for the Crown. Where Alois was brave and extraordinarily lucky, Renir was uncommonly loyal. No man embodied patriotism and national pride like the Minister of Shadows. He had been lorded by the previous Royal Family, but when the Cavender king was given the throne, the decision was made to keep the Minister. The Viehlish people trusted that he would maintain their best interests and it was a wise move on the part of King Bertold to keep Renir close. Instilling faith in him had amplified his devotion.

Sulat had no love of Viehland. It was a country like any other: filthy, prejudiced, and corrupt. The Viehlish had money in their pockets, money that could easily be hers, but so did the people of other kingdoms. What Viehland did have, however, was a bounty on her head, and the head of her only real friend. Their crimes were a matter of public record now: when they had been committed, where, and against whom. The Minister of Shadows would not hesitate to bring down the full force of the law. Yet, Sulat and Alois also had influence and connections within the criminal world. It was in Viehland's best interest to keep the two alive and operating, waging a war against crime from within.

Sulat strode through the splendid corridors and hallways with their molded walls and priceless art, her booted footsteps tapping across tile or lost in plush carpet, until she reached the stairs that led into the tunnels beneath the Palace. The tunnel was paved and well lit by wall sconces that matched the ones in the palace above, and at the end stood a large wooden door with imposing iron fittings that Alois joked had probably originally belonged to a dungeon.

'I was summoned,' Sulat said to the bewigged secretary at his desk in the small antechamber. The secretary pushed open the door on the opposite wall, leaving Sulat alone with Lord Renir, his back to her.

'Captain Sulat.' Lord Renir said.

'At your service, my lord,' she answered, clicking her heels together and bowing deeply, doffing her plumed hat. The words were bile in her mouth. *At your service.* She had vowed never to serve again in her life, but that was the script. Much more politic, as Wese noted, than 'what do you want?'

Lord Renir waved for her to straighten. 'You've been getting into some scraps lately, Captain. Do you have your papers handy?'

'They're on *Meltythia*, my lord,' Sulat said.

'They're expired.'

Sulat cocked her head. 'They're not dated.'

'Not to worry, not to worry.' Lord Renir beckoned her over and scribbled on a piece of parchment with a fluffy white quill. 'I'll write you up a new Letter now. And while we're on the subject, there's something I need you to do for me.'

'For you, sir?' Sulat crossed her arms. The more annoying the mission, the more like a favour it was phrased.

'For your king and country.' Renir tapped out his signature with a stiffness that told her it was a gently-worded order. *Do it, or hang.*

Sulat pursed her lips as Lord Renir dusted the text with powder, blew on it, and fanned the parchment through the air. 'Tell me, have you been to Rhythlin Island lately?'

'I've never been there,' Sulat answered truthfully. She preferred to get to her destination and back as quickly as possible, and made sure to never have to stop at the small islands to the west of the perpetually stormy patch of ocean, known as The Squalls.

'We've had a number of merchant and peacekeeping vessels go missing between here and Vurdia. If you please.' Lord Renir pointed to one of the maps on the table. His powdered finger landed on a tiny speck of tan surrounded by blue ink. 'This is the island of Rhythlin. It's flat and full of deep holes, which you would think would deter pirates, yet the blighters are doing something out there. I'd like you to go and have a look. Clean it out, if you can. I'm afraid the need may arise to betray some of your friends.'

'I don't have any friends.'

'Wonderful.' Lord Renir clasped his hands behind his back. 'Oh, and speaking of the friends that you don't have, take Lord Brynglas with you.'

Sulat bristled. *Alois. What good could he be on the sea?*

'I can do this myself, with my crew. I don't need Alois-- Lord Brynglas. My lord.'

'You've done well as a merchant, Foth tells me. But this is your first real mission for the Crown, and you're untested. You and Lord Brynglas work well as a team; perhaps he will be of some comfort to you.'

'You don't trust me to do this on my own.' Sulat's nostrils flared and the heat rose inside her. *Just like before, just like every employer we've ever had. What good is Foth if he's not reporting accurately?*

'Now is your chance to prove yourself.' Lord Renir leaned over his maps. 'That's an order, Captain. You may go.'

Alois poured a glass of brandy and threw himself into his desk chair.

Brandy at this hour? Johanne's voice chided in his head. He scowled at the midmorning sunshine and kicked his heels onto the desktop.

Yes, and I'll put my shoes on the furniture, too. It's my bloody desk, I can do what I want. He knocked the brandy back and it burned bitterly all the way down.

Drinking too early in the day, putting his shoes where they oughtn't be, chewing with his mouth open. He couldn't do anything right. Every step he took was met with criticism, with scolding, and this midday, a full-blown argument.

So what if he'd done it in front of Rosabel? Yes, she'd laughed and imitated him, but what of it? She knew better than to behave that way in public, not that she'd have a chance to display her manners before her peers for many more years. At the age of seven, she was far too young to attend parties, so what was the harm in a bit of buffoonery at the luncheon table?

Loose paper covered his desk, dotted with the occasional ink blot or brandy stain. He pressed the cold glass to his forehead. Rent was coming up and he'd have to collect in person. And the harvest was coming in, so he'd have to go into town and negotiate renting a stall for market day.

Alois groaned and flipped over the top sheet to hide the numbers. He'd run away from home and joined the army so that he wouldn't have to be a farmer, and now here he was, directing other people in doing the farming. And if he wasn't doing that, he was reading in the library, or playing billiards, or going to tea at a neighbour's house. Even hunting had lost its appeal after a few months, the thrill of the hunt dulled by the predictable choreography, designed to give the advantage to the most senior gentleman. Something that should have been exhilarating and primal was sanitised and reduced to little more than target practice, casually observed by gentle ladies with their fluttering sashes and porcelain teacups.

He was bored out of his mind.

His pair of dragon pistols sat on the bookshelf, gathering dust. He'd last fired them during a scuffle with a group of brigands while escorting Princess Dahna to her wedding. A smile crept across his face at the memory, nearly a year old now. Sulat had been in such a temper with the high maintenance princess, but enough time had passed that he could now remember the peacekeeping ordeal with humour. Since then, he'd only caught up with Sulat a couple of times. The shock of being away from her after three years of her constant presence still stung, but he never doubted her friendship, no matter how long it had been.

The smile faded and he set the glass down. It wasn't Johanne's fault they were in this situation, any more than his. It strained them both, and despite it and the boredom of lordly life, he was mostly happy. Even with his rosy reminiscence, he would rather be here with Johanne and Rosabel than blocked from visiting them, as he had been in the days he was living as a thief with Sulat. Life was also undeniably safer and more comfortable at Parry House. Gone were the bed bugs, the cheapest cuts of barely edible food, and the constant stream of enemies showing up unannounced and seeking satisfaction on whatever grudge they held. These days, Alois sparred with words, and often lost, which was another thing Johanne gnashed her teeth over. He was still working on judging what things were suitable to say, and which were better left thought.

Downstairs, the front door opened and voices exchanged words. Footsteps climbed the stairs and Rhustiss, the butler, appeared at the door.

'Captain Sulat is in the sitting room, my lord,' he said stiffly.

Alois leapt to his feet and bounded down the stairs. Sulat stood in the middle of the room, with a glass of brandy, dressed in a white shirt, brown breeches, and a dark blue vest trimmed snug against her slight frame. Alois pulled her into a tight hug.

'Get off me, you oaf!' She pushed him away. 'Someday, you'll just say, "It's nice to see you, Sulat."'

'It's bloody nice to see you, Sulat.' Warmth spread to the tips of his fingers and all the bad mood of the day evaporated. Despite Sulat's terseness, he had missed her awfully. He stepped around her and poured himself a drink from the cut crystal decanter set, and sat in a slender light wood chair with a floral cushion. Johanne liked floral patterns.

'How've you been?'

'Well, you know,' Sulat said with a shrug, topping off her glass and sitting opposite him.

'That good, huh?'

'How's..?' Sulat whirled a finger at the high moulded ceiling of the elegant country house.

Alois dropped his gaze to his glass and tried to hide his frustration. Sulat was rubbish at reading faces, but he didn't want to risk it. Then again, there was no need to lie to her.

'Well, you know.'

'That good?'

Alois barked a laugh. 'In truth, I'm climbing the walls. It's been too long since we had a decent adventure. I wish Renir would hurry up and extort some wickedness from us, like he promised.'

'As it happens.' Sulat swirled the brandy in her glass. 'I'm here to extort you.'

Alois shot forward in his seat, nearly dropping his glass between his knees. His mouth went dry. 'Do you mean that?'

'I do.' Sulat squinted at him. 'When can you be ready?'

'Now.' Alois stood. 'Right now.' He drained his glass. 'I'll grab some clothes and tell Johanne.'

'The good life not as good as it looks?' Sulat shouted over the rattling of the rented carriage as they pulled away from the pea green house with its symmetrical facade, pillars, and rect-angular windows painted white.

Alois didn't answer immediately, but tapped his fingers together for a moment.

'Johanne and I have been fighting a lot lately.' He kept his voice low, choosing his words, and chewing the inside of his cheek. 'We've been married almost a year and she's still not pregnant. But there's no point fighting over that, so we fight over everything else. Stupid things.'

'She's still young, you have time.'

'Then we got a letter last week. Her sister is expecting number five. Her eldest sister.'

'What does that mean?'

'It doesn't mean anything!' Alois growled, running his hands through his unusually tidy curls. 'Sometimes it's easy, and some couples wait ages. It's not a science. But you tell her that. I'm not usually the voice of sanity, but she's obsessed with having more children. It's all she talks about.'

'Don't you want more?'

'Of course, I do. But not enough to tear our marriage apart. It's a simple process. We managed it once, and that was a drunken accident. I don't know what she expects me to do that I'm not already doing. But anyway,' he sighed so heavily that he folded nearly in half. 'What's the job?'

'Pirates.'

'Fun.' He perked up a little.

'Maybe not. They've been attacking merchants and warships, and Renir wants me to investigate.'

'Interesting. Friends of yours?' He picked at a loose thread in the carriage's curtain.

'No.'

Alois laughed. 'Of course not. You have papers, why does he need me? I've been on a ship...twice, I think, in my life.'

Sulat ground her teeth. *Because you're a man who doesn't work for me.* 'I don't know. He seems to think you'll be of some use.'

'Then he's the only one.' Alois slumped against the cracked leather cushion.

'Are you up to working? I can tell him you declined my summons.'

'It's not like I'm doing anything there. Honestly, at this moment, I'd rather be anywhere else. I need a break. Maybe some fresh sea air, and a good fight.' He grinned at Sulat and in spite of herself, she smiled back.

It is good to see him again.

'Wait, why are there warships at sea?' Alois asked suddenly. 'Are we mobilising?'

'I don't know,' Sulat said. There was always sabre-rattling at Vurdia, and Cavendy didn't need much persuading to prepare for war. 'It's the usual posturing, making sure everyone stays in line.'

Alois scoffed. 'Just our ships, though, right? I doubt the Vurdence would shift from their benches, even if a real war were to kick off. It'd be over in a week, as soon as we cut off their supply of good beef and beer.'

He had always hated the Vurdence. Sulat leaned toward liking them. They were far more open-minded about people of different origins than the Viehlish and Cavenders were.

Yet, she couldn't condemn the Viehlish entirely. After all, they had granted her command of her own ship, and equality to any other captain on the ocean.

Chapter Two
Meltythia

Alois took his place behind Sulat on the top deck of *Meltythia*. The steering wheel was mounted right at the back of the ship, at the end of a long box pressed against the rail. With barely room for a man to walk between the wheel and the back of the captain's cabin, it required the huge Watani helmsman, Darib, to steer from the side of the box, facing the nose of the ship.

'Weigh anchor!' Sulat shouted, pulling her hat on over her red headscarf.

Her First and Second Mates, mutton-chopped Eaton and squinty Wese, stood casually on the other side of the steering box while the men positioned at the front of the ship heaved around the large cylindrical capstan. The heavy chain clinked and water whooshed over the rising anchor, while men on the dock untied the huge mooring lines.

'Raise the sheets! Watch how she flies,' Sulat added quietly to Alois as other sailors scaled the rope ladders and leaned across narrow beams. The sails unfurled and snapped open with the breeze. *Meltythia* slid into motion-- smoothly inching forward along the dock, rocked ninety degrees out to sea, and slipped into open water.

Alois lurched to the side and hard against the rail as the navigator, a mousy young woman with thick spectacles, stepped up the stairs. Sulat nodded curtly and signalled to Eaton. He strode on long legs to the front of the ship and rang the brass bell.

'First shift, hands to stations!' A bunch of men left the rail, where they'd been saying their farewells, and took places around deck.

'Tour?' Sulat asked Alois. Her face shone, her deep brown eyes bright as she pulled them away from the grey horizon.

'Yeah, great!' Alois said, excited.

'I'll come, too,' said a doughy, sleepy-eyed man, dressed well above the station of the other sailors, in a fine woollen suit and powdered wig.

Sulat rolled her eyes, but didn't protest, and pulled open the door to her cabin, just in front of the steering wheel.

'Who are you?' Alois asked.

'This is Elmor Foth,' Sulat interrupted. 'He's my nursemaid.' She stepped down into the dark staircase. The wind blew away one of the curls at the base of her head, revealing a small tattoo.

That's new. Alois had a tattoo; a regimental insignia from the war. The nature of a dangerous life on the road meant that he knew every inch of Sulat's body, and she definitely didn't have one before.

Foth chuckled. 'Hardly. I'm the king's man.' He put a hand out and Alois shook. 'I'm just here to observe.'

'Alois, Lord Brynglass. Observe what?'

Surely, a man like Foth wouldn't board a ship like this voluntarily. *Meltythia* rolled, slamming Alois into the wall of the stairwell, and he slid a couple of steps.

'Legalities.' Foth said blandly. 'Watch your step.'

'Ahh.' Alois pulled himself upright. 'You're here to make

sure everything's...ship shape.'

Sulat huffed.

'Exactly,' Foth lowered his voice. 'And, of course, I'm familiar with your history, my lord. You should know that the good captain's feelings of persecution are quite unfounded; my business is not personal. I am merely here in the interest of the kingdom, and that means that anyone on this ship-- officer, crew, or *passenger*-- can catch my attention.'

Alois raised his eyebrows. 'Subtle.'

'I just want to make sure we're all behaving accordingly when we represent our kingdom abroad.' Foth smiled again.

'This is my cabin,' Sulat grumbled, stepping across the narrow room and opening the door opposite to give them space.

Alois squeezed himself between a desk and a cabinet to make room for Foth, next to the narrow bed, tidily made up with a wool blanket and cotton pillow under a small round window. Opposite, was a tiny room, practically a closet, with a hole set into a white-painted bench and a ceramic bowl on a shelf with a small pitcher.

'You're lucky you're a small woman,' Alois pinched his shoulders together. He had images of putting an elbow through the glass panes of the cabinet doors or knocking over something important.

'The rest of us are not so lucky,' Foth groused behind him.

Alois agreed silently, dreading what space would be afforded his own large frame. *Probably a bedroll on deck.* 'I don't imagine you have many crew meetings in here.'

'That's what the salon is for.' Sulat stepped into the next room. It was well apportioned, with dark panelled walls and leather furnishings. Utilitarian yet tasteful; as if Sulat had planned it, and someone who anticipated long strategy talks came in later and made it comfortable.

'Very nice,' Alois said, impressed.

'Yeah, it's not bad,' Sulat said in a light, conversational tone. The expression on her face betrayed her-- more like a mother gazing at her firstborn child than a detached approval of a business asset.

A hallway led out of the salon, with three rooms on either side, ending in a glass-paned door. Alois whistled at the luxuries in the officers' pantry: cheeses and cured meats, tea and tobacco chests, a sugar loaf, and porcelain dishes.

The other rooms were the officers' privy and cabins. About half the size of the captain's cabin, Alois' room had a desk and washbasin built into one wall, a tall narrow cabinet, a stool, and a small bed against the far wall under a small window.

'It looks comfortable,' he said, with a nod. The corner of Sulat's mouth twitched. *Is that amusement or sympathy?*

'This used to be my cabin,' Foth said. 'I had to move to the map room for this journey.'

'Nepotism, Foth,' Sulat said, pushing open the door to the outside, letting a slash of light into the dimly lit cabin. 'I like him better than you.'

'Aww, thanks. I'm blushing,' Alois said. She never admitted out loud that she liked him, especially not in front of other people.

Up closer, and in the light, he squinted harder at the tattoo on her neck. It looked like a lobster with its tail split into two pointed curves, holding a lightning bolt in one claw, and a star between its antennae.

The ship pitched on a swell, but Alois managed to save himself from falling again.

'This is the main deck,' Sulat said.

There were two buildings-- the crew cabin and the deckhouse. Rowboats perched upside down on top cast shade across the narrow walkways and made it feel more like a shopping street crammed with stalls than the deck of a ship. There wasn't much space between the masts and the cabins, or the cabins and the rails; he couldn't imagine sailors running back and forth during storms or battles without running into each other, tripping over coils of rope, or crashing through the grated hatch that took up the rest of the floor space.

'Not that you will ever need to go down there,' Foth

chortled after Sulat explained the belowdeck storage. 'You're of much too high a station to haul crates.'

Sulat ground her teeth. 'My lord,' she snapped, a vein pulsing in her temple. 'We are underway now, don't you have a ledger to see to?'

'Right you are, Captain.' He bowed elaborately, screwed a quizzing glass into his eye socket, and disappeared back into the cabin.

'My own ship, that's what Renir promised me. Some days, it's all I can do not to lock that fool in his cabin or throw him over the side.' She flexed and relaxed her fists. 'Anyway, that's the tour. The raised deck at the front is the focsle. It has the crew privy and the ship's bell. We ring that to signal shift change or emergencies, so keep a listen for it.'

'So, about that tattoo.' Alois gestured at Sulat's neck, and a slow warmth spread across her face.

'The Anchor-Tailed Lobster. It means I went through rough seas and kept my nerve. I can be trusted as a member of a crew. The lightning bolt...' She tapped the drawing. 'Means I earned it crossing The Squalls. The star means I'm a captain.'

Her whole face glowed. She loved the ship, yes, but the tattoo was the real prize. The Anchor-Tailed Lobster could never be taken away. So long as Sulat had her neck, she had a way back to the sea.

Alois pestered her for details about her first voyage, how she'd earned her tattoo, and what she'd been up to since.

'I can't imagine you scrubbing decks, given your many oaths against servitude,' he said.

'I never scrubbed decks,' Sulat scoffed.

'Really?'

'I was meant to, but the second mate poached me.' She made a motion with her thumb and middle finger like plucking something out of thin air.

'The squinty one?'

'No, a woman named Dilys. You'd have liked her. She was a talker.'

'"Was?" What happened to her?'

'Nothing, as far as I know. Probably still second mate on *Martinette*. I tried to bring her with me, but she's too damn loyal.' Sulat chuckled. 'But Wese and Eaton were on that ship, too. And I poached them.'

That night, Alois joined the officers for supper at the captain's table. He dressed in the nicest thing he'd brought, a slightly more formal jacket and breeches. He wasn't sure what to bring when he packed. Obviously, a diplomatic mission, of sorts, but with the possibility of daring and violence. Who would be needed: the lord or the scoundrel?

He compromised and packed both, yielding to class for the journey to Rhythlin Island, reclaiming his fighter mantle for the mission there, and donning the lord once more to report to the king and return to Johanne.

Maybe if she misses me enough, she'll get over being angry.

Already at the table were the heavy-lidded mate, Eaton, and Elmor Foth. Foth sipped delicately at a glass of deep red wine, casting sideways grimaces at Eaton, whittling a figure that might have been a young boy over a greasy cloth.

'Must you do that at the table?' Foth groaned. 'The shavings fly.'

'They don't. I put a cloth down,' Eaton grunted. 'Light's better here than in my bunk.'

Foth sneered, then spotted Alois. 'Ahh, my lord!' He leapt up and pulled out a chair, gesturing elaborately for Alois to sit.

Sulat emerged from her cabin a moment later, tossing a rolled-up map onto the cushioned bench and pouring two glasses of brandy. She handed one to Alois with a nudge to his shoulder, and nodded at the young sailor who appeared at the door of the saloon. He bowed and left the cabin.

'Good, now we're all here.' She sat and took a deep drink of brandy.

'Wait--' Alois pointed to the empty chair. 'Isn't there another officer? The older one?'

Foth snickered and Sulat shook her head.

'On a ship this small, Second mate is crew advocate. Wese eats in the mess. We'll catch him up.'

'Doesn't like fancy tables, anyway,' Eaton mumbled.

Tall, thin and lanky, Eaton had a hooked nose, dark eyes, and stringy black hair shot through with grey. He dressed in scuffed and threadbare clothes that he probably found lying around. Nothing matched or fit properly. He was as different from Foth as it was possible to be.

Every so often, the king's man would cast a look between Alois and Eaton as though while neither of them belonged at a captain's table, at least Alois made an attempt to dress appropriately.

Alois wondered how Foth felt about Sulat being present at her own table. Aside from being an unabashed Ebian woman who made no attempt to lighten her dark skin, or hide or tame her thick fluffy hair--only going so far as to keep it pulled back out of her face--Sulat had only worn a dress on three occasions in the four years Alois had known her. She knew her place, and kept as far from it as possible.

Sulat hadn't bothered to change for supper, wearing tight breeches and flowy shirt, with a simple fitted waistcoat. She had eschewed her hat in deference to the formality of supper, but the red scarf and all of her clothes smelled of salty air and tobacco.

The door to the cabin opened and the boy entered with a tray laden with plates of fresh vegetables, meat, cheese, and loaf of crusty bread.

'Thank you, Tobin, that will be all,' Sulat said, and the boy bowed and left. 'This will be the last decent meal we get for at least a week, so take advantage.'

Dawn broke bright and sharp through the wobbly glass window across Alois' face. He groaned and sat up, rubbing sleep from his eyes and stretching the soreness in his back. As he'd suspected, his bed was slightly too short for him to lay flat. However, with some manoeuvring, he managed to put his feet up on the desk and get mostly comfortable, but as a result, he'd left his already mistreated body to the mercy of the wind and waves. And they had not been kind.

He dressed gingerly in his adventuring clothes, babying his joints and muscles, washed his face to slap some awakeness into himself and shuffled into the salon.

'Good morning, my lord,' Elmor Foth's voice shattered Alois' calm. 'Come, we're breaking our fast.' Foth gave the change of fashion a disapproving sniff.

Alois sat at the table beside Sulat. She pushed a steaming ceramic cup of coffee at him.

'Better than breaking your mast, eh?' he asked around the table. Eaton snorted.

'Oh, very good, my lord.' Foth gave an appreciative nod.

'Stop,' Sulat said, still reading the book in front of her. 'I can't kill you in front of Foth.'

'Quite right,' Foth took an imperious sip of tea.

'How's your stomach?' Eaton asked, pointing at a plate of dry crackers. The table also held a stack of toast, butter and jam, chunks of ham and cheese, a steaming teapot, and a bowl of cut lemons.

Alois concentrated. 'The least upset part of me,' he concluded, reaching for the ham and cheese.

'Good,' Eaton said, the barest flicker of friendliness passing over his long face. 'Thought you might be one of those delicate heifers.' His darks eyes flicked toward Foth, with a mound of white crackers on his plate and nothing else.

'*Heifer*?' Alois' gagged. 'If you're not a Lobster, you're a *heifer*?'

Sulat shrugged. 'I don't choose the terms.'

'I'm a Lobster, now!' Foth cried, glaring at Eaton. 'I survived the Squalls, same as anyone.'

'What's the Squalls?' Alois asked.

'The shape of the continent of Triothlon, the path of the currents, and other things, create a section of the ocean where it's always stormy,' Eaton explained. 'They say the sea claims one life for every passage through the Squalls. From what I've seen and heard, that figure is accurate.'

Sulat and Foth nodded their agreement.

Alois took a deep swallow of the strong black coffee and his mood improved dramatically, despite his new title and the perilous waters.

After breakfast, Alois headed out to the deck with Eaton. He stumbled and twisted an ankle, but recovered.

'Give me a job, Eaton. I can be useful,' he said, bouncing on the balls of his feet.

'Oh, no need, my lord.' Eaton attempted a pleasant grimace. 'We have enough men for the hard work. And I doubt we can afford to pay you a decent wage.' He clapped Alois on the shoulder and strode off to correct a sailor looping ropes at the rail.

Alois found Wese and made the same request, but got rebuffed there, as well.

In a huff, he returned to his berth and sat awkwardly on his too-small bed. Soon, that, too, rankled. He wasn't built for sitting around and doing nothing.

He tried to sit at the desk and pen a letter to Johanne, but he didn't have anything to say beyond the usual I-love-yous and a description of the ship, which she would, no doubt, find interesting, but he could as easily tell her in person when he got back. He tossed the pen and sighed.

Maybe I can stand on deck and watch the sea without being in anyone's way.

He stepped out into the bright sunlight and found a patch of rail that didn't have much activity around it. Sailors bustled around him and left him alone for a time. Then a small voice cleared its throat behind him.

'May I fetch you a drink, my lord?' the cabin boy, Tobin, asked.

Alois smiled at him and glanced around at all the men politely avoiding disturbing him.

'Do you know who I am, boy?' he asked.

'Uh, begging your pardon, yes, I do, my lord. You're Lord Brynglass.'

'Yes.' Alois waved his hand. 'But apart from that.'

Tobin shrugged, unsure how to answer properly.

Alois patted the boy on the shoulder and stomped past, going straight to the source of the confusion.

Sulat sat in her cabin, her booted feet crossed on the table, tobacco smoke curling from her pipe, filling the room with a sweet and earthy aroma. She poured a glass from the half-empty bottle of claret.

'How are your reflexes, Captain?' Alois picked a heavy pouch of shot cartridges up off the shelf and tossed it underhand at her. She caught it with her left hand and set it on the table.

'You know better.'

Alois laughed and sat on the bed. 'You didn't tell them about me.'

'I did.'

'Not that we'd been partners. They think I'm some useless noble.'

Sulat snorted into her wine. 'I thought we were keeping your personal and criminal lives separate.'

'So, you went with "lord" before "partner." Is it Weaton? Is he jealous?'

'Eaton and Wese are different people.'

'Are they the new Alois?'

'Look who's jealous.'

'I just wonder at your reasons for not telling them what I can do. I can fight, I'm strong. Lord Brynglas is rich and well-connected, and that's about it.' He poured himself a glass of claret from her bottle and winced at the vinegary tang.

'Why would I need a highwayman on my ship?'

'Why would you need a lord?'

'Because you're rich and well-connected.' Sulat's eyes met his and he saw fire there. She scowled into her glass. 'This was supposed to be my mission. Renir ordered me to bring you.'

'You should have told me!' Alois slumped back in his chair. 'I'd have come up with a reason to stay home.'

'It wouldn't have worked. You know Renir doesn't accept "no."'

'As far as I'm concerned, this is your ship, your crew, your mission. I go where you point me.'

'You never have before.' A smirk twisted the corners of her mouth. 'Just punch and shoot, as usual, and we'll be done.'

'Good. Quick job, get me home so I can fight with Johanne some more.' He chuckled and clinked her glass with his fingernail, then fell silent a moment, struck again by a sudden thought. 'But these pirates must have decent firepower, if they've been attacking warships.'

'They must do.' Sulat said.

'So? What's your plan? Do you have guns?'

Sulat nodded. 'I have twelve falconets.'

Alois choked on his brandy. '*Falconets*,' he gasped.

Falconets were ancient technology, a hundred years past their heyday. They were light and manoeuvrable, sure, but the damage they could do was only effective at close range, and only to a small, delicate target. 'I didn't know they were still in production.'

Sulat blinked slowly, taking a deep breath. 'Don't be so dramatic. We do fine with falconets. We hardly ever fire them. These pirates will be slow with their big guns.'

Alois pointed to the Letter of Marque nailed to the wall. 'Have you taken ships?'

'I have.' Sulat nodded.

'How do you manage that with falconets?'

'Strategically. We take small ships. High value cargo, small enough to carry. We can't fight a galleon, but where would I put cattle and lumber, anyway? And this is only a scouting mission. Our speed is our best asset.'

Alois had a sudden memory of a time he'd watched a falcon catch a kestrel on the wing. A small bird of prey snatching up a smaller bird of prey as though it were no more challenge than a mouse.

'Well, on that cheery thought, I'd better head back to my berth and do nothing some more,' Alois said, slapping his thighs and rising. Then he remembered something else. 'Speaking of not-jealous Eaton, what is with all the whittling?'

'Everyone has a hobby,' Sulat said, putting her empty glass in the cabinet with the bottles of brandy.

'Sulat...'

She smirked. 'He has magic, I'm sure of it.'

'That explains a lot,' Alois muttered.

'What?'

'Nothing, I'll see you later.' Alois waved and went back to his berth to try to cram himself into his bed to nap for a couple of hours, feeling even more annoyed.

So the New Alois has magic, wonderful.

Chapter Three
The Prophecy

One month earlier

King Kellac surveyed the colony from the highest cave of his limestone formation. The preparations for the bicentennial celebration were going well. Streamers of braided seaweed fluttered in the current, the slimy algae had been scrubbed from the walls of the formations- including his royal residence, and polished boulders stood in artful positions to best display their colours. The people decorated themselves extravagantly, weaving intricate hairstyles, exfoliating their scales and shells until they shone, and draping themselves in their finest adornments: strings of pearls and pebbles, sea fans in every colour of the rock pools, shells, and live anemones and urchins. The king himself draped a heavy net, studded with pearls and sea jasper about his shoulders.

He clicked his tongue. The net was too dull against his

translucent grey shell. No, he needed something brighter, something striking, something that would draw every eye. He called to his valet, who undulated to his side on eight purplish tentacles.

'This cloak is a bit drab for such an occasion, don't you think? What colours do we have?'

'We have some beanweed and dulse, that's red.' The valet twirled around the adjoining caves, tossing out chunks of seaweed in different shapes and shades. 'Velvet horn and sea lettuce are quite cheerful greens.' They were nice, but something was still missing.

'Have we got anything in...blue?'

Blue was rare in this area of the ocean. The other colonies of merfolk often had blue, either naturally, or caught from human ships. But here on the rocky shore, most everything blended in with the grey-beige formations, or else utilised colours that protected against sun damage at low tide. A blue bauble would definitely stand out against everyone else wearing beanweed and sea lettuce.

'Blue, you Highness?' the valet hesitated.

'Yes, find me something blue before tonight. I'm going to see Breen.' Kellac's ten walking legs carried him out of the cave, and his swimmerets and powerful armoured tail drove him through the water toward the rugged sea floor outside the sea witch's cave.

Every Rocky Shore celebration included a prophecy to buoy the spirits of the citizens. The last sea witch had been great at it, always delivering messages of hope, of community, of perseverance. But she had died some years ago and her young apprentice who succeeded her had her own ideas.

The cave was deep and high, with other such chambers leading off the main, though Kellac had never found the courage to explore past the first room. Even when he was young, he always stuck close to his father's legs while he instructed his sea witch on what message the people needed.

The room had a long slanted slab of rock where he often

found Breen reclining, as well as a few calcified anemones placed around the room for others to sit. Holes drilled into the sandstone walls held potion bottles, fossils, and all manner of mysterious objects that Breen presumably used in her spells.

Breen emerged from a side cave as he arrived, twisting long spiral shells into the holes in her fluted ears.

'Your Majesty,' she greeted him. 'What can I do for you? I'd have thought you'd be busy with preparations.'

'Oh, everyone is doing fine without my help.' King Kellac waved away her concern. 'It was your plans I came about.'

'Your Highness is too kind.'

'I'm just nervous...about tonight. I-- it's not that I don't trust you, but the prophecy...' the king shrivelled under her piercing golden eyes and the sudden twitching of her yellow and grey tail. 'It's just...pageantry. Isn't it?

'I don't decide the message, your Highness,' Breen answered. 'Good or bad, it's what the people need to hear.'

'Uh-huh.' The king's maxillae ticked together. 'Just...try to keep it light. "Everyone keep your chins up, the best is yet to come," that sort of thing, you know?' He cleared his throat and backed out of the cave. Breen followed, and her face softened under the cloud of amber hair.

'Your Highness, whatever is said, it's for the good of everyone. That's why I must be impartial. If I only say nice things, we may not see danger before it's too late.'

Breen was one of the only people King Kellac could trust to be completely truthful, if occasionally unkind and maddeningly stubborn. She thought him weak, and he feared she was right.

He patted her freckled pale yellow shoulder. 'I apologise for doubting you.'

She bowed her head and he scuttled away, back to his formation, his chest tight. Visiting her hadn't been as comforting as he'd hoped. Why did she have to be like that, so headstrong and imperious?

Can't she just say what I want to hear, like everyone else? Just once?

Bioluminescent algae coated the seaweed garlands in the village centre, coating everything in a calming blue light.

A band perched on staggered ledges up the side of a formation, playing a lively tune on bladderweed pipes, coral flutes, and pufferfish-skin drums. king Kellac bobbed his head along with the beat, taking his position on a smooth stone in a comfortable alcove above the heads of everyone else. A troop of mermaids filed in and danced in front of the band, twirling and fluttering on delicate fins and flippers, streams of bubbles following their movements like glitter. A young merman picked his way through the crowd, passing out algae juice sacs and tiny crunchy crabs with the tentacles he wasn't using for movement. King Kellac called for some and happily munched away as the dancers performed for the growing audience.

When the seats were filled, the dancers took seats in the stands and a group of actors came forward to enact the expulsion of the witches from Ildecoke Island and their subsequent wanderings in exile. The crowd was quiet during this somber re-enactment, but when the play reached the part where the Rocky Shore Merfolk split from the other merfolk tribes, the viewers perked up a bit, and when the little band of refugees landed at the foot of Rhythlin Island, the assembled erupted in cheers. Even the king joined in, pride swelling in his chest.

We really have come a long way. Look what we have: plentiful food, safe shelter, even thriving arts. Is that not the standard of success our ancestors had dreamt of?

After the play came another set of dancers, followed by a choir of mermaids rooted in clamshells, and then a contest for best camouflage among the chromatic citizens.

A tinkling sound fluttered over the din from the edge of the colony. A pair of mermaids, shrouded in gnarled woven cloth and netting, glided toward the town centre, the smaller of the two holding a platter of pearly grey seaweed. A hush fell over the crowd. Breen threw back her hood and picked up a pod of dreamweed from her assistant's platter. She popped it into her mouth and chewed slowly. The assistant faded into the background and all of the light from the luminous garlands formed a blue halo around Breen's beatific face.

Her mouth opened and her jaw hung slack. A wheezing noise emanated from her, followed by a stream of unintelligible words. Then her speech coalesced, her sentences punctuated by shuddering gasps.

'The new age will be heralded by a blue light, sparkling. It is an abomination, a great shame, a terrible deception. The son of the king will lead his people into a new era of prosperity, but to do it he must leave his home. The humans will turn on each other, they will make themselves weak.' Breen stiffened and convulsed for a moment, then relaxed and continued in a croak. 'There is blood in the water, scarlet foam. And those who were expelled will reclaim the island.'

Her shoulders slumped, her head fell forward, and she hung, limply suspended in the water, surrounded by her cloud of coppery hair. The village centre stood silent, and slowly, every face turned to the king.

King Kellac shook all over. All his life, he's cowered in the shadow of his father. King Aiwar had been strong, decisive, and longed to wage war against the kings of Viehland. But he knew his people were not ready, so he channelled the energy he would have used toward conquest into building the city and providing for the people. If Breen's prophecy was right, the people were ready, but the king they needed was long dead, and the quest would fall to Kellac.

He swallowed hard, his chest tight, his stomach twisting. *They're all looking at me. What do I do?*

He raised his shaking hands and clapped. A few people joined in, but the rest continued to stare, apprehension on their faces. And disappointment.

King Kellac stood and a couple of muscled mermen pulled away from the crowd to guide Breen's unconscious body back to her cave, her assistant gliding along behind her. But still those eyes were on him. He cleared his throat, stood still for a moment, then climbed out of his seat and picked his way through the crowd with as much grace and decorum as he could muster.

His walking legs trembled all the way home, but he didn't trust his swimmerets to carry him through open water.

The son of the king. The son of the king. Why not 'the king'? I am king after all, in my own right. Aiwar is dead, that makes me king.

No one sees me that way. Always King Aiwar's weedy hatchling. A shrimp in more ways than one.

Back in the quiet of his formation, King Kellac slumped against the wall.

Maybe she means a different merman, an actual prince. There were many kings since the Exile. Many of them had sons. There's Cialis, son of Deldra of the Open Sea Merfolk; Irako, son of King Lorld in the Ice Fields; Okala, son of Clyr of the Sandy Shore nearest to Ildecoke; and countless others. She could have been referring to anyone. Why tell us? Why deliver a prophecy that doesn't have to do with us?

Kellac picked at a shred of loose shell. His molt was coming soon. *Maybe when I climb out of this grey carapace, I'll be less mediocre.*

That had never happened before. He'd itch for a few days, then peel off the irritating outer skin, and emerge the same nervy, dull inefficacy he'd always been.

Why should we fight? What's wrong with this island? We have everything we need here. There's food, shelter, not many dangers we can't defend ourselves from. We're happy here. Why start something again?

He climbed out of his limestone palace and swam to Breen's cave. She couldn't control the visions she saw, but she could damn well control her interpretation of them. *I'll have her tell everyone that the prophecy is about a different tribe. Let them fight the humans, and let us stay here.*

Breen lay huddled under a thick blanket of woven fishing net, holding a cloudy white stone in her lap.

'Your Highness,' she whispered, straightening.

'I need you to deliver a statement, Breen.' Kellac stood tall and tried his best to emanate confidence and gravitas. A bit of carapace on his wrist snapped free and fluttered in the current. He ripped it off and let it drift away, his face burning.

Really? It starts now, when I'm trying to be commanding?

'Your Highness?' Breen's voice was thin and her brows contracted.

'You're going to tell people that your prophecy wasn't about us. It was about Okala or Cialis, someone else, I don't care. But not us.'

Breen winced as she tried to sit up. 'I can't control what I see.'

'But you can control how your interpret it.' His brain strained to find a logical argument, but it didn't matter. 'Look, I'm king. I'm ordering you. It's an order.' He lifted his chin and pointed an imperious finger.

Breen fixed him with an odd expression. *Is that defiance?*

'It won't change the future. If we're meant to do this--'

'Come on, it was *ages* ago! Nearly a thousand years.' Kellac's composure failed him. *Why is she always so stubborn?* 'The point of today is to celebrate how well we've done, not to re-open old wounds. What can be gained from fighting? There are too few of us, too scattered and divided, and the humans have far more advanced weapons. Shall I lead this village to Ildecoke with our sharktooth spears and urchin darts?'

'You can unite the other villages!' Breen pulled herself up straighter, her voice still weak. 'Not just the Rocky Shore folk, but the Sandy Shore as well, and the Open Sea. All of them. I can't be the only one to have had this vision. The time is right to mobilise. Appeal to that ancient pit of rage in every merperson. They'll swim behind you, I know it.'

It still doesn't feel right. 'If we fight, many of us, if not all of us, will die. If we stay here, we can thrive.'

'Thrive? You call this thriving?' Breen's voice cracked. 'Are you truly content to sit here, huddled under the rocks like a hermit crab, picking what little we can from the rocks, frightened of the light, frightened of a bigger predator? Will you climb into your shell at the first ripple on the water? Does it not boil you alive that there are humans on our island?'

All the fire in Kellac's belly died, and he picked at his flaky shell. 'I'm not the man for this, Breen. We both know that. I'm not my father. I'm not strong, nor inspiring. You have the passion, you lead the people, if it means that much to you.'

Breen slumped. 'I'm not the king. The people fear me.'

'Then perhaps the time is not right. Maybe, one day, there will be a king with your fervour, but it's not me.'

King Kellac backed toward the mouth of the cave. He had nothing more to say.

'Your Highness,' Breen called him back. She was up from her rock, and holding something out in her hand. 'I heard you wanted something blue earlier.'

She opened her fingers and in her palm was a spray of fan coral in bright, shining blue. Kellac's jaw dropped as he reached for it.

'Where did you find it?'

'Here.' Breen waved at her cave wall, bristling with coral. 'It's not natural. I did a spell to turn it blue.'

Kellac grinned at her, sorry that they were too different to be real friends. 'So, not everything you do is scary.'

Breen bowed her head and let him leave with his gift.

The moment the king returned to his formation and the

colony lay dark and quiet, Breen slipped off her rock and into her deeper caves. She waved a hand over her cloudy rock. The crystal cleared and became a window into King Kellac's caves. He slept peacefully on top of his bed rock, legs folded under him, his valet balled up in the corner.

Good.

His molt was coming, the timing was perfect. Breen gathered the supplies she needed: a sharktooth spear, a patch of kelp net, a limpet shell, two chunks of wood from a shipwreck, and a large rock from her breaching at Ildecoke Island. She kept an eye on the sleeping king while she sang her incantation and painted the wood in bright greens and reds, with swirls of yellow and dots of rare, precious blue.

Satisfied with her work, and the sticks pulsing with power, she hauled a giant crab shell out of her closet and pulled it over her head. It was hard and uncomfortable, but it might just save her life. She gripped the stone hard and tapped it over the face of the king. He jumped and woke, dazed and confused.

'Come to me, Your Highness,' she whispered. 'It's time. Come to me.'

Kellac rose on his walking legs and leapt from his cave, pedalling his swimmerets through the water. A moment later, he arrived outside her cave. His eyes were unfocused, his movements clumsy. Breen wrapped the netting over his shoulders, strapped the limpet shell to his left arm, and put the spear in his right hand, then led him into her deep cave. She positioned one of his walking legs over the Ildecoke stone, and stood back, painted wood in her hands. She adjusted her hold, moving around the rigid shell covering her torso.

'King Kellac,' she spoke the words loud and clear, her voice sounding much stronger and more confident than she felt. It was a skill that took her years to master. 'For years, you have lived in the shadows, afraid of the light. But you cannot hide from destiny, it will find you under any rock. And today, it has found you. Wake now, as the king you were born to be.'

She slammed the sticks together. A shockwave ripped

through the cave, splintering the spear, shattering the limpet shell, and cracking Breen's crab armour. King Kellac's grey carapace dissolved in a puff of dust and he collapsed under the netting.

Silence and stillness followed.

'Your Highness?' Breen whispered.

Oh sea, what have I done? Her chest froze her lungs and twisted her stomach. *Have I killed the king?*

It had been a spell of her own devising, untested. How could it not be? Who was worthy to test a kingmaking spell? She reached out a hand to the tangled heap of netting on the floor. Before she could reach it, a crimson leg ripped it back.

Breen gasped as King Kellac rose to his feet.

Chapter Four
Kyri

Okala, his sisters, and their father zipped through the royal kelp forest in a clash of colours, chasing the choicest fish, but it wasn't as exhilarating as usual for the young prince.

Nearby, Marya and the king discussed politics, moving together through the weeds to corner a small silvery school. Okala had no interest in politics, and even less in how the Rocky Shore Merfolk ideologies had shifted. He scowled at Kyri nearby, stalking a crab, who still refused to tell him anything about her day on shore. She stunned it with a smack, sat on a stone, and sighed dramatically.

Okala rolled his eyes, but Marya glided over with her catch, and put a graceful hand on Kyri's arm.

'Are you feeling unwell?' she asked.

Kyri shrugged, picking the flesh out of the crab shell. 'I think I'll go to bed early tonight.'

'Perhaps it was the potion,' Ytaso said. She was Adeto's

apprentice, and was good enough with potions that she'd made the one for her own Breaching.

'Or the sun. It can have strange effects outside the water,' Neri said.

'Maybe something bit you,' Vila muttered under her breath near Okala.

So many things could go wrong. Was it really that dangerous, just going up, not even involving humans?

Kyri put down her half-empty crab shell. 'If you'll excuse me, Father.'

King Clyr nodded, a crease between his red brows. 'Neri, go with her.'

'No, that's not necessary,' Kyri said as Neri moved forward with her fish. 'I'm sure it was just the excitement. A combination of everything.' The pouch bounced at her hip as she waved her pink tail. 'I'm sure I'll be true as the tide tomorrow.' She smiled weakly and drifted from the forest.

'Someone should check in on her,' the king said. 'Adeto's potion is strong, and she's always been delicate. Vila, that will be your task.'

Okala squirmed. Kyri was fine earlier-- smug, even-- only pretending to be exhausted. Adeto's potion was strong enough to change a body, but no one had gotten seriously sick, that he'd ever heard of.

His stomach twisted at the thought of how it might feel to have a reaction, but even that didn't quell the longing.

'Is there a way to stay more than a few hours?' he asked Ytaso quietly.

She gestured at Kyri, swimming slowly home. 'One day is dangerous enough. It was probably the sun or the excitement that's affecting her, but it could easily be a flaw in the potion, or something else she encountered. The longer you stay up there, the greater the risk you'll be seen. We know what that means.'

Neri hissed at the memory of all the stories they'd learnt about the exile of the witches of Ildecoke. 'I heard if you marry a human, you can stay forever.' She stuck her tongue out. 'There's a thousand sailors on the shore and over our heads right now. Go sing to one.'

'Ladies,' Marya scolded. Neri and Ytaso went back to their hunt.

'But is it possible?' Okala pressed his sister.

'Who would risk it?' Ytaso asked. 'I doubt even Adeto knows how to do it.'

'That's enough for today, I think.' Marya appeared again and pointed an authoritative finger at the palace. 'Finish your fish and go back to your rooms.'

Okala finished the fish in his hand and headed back for the palace moulded from packed sand. Okala's room was next to Vila's, as they had always gotten along well. He dug a finger through the sand wall and peered through. Vila was undressing for bed and brushing her hair.

'Oh molt,' she muttered and rolled the large stone away from the mouth of her cave. The sounds of her tail swishing faded through the corridors.

She's gone to check on Kyri. Okala listened hard for the sounds of her return, and widened the hole.

'How is she?' he whispered.

Vila came closer. Her lips, only partially visible through the sand, pursed. 'She's faking, of course, looking for attention. She's right as riptide in there, dancing and flitting about, plaiting her hair. I don't know what she's up to, and I didn't care enough to ask, but she certainly looks to be feeling better.'

She moved away and a flash of orange fin told Okala that she had tucked herself onto her flat bedstone. Okala sat on his own bowl-shaped stone and pulled out the mirror he carried with him. A tangle of blue hair had formed under one of his ears and his orange eyes looked worried.

He and Kyri had been close once, when they were very small. They were the next closest in age, after Neri and Ytaso, who were practically clutchmates. They used to play sharks and prey all the time, hiding and pouncing on each other through the halls. It all changed when she started her lessons, and though he was well into his studies now, the little gap that formed between them had been hard to bridge. As a mermaid, she was a political asset, preparing for an advantageous marriage. Princes were really only worth anything if they were born first, and Okala was last in line. He was just trying to stay alive and not embarrass the clan too much.

Yet, there might be something there still, some quiet forgotten ember of the old bond they used to have, deep under the sophisticated mermaid and the pariah. Maybe he could throw himself on it and get her to tell him something --anything-- that could keep him going until his own Breaching. It would mean so much.

He waited until Vila started snoring before rolling back his own door stone and hurrying down the hall. Kyri's lay was quiet and still. Okala edged the door stone away, just a crack. She wouldn't thank him barging in. He peeked inside, but it was dark and still. No pink and purple shape sleeping on the stone. No dancing mermaid, nothing.

She was gone.

A chill spread through him. His first impulse was to raise the alarm, to speed down through the halls, shouting. Wake his father, wake Marya and Vila, Neri and Ytaso. Had she gone out for something, or had she been taken?

But something still wasn't right. She had been so smug, so excited. Then suddenly completely depressed, then Vila had seen her dancing. And what was in her purse? Why was she so secretive about it?

Okala slipped into her room, careful that she wasn't in the hall behind him, and sifted through her things. She had something from the surface, he was sure of it. He searched all around her bed stone for a clue, and in her little cubby holes and behind the chunk of glass from a shipwreck that she used for preening.

Something shifted outside in the tall seaweed. Something was moving, disturbing the weeds. One person. A flash of pink.

Okala gasped. *She hasn't been taken, she's running away!*

He slipped from her window hole, slid down the sand wall, and dove into the forest of weeds. But they were swaying and dancing too much in the currents. He crested the forest once, twice, three times. *Yes! There she is!* He kept up his leap and dive like a dolphin, to keep her in his sights, while staying out of hers.

Then she was gone. He froze in the water, searching the wide grey expanse. *Where is she?*

There! He spotted a fin, a little purplish spot against the shadows, and sped after her. She was heading for a break in the rocks, The Shelf. His heart hammered. The ocean floor fell away sharply and it was open sea for miles after that. Would she waste time to find cover, or speed across the vast expanse to wherever she was going?

He thrashed in aggravation. His bright green tail and yellow fins would stand out against the water like a giant banner with his name printed on it.

Keeping one eye on his sister, he tore long strips of seaweed out of the seabed and tied them around his waist. There was a cracked and abandoned snail shell that he jammed onto his head. A deflated puff bladder drifted past him and he seized it and shoved a couple rocks in. He couldn't hide his tail, but dressed like this, from enough of a distance, he could be any old merman on his way somewhere. Kyri surely didn't expect him of all people to be following her. By the time he finished, she was little more than a speck in the distance.

He swam after her, careful to keep a good few fathoms between them. She stopped abruptly and watched him for a minute. He didn't slow-- random traveller wouldn't-- but his heart hammered in his chest the closer he got.

Go, he begged. *Go again.* How close would he have to be before she recognised him?

She waved her tail, but she was still too far to read her expression. Then, mercifully, she sped away, even faster than she had before.

She didn't recognise me. His chest eased. If she had, she'd have gone crazy. He actually didn't know what she would have done, but she certainly wouldn't have kept going on this journey. He kept his head down, careful to act like he was exactly where he wanted to be for his own business, and kept her in his sights.

She suddenly shot straight up. Okala's eyes rose above her to the ribbon of fish and detritus moving quickly overhead. *She's going for the Lenord Current! Where are you going, Kyri?*

He let her get a little ahead before he joined the stream, as well. They sailed through the empty expanse for what felt like hours, her ahead, him careful to keep a leisurely pace.

She dropped abruptly out of the current and he almost shot right past her, but caught it in time, and fell behind her.

Where are we now?

The sea floor came into murky view, the profiles of rocks and reefs disrupting the smooth grey haze. The ground became more and more textured and weeds reached up, their finger-like leaves grabbing at them. Kyri dove into the cover of the forest, her progress creating ripples between the ribbons of weeds. This patch of sea was unfamiliar to Okala. How did Kyri know about it?

Up ahead, a huge limestone formation appeared out of the gloom. It was still miles away, but it had to be big enough to support a whole colony of merfolk. And with all of these rocks, so much more than the smooth land where he lived, this had to be Rocky Shore Merfolk territory.

What are you doing with the Rockies?

The nerve that ran along his spine tingled in the unfamiliar currents and the tiny scales on the back of his neck stood up. The Rockies and the Sandies weren't exactly enemies, but they were far from friends.

Sandies were peaceful, content to live where the fish were plentiful and life was easy, if a bit too close to humans. Rocky

Shore Merfolk preferred to live in places too rough for humans, in the sharp crags, where life was stubborn enough to cling to the rocks. They were far more warlike, settling their differences with violence and brutal magic.

Other structures were coming into view now, and shapes moved around up ahead.He skimmed the tops of the weeds, sticking as close as he could, but still keeping Kyri's brown hair, unadorned by her usual circlet of pearls, in his line of sight. She burst through the forest of weeds into the short stretch of rough ocean floor, still heading for the formation. Okala darted for a stone wall and edged along, careful to keep his weeds about him.

The few shapes moved in the darkness, clad in hard shells. Many of them had multiple legs and skittered into and around their homes, pulling snails and mollusks from the rocks and eating them, shells and all. They were dull and dark, greys and beige, sometimes only their movement alerted him to their presence. Okala no longer put faith in anonymity-- no one but he and his sister had the long scaled tails of the Sandy Shore Mer-folk, nor the bluish skin tone of the line of King Clyr. Okala, with his bright green and yellow tail and his blue hair, would stand out sharply in daylight and he was deeply relieved for the dark-ness, amplified in this shadowy world. At home on their sandy shore, there were few structures to hide the clear light of the moon.

Kyri darted straight up the largest peak of the forma-tion. Long hair and a blush of pink against the blackness. Okala dashed behind her. She had gone too far, she was in danger. But he knew by the thrashing of her tail and the stiffness of her limbs--she was determined.

Kyri, what have you done? She was always selfish and im-petuous, and she had a dramatic streak, but this was by far the most danger any of them had ever been in. She disappeared into a lit cave near the top. Okala didn't dare enter behind her, so stayed in the shadows below the mouth, listening hard.

'Who are you?' a high reedy voice asked. 'How did a Sandy

Shore Mermaid get in here? Guards, seize her!'

'No, please! I come with a gift!' Kyri's voice was a little too loud and shrill, but excited and breathless.

'Show me.'

'Your Grace, I have heard of your plans, about the war. I come to offer you our support.'

There was a long pause and the clicking of hard shell against the stone.

'Why, you're a princess, aren't you? Are you Manal's girl?'

'Kyri, daughter of King Clyr.' Her voice shook. She sounded frightened. Okala's chest tightened. *Oh, Kyri...*

'Clyr! Breen, do you hear that? Clyr's on our side. I'd never have imagined--'

'Please, your grace' Kyri interrupted. 'He isn't. But I think I can persuade him.'

There was another, longer pause.

'Kyri,' Kellac breathed slowly. 'I don't recognise your name. It's Marya who's next in line, isn't it? Or is it Okala?'

Okala flinched at the sound of his name so casually dropped by someone he'd never met.

'Marya is my father's heir, yes. And she agrees with him. I am the youngest of the daughters, and Okala is after me. My middle sisters don't care much for politics, and Okala is a fool. He's a split-fin, he loves humans more than his own people.'

That stung. It hurt that she would insult him to a stranger like that, and it wasn't true. He was fascinated by humans, that was no secret, but he didn't love them more than his family.

The king and someone else in the cave made noises of disgust.

'Disgraceful,' the other voice, a female, said.

He had the urge to burst into the cavern and defend himself, but he held his nerve.

'Yes,' Kyri agreed. 'Okala is not a part of this. But I can be. I see the future and I am proud to stand beside my fellow merfolk, wherever they live. I can persuade my father.'

'There was mention of a gift,' the female cut in.

'Yes,' Kyri said quickly. 'I had my Breaching today and I found something I hear you've been looking for. Sometime last year, there was a conflict amongst the humans at the palace they stole from us. One fell to her death in the sea. She was wearing this. It is very blue, isn't it?'

Someone gasped as a blue light flashed above Okala's head.

Chapter Five
Rhythlin Island

The tone of the table at breakfast was tense when Alois joined Sulat, Eaton, and Foth in the salon.

'So, the plan,' Sulat said, sitting with her glass of brandy. 'Scout the island, see what's going on. If they engage us, we defend ourselves and get back to *Meltythia*.'

'What if they flee?' Foth asked.

'We can make a plan to disable their ships and boats. Keep them there until the king can send reinforcements.'

'Maroon them on their own island,' Eaton said.

'We go in on boats, we look around and then we come back. If we can take prisoners and fight the others, we do. If not, we blast their ships before they can stop us, and go back to tell the king.'

Eaton and Foth nodded quietly.

'Good. Foth, you may want to go make a note in your log before you forget,' Sulat said, digging into her plate of buttered rolls.

Foth hopped up and snatched a fistful of crackers. 'Quite

right, Captain.'

As soon as his berth door shut, Sulat leaned forward and Alois and Eaton leaned closer. 'We don't have to destroy all the ships. If they have any in good repair, we can take one, maybe even a bigger one. Eaton, I'll give you a skeleton crew and we can take it back with us. Two ships at least is a fleet, start of a proper shipping company. We could expand into heavier cargo.'

Eaton sat back and Alois whistled. 'Look at you, getting ambitions. Whatever next?'

Sulat lifted her glass with her pinky finger out. 'Think I'm aiming too high, your lordship?'

'Not I, Captain. What would I know of it?' He emitted a pretentious nasally chuckle, imitating one of Johanne's friends. Sulat choked. 'Are you all right?' He pounded on her back, his normal lowly accent back in place.

'Ass,' she croaked.

Alois opened his mouth, as a voice outside cried, 'Land to port!'

Sulat leapt to her feet and Foth rushed back into the salon, a book clutched to his chest.

'Are we there already?' Alois asked, standing. His hands went instinctively to his hips where his guns and swordbelt used to be. 'I need to get my stuff.'

'Nearly,' Sulat said rushing up onto the steering deck where Alois, Eaton, and Foth queued up in the stairwell of her cabin. Darib's face was stern as he nudged the steering wheel gently to the left. Whatever the lookout had spotted, it was still far away.

Sulat dashed to her cabin and seized the spyglass from the drawer in her desk, then rushed to the bow of the ship, where they young brown-haired woman already stood, Alois and Eaton close behind her. Sulat snapped the spyglass open.

Yes! There, on the horizon, still a long way out, was a speck, barely perceptible against the murky lavender of pre-dawn.

'Is that Rhythlin, Ashryn?' she asked. The navigator pushed a pair of spectacles up the bridge of her nose and tightened her hold on the ledger in her arms.

'I think so, Captain,' she said slowly. 'If my calculations are accurate. But I've never tried to get to one of these islands on my own before.'

'I trust you.'

Ashryn adjusted her shoulders. 'I am prepared to say that it is, Captain.'

Trust your crew. You have them for a reason.

'All right. Eaton, make ready to drop anchor when it's safe to, and ready the boats.'

Eaton nodded and moved away, barking orders.

Sulat leaned against the railing. Eaton's voice faded into silence as she watched the island against the horizon.

Sulat approved the order to drop anchor far out from Rhythlin. The ocean floor was rough this close to so craggy an island and she didn't want to risk running aground. Alois, Sulat, Wese, and a couple of other crewmen climbed into a boat and lowered into the choppy water. Alois' muscles ached almost immediately as he rowed on the bobbing waves to the island.

I've gone soft at Parry House.

The boat bounced hard on the icy grey water, salty spray and small waves battering the passengers. The party tied the boat to an outcropping of rock and climbed onto land.

Alois checked his weapons and followed the others. A cool wind ruffled his stiff hair and the damp folds of his shirt. Weak sunlight struggled to break through the clouds as they picked their way over the jagged rocks and spread out in different directions. Alois wanted to stay with the group, but the plan was to split up. They all had fighting experience and could handle themselves until the sounds of a struggle called the others to their aide.

Rhythlin Island was made of chunks of limestone rock wedged together with deep crevasses and dark pools dotted about, nearly invisible until it was too late. There were no trees or grass, or apparently any living thing larger than the tiny fish and mollusks trapped in the tide pools.

An eerie stillness blanketed the island. Nothing moved, save for the other crewmen and *Meltythia* swaying out at sea under the grey sky. No pirates, no pirate ships or shanty towns. Nothing.

Then a sound-- soft, a wisp of something high and sweet carried on the breeze--a woman, or a young boy? Was it someone on the ship, their voice carrying all the way here?

No, there it was again. It sounded much closer.

Alois' heart leapt. If it was a woman, she might be a captive and she might be willing to betray the pirates who held her. If it was a boy, he might be tempted away. Or intimidated, or even used as ransom.

Alois listened hard for the voice again. *There*! He set off in the direction it came from as fast as he could while keeping careful not to slip.

He climbed down and down, ever closer to the voice. It sang a haunting and sad melody, yet with a bit of a dance in it. Perhaps it was a love song, some lament for a girl left at some faraway port town.

Johanne's face flashed across Alois' mind. He could relate. He didn't want to be here on this cold bleak island so close to a cursed area of sea. He himself wasn't sure if he'd make it back to her alive. But, at least, he had something in common with this boy. If he spoke Viehlish, he had a chance at creating a bond.

He'd followed a singing voice a few times before, the last time to a tower in the woods. A magic girl lived up there and he had rescued her, setting her up with the landlord at his favourite tavern. She had become a good friend since then. And, many years previous to that, he'd realised that he was in love with Johanne while she sang and played guitar, one lonely night. Good things live at the end of sweet songs.

Alois followed the voice for what felt like forever, splashing through cold streams and picking his way over slippery and ragged rocks, and didn't seem to get any closer. The voice followed him, yet stay ahead, filling the air rather than coming from one place. He stopped, trying to decide where to go next. He'd lost sight of the other men from the crew and he was all alone in knee-deep water.

The world spun like he was dizzy or drunk, the air suddenly thin. Even the sound of the waves lapping at the craggy shores had faded, leaving him alone in this silent grey fog.

Something like a face flickered in the water and disappeared. Alois dropped to his knees and groped around, lurching forward as he stumbled across an underwater cliff. He kicked out and backwards, resettling in the shallows. The face rose out of the pool, attached to the long copper hair and slender tangrey body of a young woman. Her nude torso, covered in a shimmer like sand, rose out of the water as she continued to sing.

Alois stared at her, mesmerised. Her voice was clear and sweet and filled Alois' ears, blocking out the rest of the world. No seagulls cried, no wood creaked-- only her singing.

The woman's lips moved slowly and her gold eyes never strayed from his. She leaned forward, he couldn't turn away. She wrapped a cold, wet arm around his neck and drew him close. Their lips met and Alois' head swam as he closed his eyes. She smelled of the sea and the cold wind of the island and something else he couldn't quite...

'My lord!' a shout broke through Alois' mind and the woman jumped violently.

'Ow!' Alois cried as something sharp cut his lip. In a flash of yellow and grey, the woman was gone and Alois realised that he had sunk to his neck in the deep ravine beneath the tide pool.

Wese rushed over to him and he and Eaton hauled Alois

out by his arms. The cut on his lip stung, hot blood pouring down his chin. He dabbed at it and found a pearly substance mingling with the crimson blood.

'The kiss of the mermaid,' Wese murmured solemnly.

'The what?' Alois asked, dazed. *Was Eaton always a twin? How is he able to stand when the world is moving so? Why am I wet?*

'A mermaid, my lord. She has claimed you as her own. It's lucky we found you, or she'd have taken you with her.'

Muffled voices rose over the silence and Sulat trained her gun in their direction. The plan was to come running if someone raised the alarm, but she couldn't tell where the sound was coming from. It was creepy out here, everything strange and distorted, nothing fixed or certain. For a barren island with no trees, sound surely didn't travel as it should.

Suddenly, Wese and Eaton burst over a crest of rock, dragging Alois between them.

Bloody idiot! What did you do? She rushed toward them as quickly as she dared, careful not to drop her gun, in case someone saw their opportunity.

'Not...pirates,' Wese panted when he spotted her. 'Gotta...the ship. Not...safe.'

'What happened?' Sulat asked.

'Mermaid kissed him,' Eaton gasped. Alois' eyes slid out of focus and his legs twitched under him.

Shit. I knew something like this would happen.

'Gotta go, Cap'n,' Wese spat.

Sulat beckoned them back to the boat as the other two crewmen came running toward the commotion. The word 'mermaid' was whispered back and forth all the way to the ship. They all helped Alois climb the wooden stairway that jutted from the hull up to the deck.

'Weigh anchor!' Sulat shouted at the men on the focsle.

They leapt into action, heaving the capstan. 'Hoist sails! Hard a'starboard and set a course back for Viehland!'

'What happened out there, Captain?' Ashryn asked, jotting notes in her ledger, Foth close behind her. Three men dashed to the capstan to haul up the anchor and two more scurried up the masts to take down sails.

'Mermaid,' Sulat said quietly. 'I'll tell you more once we're underway. The king's information was wrong, no need to stick around. Take us west of the Islands. I don't want to bother with them and I don't want to risk the Squalls.' Ashryn nodded and dashed for the stern deck and the helmsman.

'What'll we do with him, ma'am?' Wese asked stepping close. 'Meaning no disrespect, but he's a liability, being Kissed and all.'

'Lock him in the hold,' Eaton grunted. The other crewmen nodded. Alois' head lolled.

Sulat ran a hand over her headscarf. *Think, Sulat.* The clink of the anchor chain picked at her nerves. 'Put him in his cabin. Lock him in, and bring me the key. I can handle him, if I need to.'

Wese knuckled his brow and the men led Alois away. Sulat checked everyone was going about their duties, then went to her cabin. She could really use a glass of brandy to settle her down. The ship rocked and swayed as the anchor disengaged. Sulat uncorked the bottle, poured a glass, and raised it to her lips.

'On deck, all hands!' Eaton's voice shouted from across the ship, ringing the bell loud and hard. The clatter of footsteps thundered all around her. Something heavy rolled under the ship.

'What now?' she whispered, heading up the stairs. The ship's bell clanged loud and urgent.

'Ma'am,' Wese knocked outside, his voice shrill. 'Ma'am, you'll want to come out now. Somethin's happenin'.'

Sulat dashed out onto the deck. A hundred shapes swirled around the ship and sharpened into lumps that rose up out of the water. Some were the green of sea moss or the grey of stone or even the reddish brown of seaweed. They exposed their faces to Sulat and her ship.

The armourer started distributing muskets and the quarter gunners shouted commands. The men pointed their guns down into the water, but the people in the water grinned with mouths full of sharp teeth.

'Merfolk,' Wese breathed beside her, pulling off his hat and clutching it to his chest. 'By the souls and all the stars...'

'What's going on here?' Sulat asked no one in particular. There was something strange and menacing in the way the merfolk remained still and silent, surrounding her. The clinking of the anchor chain continued in the background, rattling her teeth as she struggled to find the right words.

'I am Captain Sulat. I have been sent by His Majesty King Bertold of Viehland to investigate the disappearance of ships in this area and I believe now that you are the cause. So, I ask you, why are you attacking our peaceful merchant vessels, and what can I offer you to make you stop?'

Sulat gripped the smooth wet wood under her fingers as the sea lurched. A great mount of water swelled before her, rising and rising before finally breaking over the back of an enormous grey shark. It breached the water and dove back down, releasing a shell ridden by a horrifying creature: a man with orange and white speckled skin, joined at the waist to a body like a lobster stretching out behind him, on at least ten spindly red legs and heavy green and blue armour. From his neck glinted a dazzling star sapphire: the Day Star.

'What the shit is that?' she screamed, her voice lost over the crashing of the waves and the shouts of the men on deck. A cacophony of booms erupted as those with loaded guns fired on the apparition, but the shots fell uselessly into the water. The creature before them held his arms wide, a wicked spear with trailing seaweeds in one fist, his blue lips spread wide in a manic grin.

He brought a second pair of fists together in front of him in a loud booming clap.

The air sparkled and rippled. Meltythia exploded beneath Sulat. She flew through the air and dropped into the freezing water. A splintered beam fell on top of her, pushing her deeper. She reached and pulled for the surface but sank lower and lower, tangling in rope and shredded sail. She kicked her legs, straining every muscle as the water around her filled with bodies and debris. Rope, chunks of wood, hunks of twisted metal. A hand drifted past her, still clutching a cutlass, and trailing blood.

The beam pulled her down deeper, she couldn't fight it. Sharp shapes flipped all around her. A flash of bright green nearly caught her in the face.

I'm going to die. I'm going to die. I won't die like this.

Her lungs screamed. Only her will prevented her from giving up and breathing in a lungful of saltwater. She fumbled with the rope at her waist, twisting and wriggling. It loosened and slipped from her and she pumped her legs back to the top. But the strain of the struggle tired her and she drifted the last few feet. Her vision blurred as the water broke over her head.

'Sulat!' a voice called her name, but she couldn't respond. She sucked in as much icy thin air as her lungs would allow. They expanded to the point that she felt they would burst.

And she knew no more.

Chapter Six

Okala

Okala had been awake all night, hovering vigilant close to Kyri's room. He wasn't sleepy at all, despite the travel and lack of sleep. Kyri was in trouble, whether she was treated like visiting royalty or not, whether she knew it or not.

He was hiding in a gravelly alcove, shielding his bright fin with algae, when the call went out. At first, it was a low hum, then came the grinding, followed by whoops, chirps, clicks, and screeches as merfolk came out of their homes and congregated in the village square. Something vibrated the water, and Okala's dorsal nerve hummed.

What is that?

He poked his head out as far as he dared, pulling it back in like a turtle when a group of black-and-white sea snake-bodied merfolk wriggled by, chattering excitedly.

'Humans,' one of them whispered as she dove straight out of a hole in the limestone.

Oh no!

On the surface of the water, to the west, floated a patch of black in the sun streaked grey-- a slim rectangle, pointed at one end. A ship.

His heart shrank.

As one, the assembled merfolk rose up, some sliding into holes in the limestone, some hovering beneath the surface in open water.

Oh no, what do I do?

How could he save them, or even help them, when there were so many merfolk heading for them? And he couldn't leave Kyri, that's why he was here. Thankfully, she hadn't joined the others. She was still enough a Sandy Shore Mermaid that she hadn't descended to eating humans.

But what could be done about the humans? Perhaps, if he saved a few, saved some, it might soothe his guilt.

He had to try.

It was the hardest thing he'd ever done, or ever hoped to do again, to wait as the water vibrated so violently around him that he thought he'd lose his scales, his nerve so tight he wanted to scream.

But that was nothing compared to what happened next. When King Kellac rode to the surface, the tension sharpened, and when that terrible explosion destroyed the ship, Okala thought his head would explode and his heart would break at the same time. Bodies fell all around him, the closest he'd ever been to real humans. And if they'd opened their eyes and seen him, they'd have thought him one of the others. He couldn't bear that.

He wanted to run away, to get Kyri while the king and most of the court were feeding, to go home and sob until he couldn't anymore.

Merfolk darted around him, catching their prey, sometimes fighting over pieces. He fought the urge to throw up as an arm floated past, clutching a sword. The smell of blood lingered in the current and soured his stomach.

Someone fell right in front of him, nearly on top of him. A human woman dragged down by a piece of wood. She kicked and struggled, but the rope was tight around her. He rushed forward and helped, staying out of the way of her wild limbs. Eventually, she got free and made it back to the surface, where she went limp and floated. He wanted to go to her, to help, but he couldn't risk it. He made a silent prayer to the tides and backed away from the carnage.

Back in the hallway outside Kyri's room, he wept. It was disgusting to Sandy Shore Merfolk that Rockies ate people, but he'd never imagined it in detail.

The court slowly returned, wandering right past the limpets clinging to the rocks, picking their teeth and preening. Some wiped blood from their faces and others left it there like macabre adornment.

Okala cast his eyes back to the surface, at the specks of wreckage floating on the surface.

Maybe, maybe someone survived. Maybe...

But how? How could someone have gotten past that bloodthirsty hoard? He thought of the woman he'd helped and a wave of grief washed over him again.

I have to at least look. Be brave, Okala, for once. Get past your grief and disgust, you might be able to save one.

He waited for his moment and went back to the wreck site.

Flat chunks of wood, tangles of rope, and shreds of fabric blanketed the water, stained red. He choked back tears as he waded in, overturning anything flat, thrusting his hands into anything soft.

Is that? Yes!

He felt flesh-- smooth, firm, warm flesh. He pushed the plank back and swallowed a gulp of sea water, not even wincing at the metallic taste.

It was the woman he'd helped, and she was alive!

He pushed her up by the waist and threw her over his shoulder, pounding his tail to keep them both above the water.

'Nearest island,' he muttered, scanning the horizon. There was one close, but close by merfolk standards.

Her face was peaceful and relaxed. He opened her mouth and forced air from his lungs into her, then pinched her lips and nose closed before diving underwater and swimming fast for land.

Hold on, please hold on. She thrashed against him and he held her tighter.

Finally, they reached the beach and he threw her as hard as he could. She didn't go far, his arms weren't strong and he couldn't leave the water. But her head landed above the waves, and that was what mattered. She coughed hard, and lay still.

Oh no.

He pulled himself as far up the beach as he dared and put his head to her belly.

Heartbeat! She's still fighting.

His own heart swelled. If he'd found her, there might be more.

He said another prayer and flipped back into the water.

Sulat's eyes fluttered open to blinding white light. She lay still on her back, a breeze chilling her wet skin.

The memory thundered through her mind like a cannon-ball.

Meltythia. Alois.

She sat up, her breath caught in her chest. It was like being underwater again, gasping for air. Her heart pounded in her chest, thudding against her ribcage. She kicked at the gravelly grey sand and surf, struggling to stand, and fell over with a splash.

Where am I? A tall peak of sandstone loomed like a mountain behind her. *This isn't Rhythlin. I have to get away. I have to find Alois.*

She splashed onto unsteady feet and stumbled deeper into the sea. Splinters of hull floated on the water, tangled up with rope and shreds of canvas. The ground fell away from her and she stood in the icy surf lapping and foaming against her calves.

My crew. A parade of faces flashed across her mind. Dependable Eaton, legendary Wese, brave Ashryn. Even the new men she hadn't gotten a chance to know well yet.

Alois. Where is Alois?

She thrashed into water up to her knees, staring wildly around for any clue.

'What are you looking for?' a voice asked. Sulat whirled around, ripping her blunderbuss from her thigh holster. The undertow caught her and pulled her legs out from under her, and she fell back into the water. Something green flipped over a nearby rock and hid, peeking over the top: bright blue hair over a young face, and broad, muscular, bluish-pink shoulders.

Sulat rolled onto all fours and splashed to drier stones. He held up his hands.

'I'm a friend!' he cried. Water flew from the blunderbuss as she ran. *Shit.* It was too wet to shoot, even if she wanted to.

'Who are you?' she snarled, tossing her gun aside and drawing her rapier.

'I'm not the one who kissed your friend. Her name is Breen. I'm not like her.'

'Who are *you*?' Sulat asked again, shaking.

'My name is Okala. My father is King Clyr. I'm a sandy shore merman.'

'What does that mean?' Sulat panted, the cold air stinging all the way down.

'We're peaceful, friendly. I saved you. And him.' The boy gestured a webbed hand at something behind Sulat. She hesitated, in case he would use her distraction, but she couldn't resist.

Some way down the beach lay another figure half in the surf; large, with shaggy brown hair and a blue-grey leather coat. Sulat sprinted to him, ignoring the pain in her calves, and threw herself beside his body. She rolled Alois toward her and peeled open an eyelid. His pupil shrank in the sharp light and she didn't fight the sob-laugh. She rolled back onto her heels and hugged herself until she got her breathing under control again.

'He was under a piece of wood,' the merman said. He had followed her, keeping to the water, holding a chunk of hull in front of him like a shield.

'What happened to the rest of my men?' Sulat asked, her throat tight. The boy didn't answer, but continued to stare. Sulat wasn't much good at reading faces, but she could guess what that meant.

She pressed a wrist to her mouth, unsure if she would scream or throw up. Merfolk were reputed to eat people. Is that what happened? Part of her needed to know, but another part desperately did not want to.

This is my fault. This is all my fault.

Alois' skin was cold and a trickle of blood leaked from a wound somewhere under his hair.

'Is he important to you?' the merman asked, edging a little closer.

'They were all important to me,' Sulat choked, blinking back hot tears. 'Were there any other survivors?'

'I'm sorry.'

I have to get him out of these wet clothes or he'll catch a chill. I need a fire, but... She patted herself all over, but she had left everything on the ship. Why would she have taken a flint with her to scout the island? She searched Alois' jacket pocket, he usually kept one on him when they were on the road. Nothing. Probably the same logic. She smacked the hard leather of his shoulder armour. *You're even more useless than you were before. How did you manage that?*

'What are you looking for?' the merman asked, still hiding behind his wooden plank in the shallows. Sulat huffed, her nerves straining.

'You ask a lot of questions.'

'I'm sorry, I want to help. I've always been fascinated by humans.'

Sulat rolled back onto her heels and rubbed her boots to keep her anger in check. 'You want to help me? Go find me a piece of flint or a flat piece of glass.'

That got rid of him. He said he was a nice merman, but they probably all said that just before they Kissed you or ripped your flesh off with their sharp fish teeth.

She shivered. The breeze pierced her emotional agitation and the heavy wool captain's coat. She unbuttoned Alois' shirt and pulled it back, exposing the pale hairy skin to the grey sky. He'd be cold, but he'd be dry. She pulled one of his pistols from his holster and examined it. The flint was still good.

There was a bundle of sail nearby that had dry patches. She drew her dagger and cut a tiny piece, a little bigger than the powder pan of Alois' gun. She dug a hole in the gravel behind a pile of rocks that looked like an eroded ancient wall, hoping the structure would provide a shield against the wind. She filled the hole with driftwood and bits of dry rope, and prepared the gun. She pulled the hammer back, scooped the wet powder out, laid the sailcloth across the pan, and lowered the pan cover. She pointed the muzzle straight at the ground in case the gun was dry enough to actually fire, and pulled the trigger. It made a small click as the hammer fell, scraping flint against the steel frizzen. Sulat pulled out the smouldering linen and laid it against the rope, blowing on it to keep it alive. The red glow expanded and engulfed the rope. A flame leapt up and soon all of the rope was ablaze. The driftwood crackled and popped, and ignited as well.

Sulat sat beside it, poking at it with a longer stick until she was satisfied with its height. The prospect of dragging Alois' body closer and pulling wet clothes off his limp, heavy limbs didn't appeal, but it distracted her, and he couldn't do it for himself.

She stood with a groan and hooked her arms under his. She dug her heels hard into the stones and little by little got him within a safe distance of the fire.

'Sorry about the cuts and bruises. You'll forgive me,' she muttered.

'Is this a good enough piece of glass?' The merman was back, holding up a quizzing glass on a long gold chain. Foth's. 'I'm sorry, all the rest either wasn't flat or was too big.' He held his hands up to about the size of a porthole.

Sulat blinked at him. *Souls, he did as I asked.*

'Thanks, but I don't need it now.' *I was only trying to get rid of you.*

'Now what are you doing?' The merman put the quizzing glass in a slimy brown pouch at his waist and cocked his blue head at her.

'He needs to get out of his wet clothes.'

'It looks difficult.'

'Yeah.' Sulat grunted, hauling off the dripping leather jacket. She puffed out her cheeks and contemplated how to get the shirt off without ripping it. They wouldn't be able to change clothes again for a long while.

'I wish I could help you,' the boy said. 'But I'm not much good on land.'

Thank the souls for that. 'You're fine where you are.'

Sulat pulled Alois a little higher up the shore and yanked off his heavy boots, tossing them aside. Depending on how high high tide was, they might be safe from the merfolk for a while.

'I won't hurt you,' the boy said, edging closer. 'I would never hurt a human.'

'Tell you what.' Sulat was near her wits' end with his incessant chattering. 'What's your name, again?'

'Okala,' the merman said eagerly.

'Okala, good. How about you catch a couple fish? You lot can catch fish, right?'

Okala nodded enthusiastically and dove into the surf, his

green and yellow tail flashing.

Sulat pulled off Alois' stockings, 'He wouldn't have wanted to see this next bit anyway, no matter how much he loves humans.' She took hold of the waistband of Alois' trousers and pulled.

Okala returned a little while later, after Sulat had laid a bit of dry canvas over Alois. He held up a couple of fat fish and Sulat motioned for him to throw them at her. She sliced them open with her utility knife, gutted them, and propped them on sticks over the fire.

Sulat hung Alois' clothes on the wall of stones near the fire to dry, then stripped off her own. She tried to use another piece of sail to hide her own modesty, but it was cumbersome and the wind made it more of an ordeal than it needed to be. Okala hovered in the shallows, watching her, but in the same way as an animal or small child would do.

'My people think I'm odd because I'm so interested in humans.' His tone was conversational as he sectioned chunks of his blue hair and braided them together.

'There are probably humans who study your folk,' Sulat said, belting her sheet with a length of rope and hanging her clothes next to Alois'. 'People are interested by what's different.'

'Oh, I forgot, I brought you something else!' Okala cried, digging in his pouch. Something shiny landed at her feet in the sand-- a flask.

'I don't know what's in it, but every human I've ever seen has had one. I thought it might cheer you up.'

Sulat opened it and sniffed--brandy. Cheap, but strong. She took a deep swig and her muscles relaxed. Then she tensed again, her stomach suddenly sour. 'Did this come from the wreck?'

'No. It came from an island nearby. The smugglers use it to

hide things.'

Her heart leapt. 'How far away, Okala? What else is there?'

'Loads. There's gold and weapons and barrels.' Okala answered enthusiastically. 'There's a boat, too! I can bring it!' he said, flipping away.

'No. Wait until he wakes up.' She jerked her chin at Alois. 'I don't want to leave him here alone. And naked.'

She cast her eye out to sea, and she remembered something.

'Where are we? This isn't Rhythlin Island.'

'This is Decombre Island. I wanted to get you away from the Rockies. The one the smugglers use is Grocachee Island.'

'So we're going closer to Vurdia,' Sulat said. *Alois is not going to like that.*

Muffled voices rumbled nearby and Alois smelled smoke. Something cool brushed his skin and he opened his eyes to the dark night sky. The cut on his lip had gone cold, like he had a piece of icy stuck there. He sat up and jumped as the stiff canvas sheet fell away from his bare chest and he found he was completely naked under it. He pulled it tight across him. Sulat sat a little way away, next to a roaring bonfire, talking to the sea.

Oh no, she's really lost it this time.

'Sulat?' he called, his voice hoarse from disuse and salt water. She stood, also wrapped in sailcloth, and helped him to stand. He clutched his covering tighter as he leaned on her and stumbled closer to the fire. 'You lost your clothes, too?'

'Idiot,' she said and dropped him in the gravel. Something soft hit him in the face. It was his shirt. He gratefully pulled it on and noticed the wall with the rest of their clothes, and the fish skewered on stocks over the fire.

'What would I do without you?' he groaned.

'You'd be safe at home with Johanne.'

'Oh Johanne, *souls*. She'll be worried sick when she finds out.'

'Who's Johanne?' a male voice asked. A head bobbed in the water. Alois leapt back, scooting through the stones as fast as he could, away from that blue hair and orange eyes.

'Relax,' Sulat said, jabbing the fire with a stick of driftwood. 'This is Okala, he's the good kind of merman. He saved us and he's been helping me. Have some brandy.' She held a flask out to him and he drank deeply. It eased the tightness for a moment, before turning to disgust.

'Is this from the ship?'

'No, it's from a smugglers' cave,' Sulat said. Her tone implied she'd already had this conversation once.

I was unconscious. How was I to know? Or that there are different kinds of merfolk. Or that we've made friends with them.

'Do your people bite?' Alois asked, as the cut on his lip throbbed.

The boy hesitated. 'All merfolk *can*, technically, but no one really does, except the rocky shore merfolk. Breen is one of them.'

'Who's Breen?'

'She's the one who Kissed you.'

'How do you know?'

'We know when a human has been claimed. We can't harm you now, even if we wanted to. You are hers, for good or bad.'

'Well, there's a blessing, I suppose,' Alois grumbled, and picked a chunk of fish off the stick. It was salty and firm, and tasted delicious.

'Did you say there was a boat in the cave?' Sulat asked.

'Yes!' Okala perked up, his orange eyes shining. 'I can bring it.'

'We should go to the cave, now we're all awake. It's less exposed.'

The merman dove under the waves and disappeared.

Now that Alois was awake and didn't need Sulat fussing over him, there was nothing for her to do, nothing to hold back her thoughts. The dam broke and she spiralled into the familiar blackness.

Alois scooted closer to her.

Souls, please don't talk.

'It's not your fault, you know,' he said softly. He turned to her and his fingers twitched like he wanted to touch her. *Don't.*

She wanted to speak, to correct him, but her throat tightened, a hard lump rising. Her eyes stung and the tip of her nose felt swollen and hot. She shook her head, keeping her attention on the steady waves.

'Just because you're captain doesn't mean everything lands on you.'

'Yes, it does,' she croaked, rubbing the tattoo on her neck. She wanted to scratch it off. The captain goes down with the ship. Crew before captain. All of the other expressions that illustrated the duty the leader had to the men under her command. All of those lives.

'Renir didn't know what was out here. All you were meant to do was come look. You tried to run, to get everyone to safety. What could you have done to save them?'

'I could have brought another ship. What were we doing, just my little twenty-crew Courser? Even against human pirates, what was I thinking? We only have a dozen falconets. *Had.*'

'You were just a scout. Renir needed an answer quickly. Killing the pirates would have been a bonus.'

'And now he won't get his answer at all. Bloody waste of twenty good lives. Do you know how Wese got his star? Another ship he served went down in the Squalls, and he rowed the crew back to Viehland in a lifeboat. Ashryn was an orphan and had a little brother she was providing for. Now he's all alone. Eaton--' The lump in her throat choked her.

'I'm sorry you have to carry all of this.' Alois moved closer and put an arm around her shoulders. She wanted to throw him off, to storm away. But she also didn't want to be alone. She wanted to put her head on his shoulder and sob until she fell asleep. The conflict ate at her, gnawed her insides until she was hollow and numb. 'But they chose their fates, you can't take that from them.'

'No one chooses to be blown up and eaten alive.'

'They chose the sea. They could have been farmhands or innkeepers or servants. But they were men of the sea, all of them. They knew the risks, and put freedom and adventure over safety and stability. You and I know that struggle. When you love someone, you want to keep them safe. But you can't take away their freedom to make their own choices. You have to love them anyway and do what you can for them. And you did. You locked me in my cabin.' He chuckled and rubbed the back of his neck. 'Because I'm bloody useless and I would have been a danger on deck. But those men were good, and they died with honour.'

Sulat snorted. '*Honour*. What's the point of honour? Honour is what you tell yourself to feel better for being stupid.' She threw his arm off her shoulder and stomped away.

The faces paraded mercilessly before her. Ashryn's sheepish toothy smile, Darib's noble stoicism. Wese, Eaton, and all of the others who had shared her ship with her. Even Foth, annoying as he was, didn't deserve to die like that.

She had been so full of hope. Her ship, her first mission. She would do this job for Renir, then she would be free to sail as a merchant, and she would specialise in tea and spices, maybe smuggle a little up and down the coasts. She might even trade in information, if she had to.

But now it was all gone. *Meltythia* was in splinters and shreds. The crew was dead, all of those hopeful lives snuffed out like they'd never existed.

It was cold away from the fire. Autumn was coming, the chill much swifter at the waterline than it was inland. The stars shone bright in the diamond clear sky.

It was said that when someone died, their soul became a star in the sky, and that's why it was milder to swear on stars than souls.

Sulat liked that idea, to die and join the other points of light, so far above humanity, so far removed from all the turmoil and cruelty, to remain forever in that still silence.

The moon was thin, but still there was plenty of light to see the waves and avoid wandering into the sea. They soothed her, the rush and hum of the foam cooling the rage bubbling inside her.

She hugged her arms around herself. Alois was still sitting by the fire. He shouldn't even have been there. If he hadn't come, who else might Okala have saved? Or would she be on this island alone? Or dead?

Quiet splashing heralded the merman's return, a small rowboat bobbing in the water between the two big boulders. Sulat kicked at a shell and started slowly back.

'Where's Sulat?' Okala's voice asked.

'She needed a minute,' Alois said. 'She blames herself for what happened.'

'It wasn't your fault,' Okala said to her as she came closer to the fire. 'It was King Kellac's fault.'

'Who's King Kellac?' Sulat asked.

'He's the merman who broke your ship. He's the Rocky Shore king, or rather, one of them. He wants a war with the humans of Viehland to win back Ildecoke Island.'

Ringing filled Sulat's head.

'A war. Perfect. This keeps getting better.' She splashed into the water to drag the boat in.

Alois stood a little taller, adjusting the gun belt at his hips. 'Tell me everything, Okala.'

Alois and Sulat climbed into the rowboat and Okala helped steer them through the dark water, chattering all the while about merfolk, about the history and other colonies. Sulat was only half listening, her eyes fixed to the stars sparkling over inky black waves.

'I'm Sandy Shore. We live near sandy beaches and we're the friendliest to humans. Then there are the Rocky Shore--you've met them, this is their territory. The Open Sea merfolk mostly leave people alone and they like to be left alone. They live in the Squalls and out west. They don't even eat fish, really, mostly krill and seaweed. Then there are the Deep Sea merfolk. And they're...odd.'

'Odd?' Alois snorted. 'Odd objectively, or odd for merfolk?'

'Both?' Okala said. 'Some of them glow. They talk in riddles and pictures. Sometimes they come to shallower water to deliver prophecies and whatnot. We try to avoid them if we can.'

'What are you doing here, then? In Rocky Shore territory?' Sulat asked.

'My sister snuck out of our colony to come meet with King Kellac. She's trying to form an alliance.' Okala said. A round shape leaned out of the darkness. 'That's Grocachee Island. I'll take you into the Smuggler's cave.'

The new island, further south, was a rock cave, poking out of the sea, a pyramid of black against the stars. Crates, barrels, and sacks lined the walls like a crescent shaped warehouse.

'We could fill our pockets with all of this stuff and no one would be the wiser!' Alois puffed his cheeks out, jumping onto the makeshift jetty and strapping a rope around the belaying pin to moor. 'If only there was food.'

'There might be hard tack--*might*.' Sulat wrinkled her nose. 'This cave is damp, food won't last long here. How close are we to land, Okala?'

'Not far,' Okala said enthusiastically. 'It's a couple of hours south for me, so maybe half a day for you.'

Alois froze and turned slowly. 'South?' *Oh no, I won't deal with the Vurdence, on top of everything else.*

'We're closest to Vurdia.' Sulat tensed, sensing the fight. 'You're going to have to bite your tongue for a couple of days. It may be a long shot, but we'd be on solid land, and that's better than being in the middle of the ocean with no food. And I'm not going past Rhythlin again. Not right now.'

'I can get you food,' Okala offered. Alois and Sulat both ignored him.

'Why can't we row back to Viehland?' Alois asked, heat rising in his face.

'Do you know how to navigate?' Sulat put a hand on her hip.

'You said you made charts on your last ship.'

'I had my sextant and other charts. I can't do it by the stars alone.'

'I could help,' Okala offered.

'No.' Both humans said at once. He had helped get them from one island to another, but getting all the way back to Viehland required more trust than either of them wanted to put in a merman who may or may not eat people.

'My ship is destroyed, my crew is dead,' Sulat said. 'Your wife will find that out soon, and we have a war to prevent.'

'Sulat, I have been through a war, a war between humans and a race of magical creatures. I can tell you right now that the Vurdence will not help us, because they *bloody* didn't last time!' Alois shouted, waving an arm in a vague direction. 'It wasn't centuries ago, it wasn't back in the mists of time, it was eight years ago and it was the same kings. It's how they are. If they're not affected, they won't lift a finger to help.'

'This affects trade. They still rely on Viehlish and Cavender goods, it's in their interest to help us deal with the problem.'

'And what, trade only happens across water? There's no need to help with a war on land?'

'This is not about the bloody ettins!' Sulat shouted back, throwing down the linen in her arms. 'This is about you being pig-headed and angry.'

'No, this is about you being stubborn and bossy!'

'All right, look. I'm taking the boat and I'm going to Vurdia.' Sulat's voice turned matter-of-fact, the fire gone.

'And leave me here to starve?'

'No, you're choosing to stay here and starve.'

'I can get fish,' Okala tried again.

'What if I took the boat and went back to Viehland?' Alois asked.

'My ship, my boat.'

'This boat didn't come from your ship.'

'Well, I'm the only one licensed to captain a ship.'

'No, your license--' Alois stopped himself. *Too far, too far. It's not worth that.* Sulat's face blanched, her eyes huge and hurt, her lips parted in shock. *Too far.*

A sweet, ethereal sound filled the cave, lilting and melodic. Sulat's whole body slackened and her expression cleared as she turned to gaze at Okala.

Alois' throat went dry and the cold spot on his lip throbbed. He ripped a pistol from his jacket and pointed it at the merman. It was probably still too damp to fire, but perhaps the boy didn't know.

'Stop that. Let her go,' he snarled.

Okala's lips snapped shut and he sank into the water. 'I was only trying to stop you fighting.'

Sulat shook her head like she had water in her ears, and the emotion returned to her face. Alois dropped his head and reached out for her. She slapped his hand away. He pulled her into a hug, but she held her arms stiff against her sides.

'All right. I'll row. We'll go to Vurdia and I'll see if I can get an audience.' Alois swallowed the bile climbing his throat.

'With...someone.' He pulled back and took her hands. She wouldn't look at him. 'I'm sorry. I shouldn't have said that.'

Sulat pulled her hands away and stomped deeper into the cave, throwing an acid glare at the merman.

'Will she be all right?' Okala's voice was low and soft, his young face anxious. He was a merman, and therefore dangerous, but there was something about the earnestness in his eyes that Alois just couldn't hate.

He's just a kid. A really big kid with lots of sharp teeth. He could have eaten one of us by now and hasn't. He's just a clumsy kid.

'Yeah. She's tough,' Alois said. *But not for a while.* 'Don't you ever sing again.'

Okala nodded. 'So you're going to Vurdia, for sure.'

Alois cast another long look at Sulat, angrily throwing crates around. 'Yes.'

It took all night to sort through the stash and load the small boat with supplies: a couple of valuables, and a couple of tinderboxes, as well as extra shot for the guns, a small barrel of fresh-enough water, and some oilcloths to keep everything dry. Then they pushed the boat out to sea and jumped in. They both took up oars, sitting awkwardly side by side, and rowed across the open ocean, following Okala's bright fins.

Chapter Seven
Bait

'The question is how we're going to do it.' King Kellac paced back and forth on his red legs.

'I'm still in favour of invasion,' Breen said, picking at her fingernails. Her claim had gotten away, and though she'd fed handsomely on that shipwreck, it did nothing to soothe her hunger for revenge.

'No, negotiation is the wisest course,' Kellac said.

Breen scoffed. 'Negotiate with humans. To what end, Your Highness? They don't see reason...they did this to us to begin with. You'll go to him in the name of diplomacy, but he will take your respect as subservience and he will brush you off, or worse. Perhaps he'll call you a threat and kill you. Then they'll come out here and kill us.'

'They may want to kill us all, but they can't reach us here with their spears and arrows. And their guns are less than useless in the water. They may have the will to kill us but it's their own fault that we're beyond their reach.'

'And if we send a delegation? There will be blood-- I have

seen it.'

'There may be, but why not try peace first? It is a better plan for lasting change. If we extend the hand of peace and they do--on the slight chance that they do-- *accept*, it will be a peaceful treaty and it will be treated with grace. There will be an adjustment period, but it will be successful. If we begin with violence, we will go forth with violence forever. There will never be peace.'

Breen glared at the king. The spell had held, his body remained bright green and scarlet, but where was the bloodlust now? Had it faded? Was it ever there, or did she want it so badly she convinced herself he'd truly changed?

'For the minority group,' Breen corrected. 'If we invade successfully, we become the dominant and we decide when there is peace and when there is conflict.'

'Will there ever be peace, Breen?' Kellac asked slyly.

'Perhaps, once they accept their place. Or leave.' Breen shook her head. *Enough of this banter*. 'The time is now. I have seen it. We will be successful. But we must strike decisively. There can be no hesitation.'

'I will not storm the island, Breen, not without assurance.'

'Assurance of what?'

'The king must be on the beach when we arrive. We must at least try peace first. If it fails, you may have your invasion. But we will try peace first.'

Breen thrashed her tail, but inclined her head and retired to her cave.

She combed her hair as she paced, frustrated and angry, going over the things she should have said, points she could have made. The fact remained that Kellac was king and she had no choice but to obey if she wanted to stay close to him. Her power evaporated if she were expelled for being a problem.

How am I going to negotiate peace?

Please, Mr King, sir, we'd like our island back. We know that you're living in our palace and there's a city here now and that you run your entire country from our home, but can we have it back, please?

She snorted. How could a mermaid, or even King Kellac, effectively negotiate? They were waves crashing against a cliff. They may make change eventually, but it would take a long time.

Unless there was a fissure in the rock. Something there already, a flaw that weakened the structure.

That's it! She needed someone already there, another human to argue for them. *THE HUMANS WILL TURN ON EACH OTHER.*

She screamed a laugh and sat herself at her chair, throwing her face to the surface.

'Where are you, my pets?'

Flashes of what her claims saw passed across her vision and voices chattered over the top of each other: the interior of a house, a child with a gappy grin, the hold of a ship, the open sea from a dock, blank blue sky, the face of a dark-skinned woman, a plate of food, a ceramic pot; 'souls I'm tired,' 'Who's a good boy, then?', 'storm's coming in,' 'good day for sailing,' 'political equivalent of Bertold's pet monkey,' 'I paid six crivas for this?' 'I'm never touching brandy again.'

What was that? It went by too fast. Did I hear Bertold?

Breen focused closer. It has been a woman's face. Which one of them was with a woman? There had been one...

There she is! That red headscarf, the defiance in her brown eyes...she was familiar. Where had Breen seen her before?

A memory flashed of the woman on the deck of a ship, shouting. It was recent.

Was that Rhythlin Island?

'You don't have to be so dismissive,' a man's slow, gravelly voice echoed in her head. He was her claim, Breen knew by the tingle on her tongue as he spoke.

'You got what you wanted,' the woman said. '...basic requirements to marry...too much responsibility.'

Breen focused in on what the man saw through his own eyes. A large human house and a fat man who didn't understand their language.

The mayor? The claim and the woman with him were talking about the attack and the merfolk.

He's the one! 'Oh, he's perfect!' Breen crooned as she watched his interactions with the two other humans. *He has political sway, he's easily manipulated and controlled.* That dark woman had some kind of control over him. He clearly didn't want to be a part of anything that was going on, but he obeyed her every command.

'He's the one!' Breen moaned.

She pulled herself out of his mind and sped back to the palace.

'I have the answer, Your Grace,' Breen said breathlessly, throwing herself into the throne room. 'One of my claims has ties to the king and he's weak. We can use him.'

'For what?' Kellac asked.

'To get the king to the beach, to bargain on our behalf, whatever we need. *The humans will turn on each other.*'

'Where is he, Breen?'

'Vurdia, your Highness.'

King Kellac hissed in annoyance. 'Where? For how long? You spend your whole life avoiding humans, then when you really need one, he's in Vurdia.'

'He's in a small fishing village, for the moment. The authority is rebuffing his attempts to rally the people, but he is making plans to leave soon.'

'Keep a watch on him. When he leaves, alert me immediately. That's good work, Breen.' The king beamed. 'Have you also found a solution to our other problems, the matter of financing our invasion? We are not the wealthiest colony, in resources or people. We can't afford your war.'

'What if we reached out to other colonies, made deals with them?' Breen asked.

Princess Kyri sat nearby, in a position of honour as was her right, her pink tail tucked neatly under her. She fiddled idly with the braids in her brown hair and gazed at herself in her mirror, patting at her facial markings.

Allowing her in on these meetings annoyed Breen to no end, but perhaps she had a use, after all.

'Princess Kyri.' Breen swept into a low bow. 'What would we have to do to convince your father to join us?'

Kyri sighed. 'If I knew, I'd have done it by now.'

'When you arrived here, you said you could convince him,' Breen said.

'Well, I can, if I have a plan to work with.'

'When you first came here, didn't you say that your brother loves humans?' King Kellac asked slowly.

'Yes.' Princess Kyri squirmed and crossed her arms.

'Could he sway your father against a war with us?' Breen asked.

'Maybe.'

'Kyri, what would happen,' Breen began, struck by a sudden idea, 'if your brother went to live with humans? Let's assume that that's possible.'

Kellac's eyes widened, his expression excited.

'Father would be livid.' Kyri shivered.

'Perhaps even livid enough to go to land to get him back?' King Kellac said.

Chapter Eight

Legs

Okala left Sulat and Alois on a beach in Vurdia and made his way back home. He feared for them, but they were safe on land now, even if they were as out of place as a Sandy Shore merman on a rocky shore. But he had to trust that they knew what they were doing. Okala had to get home to his family.

He sped along, skirting the Rocky Shore colony, back across the weed field, joined the Cavendy Drift through blue water, to his own lands. Bands of merfolk spread out and soon a cry of 'he's found,' 'Prince Okala,' and 'he's back' rose up on the current to him.

His stomach twisted. They had been searching for him.

Out of nowhere, a dark purple shape tangled him up in pale bluish-pink arms. The scent of Marya's anemone perfume engulfed him and he relaxed into the hug from his eldest sister. She shook against him and when she pulled back, the furious vibration of the water around her burned his skin. He couldn't face meeting her eyes.

'Where were you?' her voice trembled, thick with emotion, and her fingers dug into his arms.

'I, uhh, I was--'

'*WHERE?*' Marya shook him hard, her anger hitting him in a wave. Her brows pinched low over her eyes, her square teeth bared.

'Kyri ran away to treat with King Kellac. I followed her.'

Marya's face opened wide, and she blinked in disbelief. A shape loomed in the gloom behind her. 'Tell me later,' she whispered, then raised her voice to a normal volume. 'I've a mind to lock you in your chambers and never let you out. Have you any idea how worried we all were?'

'I-- I'm sorry,' Okala stammered, trying to keep up with her. 'I didn't think. It won't happen again.'

'Yes, it will.' Marya tugged his ear and gave him an indulgent pat. 'Go to the throne room and I'll find Father. He's been out looking for you with everyone else.' She knocked him on his backside with her fin and bent her head toward the merman who had come up to her, speaking in a hushed voice as Okala sped off to the palace.

He wasn't there long before his father burst through the walls, a cloud of bubbles frothing in his wake. Marya followed and pulled the heavy stone to cover the entrance hole.

'Tell him,' she said.

King Cly's golden eyes bored into Okala, and there was more pain and fear there than Okala had ever seen.

Okala recounted the events of the night Kyri went to the Rocky Shore colony, and stopped abruptly before the part where the Rockies attacked the ship.

'Well?' Clyr pressed. 'What happened to her? Is she all right? Why didn't you bring her back with you?

'She didn't know I was there. I...' Okala didn't want to tell the rest of the story, but had to find a way.

'What happened after you found her?' Marya pressed.

Okala hesitated. 'A little after all of that happened, a human ship landed on the island. They were looking for pirates.

They think it's other humans who have been attacking ships, but it was Kellac and his people. Breen kissed one of them. So they all ran back to their ship and made to go back to Viehland, but Kellac went up to the surface and destroyed the ship.'

Marya and King Clyr exchanged perplexed looks. *They don't know. They think he's a grey shrimp like he used to be.*

'Destroyed the ship? Destroyed it how? You mean he commanded his men to do something?'

'He clapped his hands together and the ship exploded. He's changed, Father. He's...I don't know how to describe it. He's *changed.* His chitin is colourful and he's completely mad. I don't know what happened.'

Marya and King Clyr recoiled. 'He was always so timid and meek,' the king said. 'If Breen did something to him, that would explain all this unification nonsense. But if you weren't captured, how did it take you so long to get back?'

Okala twisted his fingers together so tight he strained the webbing. 'There were, uhh, survivors.'

The king and Marya groaned and their shoulders slumped.

'Okala...' Marya rubbed the bridge of her nose.

'I had to save them!' Okala pleaded. 'I couldn't just leave them to drown or be eaten! Honestly, do you expect for a minute that I could?'

'I appreciate that you have such a caring heart,' Clyr said. 'But this isn't our fight. What is between the humans and the Rocky Shore Merfolk, as I have told Kellac's emissaries myself, is between them. We do not get involved. We certainly don't risk our own safety, without telling someone where we've gone.' He deflated. 'I'm not angry. I'm more glad that you're back than you can imagine. I just wish you had told someone where you went, and that you'd have some sense when dealing with other merfolk or humans. Better still, that you refrained entirely.'

'What did you do with the humans?' Marya asked.

'I took them to Decombre Island, and then helped them get to Vurdia. That's what took all the time. But then I swear, I came straight home.'

The tension had gone from the room, replaced with the heavy torpor of exhaustion. Marya's shoulders drooped, King Clyr stared absently at a patch of smooth floor, the skin of his face hanging from his bones, and Okala hovered, watching them both. Clyr held out an arm and Okala went in for the hug.

'I'm glad you're home, son. Get some rest. Your sister and I have much to discuss. And don't leave the colony.'

Okala retreated to his room. One by one, his remaining sisters paid him a visit throughout the day to check on him. Slowly, the merfolk out searching retreated to their homes, and silence fell.

It was eerie, here on the brink of war. The prince had returned, but a princess had sided with the aggressors, and so whether they wanted to be or not, the Sandy Shore Merfolk of Ildecoke Archipelago had joined the fight.

Okala found Marya and told her that he would be going to his cave. She gave him a disapproving grimace, but didn't stop him. She hated that he was leaving the palace on his own, and that he was going to spend time with his obsession with humans, but at least he stuck to his bargain. And they all knew where his cave was.

He sped along the sea bed over the rotting wood, under the rocks, and into the tunnel he'd built. The plankton were still glowing but needed a top up. He smeared more fish paste on the walls, humming his tune. Then he moved things around to make a space for his new trinket, the circle of glass Sulat had asked for but ended up not needing. In a way, it felt like she had given it to him, a gift from a real-life human! It would have pride of place in his collection, and he would cherish the memory forever.

'Greetings, Your Highness,' a voice spoke behind him and he spun around to find Breen, the Rocky Shore sea witch, floating in the dark cave behind him, a sack over her shoulder.

'What do you want?' he snapped. Of all people to come unbidden into his private sanctum, she was the least welcome. Breen flashed her yellow eyes and her lips parted in a wide grin.

'Is this the welcome an emissary receives from Sandy Shore royalty?'

'I know what you're here for, and you can forget it. You have no chance of treating with my father without giving my sister back.'

'We didn't take her. She came to us of her own free will.' Breen said smoothly. 'And anyway, I'm not here in this...'She waved a hand in obvious disgust, 'grimy little cave to treat with your father. It's you I want to talk to, about what *you* want.'

She picked up a length of rusty metal and drew something in the sand: a circle for a head, two arms, and where there would be one long squiggle for the tail, she drew two short legs. Okala set his jaw.

'You can't do that. It's illegal.'

'For Sandies. Rockies are more forgiving of raw, selfish ambition.' She swam a little closer, a menacing thrum in the water around her.

'Why would you come here and offer me that? And why would you think I'd want it?'

'You do.'

'What's in it for you?' Okala asked warily. 'You wouldn't offer this out of the goodness of your...do you even have a heart?'

Breen placed tan hands over her chest. 'You wound me, Your Highness. I *am* doing this out of the goodness of my heart. I'll not ask anything of you. All I want, all *you* want, is to go away and never come back. What happens down here is no longer your concern. You can live with the land people, with their cows and trees and sunburns, and all the rest of it, forever and ever.'

Breen's eyes sparkled like gold in the shifting light of the cave and her sharp teeth glittered. Okala tugged at his hair as he cast his eyes over his treasures, the little bits of garbage he'd collected over the years, watching trends come and go. The smoking pipes changed shapes from one decade to the next. The jewellery, the faces stamped in the coins, the curves of the glass bottles, even the liquid inside them evolved. Humans were so fascinating in how they shifted so quickly, and still never really changed. They still did the same things their ancestors did, how his ancestors did, but subtly different.

He wanted so desperately to be up there with them, to watch them, to be one of them.

'What's the catch?'

Breen cocked her head. 'I thought I said.'

He didn't trust her at all, but her logic was sound. She was crazy and zealous, but she was also powerful, and she wasn't stupid. She wouldn't kill him. The Rocky Shore Merfolk couldn't fight the humans and the Sandy Shore Merfolk at the same time. And it was logical that she'd want him out of the way. Permanently on land was a perfect way to do it.

'I don't know what's taking you so long,' she said, the water vibrating around her. She glided along the shelves, and picked up a string of blood-red stones set in blackened silver. She held it against her slender tan neck. 'I'd have thought you'd jump at the chance. Are you debating whether or not you can trust me?' She hovered close to him, close enough that he could see the vein pulsing along her neck. He recoiled a little, but she followed. 'Or are you wondering if you'll miss your family?'

She tapped him between the eyes and memories flooded his mind. His father shouting at him about loyalty and pride. Marya surveying the cave with a perplexed expression. Kyri smashing a green glass bottle against the side of the cave. Vila and Neri sighing every time he mentioned humans. Ytaso whispering to Adeto that perhaps they should increase the guard for Okala's Breaching, in case he tried to run and got stuck when the potion wore off.

'You know what they call you,' Breen whispered.

'Yes.' His face reddened and he squeezed his eyes shut, fighting back the tears.

When he opened them again, Breen was almost nose-to-nose with him, pity on her face. 'Strange. Poor baby Prince Okala. With his funny little toys and his fascination with the humans. It's a good thing you're so far down the line.' She made six little ticks in the water between them. 'Right at the end.' She quirked her mouth in a savage pout.

Okala pushed away from her and nearly ran right into the ancient figurehead. The wide round features, the thick curly hair fixed in rows along the scalp.

Sulat. She likes me. She thinks I'm strange, but she's different too, she said so. Humans are so much more accepting.

A shard of green glass winked in the doorway, part of the bottle Kyri had smashed.

Okala turned to Breen, watching him.

'When and where?'

A grin spread across her dark grey lips.

'We can go now, if you want.'

Okala followed Breen for hours. Their tails beat the water hard and fast, speeding through the Lenord Current across open sea.

'Where are we going?' he shouted ahead.

'Vurdia,' she called back over her shoulder. 'Unless you want to become a man on Rhythlin Island. But there are no humans there, only us Rocky Shore Merfolk.' She ran her tongue over her sharp teeth.

Okala swallowed hard. *No. I don't want that.*

The sea floor came up to meet them. It climbed and climbed and soon oblong shapes appeared along the surface of the water. Breen pointed.

'See, there are your people, returning home and heading out on their jaunts. Perhaps one day they'll take you out on a boat, too.' She gave her cruel smile and pressed ahead. Okala sped to keep up with her, trying to contain the surging of his heart. She was taunting him, but she was right. He yearned so dearly to be up there with them.

Breen suddenly changed direction and sped into darkness, away from the boats.

'Where are you going?'

'I know a quiet spot up here. We don't want to be seen.' She shot a wink back at him and he followed. 'I hunt along this coast all the time. I like Vurdencemen. The plants they eat season them better.'

Okala gagged as Breen poked her head above the water. He remained below until her slim yellow hand beckoned him to follow. He broke the surface and wiggled along until there wasn't enough water, then inched up the beach on his hands and tail. Breen remained waist deep in the water, her striped yellow and tan tail curled under her. She flipped her fluke, splashing water over herself as she waited for Okala to situate himself comfortably.

'You ready?' she asked, her face splitting in a wide grin. *I wonder if she smiles like that before she tears into a man's face.* He swallowed hard, steeled his nerve, and nodded. 'Then let's begin.'

Breen opened the sack and tossed some things across the surf at him: a waterlogged and rotten leather shoe, a cracked ceramic cup, and a hat with the brim folded in three places. He put the hat on his head, placed the shoe on top of his fluke, and held up the cup, feeling exceptionally foolish.

Is this part of the spell, or is she trying to humiliate me?

Breen pulled a cracked crab shell out of her sack and propped it across her chest. She lifted onto her hips and held up two brightly painted sticks.

'Prince Okala,' she said, her voice thin as the wind whipped it away. 'For years, you have lived as an outsider in your own clan, one fin in our world, one foot in the world of Man. But you cannot keep your balance on rolling waves. Step fully onto land, and stand as the man you truly are.'

She brought the sticks together with a deafening crack. Okala shrieked as pain ripped through him. It climbed from the tips of his fins up the centre of his tail, and spread through the bottom half of his body. It crept up his belly, to his chest, down through his arms, and up his neck into his head. It tingled with terrible strength and ferocity, like every cell of his body was breaking free, dissolving. He was coming undone, to the smallest particle of himself. There was no sky above him, no sand beneath him. Only pain. He couldn't even make noise to focus on. All he could do was try to breathe.

He couldn't even do that. He came back together, fusing once more. His tail split as though someone had taken both fins and ripped him straight up the middle. Something in his gut shrank and popped out of existence, leaving searing heat where it had been. A streak of fire climbed up his spine, and his neck felt like it was melting as his gills fused into smooth skin.

Then it was over. He was on his side, legs splayed, arms held wide, fingers buried in the sand. He stared up at the cloudy grey sky, still screaming. His voice fell away and he lay there, panting, until the pain subsided enough to roll onto his side. Each grain of sand was like a sharp stone cutting into the new skin on his legs and feet.

The shoe and hat had fallen off and the cup sat on its side in the sand beside him.

Breen swayed in the water, splinters of crab shell floating in the water around her.

'You didn't tell me it would be that painful,' he croaked.

A smile flickered across her face as she tucked the sticks back into her bag. 'What did you expect? A pleasant tickle? It's not like the Breaching Potion that lets you walk on land for a day. I've changed your whole body to withstand life on land. No gills, no swim bladder, no dorsal nerve. Your hair will tangle and mat, your feet and legs will ache if you walk too much. You'll be more resistant to sunburn, but it will be worse and last longer.'

'Why wouldn't you tell me? What did you have to lose?' *Are you really that insanely cruel?*

'Would you still have gone through with it?' She adjusted her tail and scooted back to deeper water. 'It'll be worse in reverse. Consider that if you ever decide to come back.' She flashed another grin and dove beneath the waves.

Chapter Nine
Vurdia

Alois and Sulat rowed all the way to Vurdia, and put in at a fishing village, where Okala had found them a quiet cove to tie up the boat.

'Souls, it even looks Vurdence,' Alois grumbled.

'Funny, that,' Sulat said.

'I need to go home,' Okala said from the water. 'My family will have been searching for me for a while, now. They'll be worried sick. Leave this boat here for as long as you're in Vurdia, so I'll know if you got away all right. I'll come back and check in a couple of days.'

Sulat waved, but that felt too little for all the boy had done for them.

'Okala, we couldn't have made it without you,' Alois said. 'You really saved us.'

Okala blushed bright pink and gave a goofy laugh. 'I don't mind. I love humans.' He extended webbed hand and Alois shook it. It was cold and slick, and a little slimy, with a dusting of fine scales like sandpaper.

That's new. Alois rubbed a thumb over him palm.

'I shook hands with a human,' Okala chuckled, a giddiness in his voice. 'I wish you the best of luck.'

He waved as Alois and Sulat climbed the beach to the road that ran alongside, up toward the little village. Alois scratched his head. The saltwater was almost dry, making his hair stiff and strangely greasy.

Maybe I'm not cut out for life at sea, after all.

Sulat pounded her hat back onto her hair and strode ahead of him.

'What a delightful young merman,' Alois said. 'What do we do now?'

'We can't send a letter to Bertold because it will be taken on ships. So we need to talk to the king here.'

'We're going to talk to King Ranwar?' Alois asked, an incredulous chuckle shaking his voice. 'We're just going to walk up and talk to the king of a country we've hated since...forever?'

'We walk up to the lord mayor or sheriff of whatever stinking dock this is, and ask for an audience,' Sulat snapped. 'You know how this works. You're being petulant.'

'Oh, easy,' Alois grumbled. 'Just like last time. They're our allies, after all.'

Sulat ignored his quibbling and hoisted her pack higher. The Vurdence may have been more progressive, but they were also notoriously haughty. Their hope rested on Alois' charm and his ability to set aside his deep-seated prejudice, or worse--her ability to be diplomatic.

They found a tavern on the beachfront with a handful of patrons milling about outside, its swinging wooden sign depicting a fishing boat with a net slung over the side. Alois clucked his tongue at the wide-legged trousers and knitted neckties the men wore.

Sulat strode up to the bar and doffed her hat. No one so much as raised an eyebrow. Alois understood why she was so comfortable here. Apparently, an Ebian woman in breeches, armed with guns and a sword was no remarkable sight.

What kind of place is this?

Alois loved her the way she was, and he had grown to respect her, but he was almost unique in that. Most of Viehland regarded her with grudging tolerance, if not outright mistrust.

Maybe she's right. Maybe they are more accepting of people like her here.

The heavily-muscled, dark-skinned barman came over as they approached.

'*Ke es seh village?*' Sulat asked.

'*Seh Pischum,*' the barman said in a deep rumble.

'*Oo ey le mair?*' Sulat asked him.

A crease wrinkled his brow. '*Pour le momo?*' he asked.

She pursed her lips and jiggled a leg before asking, '*Oo ey son buro?*'

'Ahh!' the man's face lightened and he rattled off in rapid Vurdence. Sulat's eyes glazed over and she nodded slowly as the man gesticulated with a beefy hand.

'*Reconisant,*' she said at last, jerking a thumb over her shoulder at Alois as she stepped toward the door.

'*Eh eh.*' The man reached out at her. '*Kee eteh voo?*' he asked, gesturing at her and Alois.

She responded fluidly, and Alois picked out both of their names.

'Whoah, hey, what's he asking?' he hissed, but Sulat waved him silent.

'*Ke fe voo issi?*'

Sulat opened her mouth, then closed it again, her eyes flickering as she tried to find the words. Her face darkened and her jaw sharpened.

'*Nofrash.*'

The barman's shoulders fell as Sulat tugged Alois' sleeve and led him out of the tavern.

'What happened in there?' Alois whispered, coming up alongside Sulat.

'I asked where the mayor lives, and he told me. Then he asked me who we are and what we're doing here. I don't imagine this village gets many Viehlish.'

'So what'd you tell him?' Alois cast a glance over his shoulder in case they were being followed.

'I don't know enough Vurdence to explain what's going on, but there's one word you learn to say in every language, just in case.' Her dark eyes rose to meet his, and angry tears trembled on the waterline. 'Shipwreck.'

'Shit, Sulat.' Alois reached for her shoulder, but she sped away from him.

'Let's get this over with.' She wiped her eyes with the back of her wrist and pressed on.

'I wish I had my nice clothes,' Alois grumbled as they walked along the cobblestone roads, following the barman's directions. 'And that I didn't smell like a fishmarket. It would be a lot easier to talk to a mayor that way.'

'You shouldn't need you nice clothes. Let's see how useful my rich, well-connected lord friend really is out here.'

'I don't think Renir expected us to end up in Vurdia. I'm at a disadvantage. Do you think the mayor will recognise the signet?' Alois spun the ring on his finger with the coat of arms he'd been given along with his title and land. It was gold with a flat top, stamped with the twisting beanstalk stretching between the ground and a cloud, a spider on one side, and a harp on the other.

The world tipped and Alois nearly toppled over. He put a hand out to steady himself.

'That's strange. I went dizzy all of a sudden,' he said.

'You got water in your ear. Anyway, I doubt many people

over here will recognise the Greenstalk name,' Sulat scoffed, some of her darkness clearing. 'It's a made-up honorary title from Viehland. You're the political equivalent of Bertold's pet monkey.'

'You don't have to be so dismissive,' Alois grumbled, tipping his head and pounding on his ear. He still felt strange, like there was someone watching them. He peered around into the shadows and squinted up at windows.

'You got what you wanted,' Sulat said. 'Anything more than the basic requirements to marry Johanne would have been too much responsibility.'

'True.' Alois had to concede the point. 'Is that it?' He pointed ahead at the house that was slightly larger than the others nearby.

It wasn't much, for a mayor's house, with a shabby thatched roof, plaster walls streaked with dirt, and a small fenced garden overrun with weeds, a couple of pigs snuffling in mud. It might have been abandoned, but for the smoke rising from the chimney.

Sulat stomped through the puddles up to the door and knocked.

'*Mosier le mair*, uhh...' She paused. 'Shit, I don't know how to say we need help. *Parleh voo Viehlish?*'

'Is "Viehlish" the word for "Viehlish" in Vurdence?' Alois asked. 'That's handy.'

Sulat scowled as the sound of shuffling footsteps approached from behind the door.

'*Kee eteh voo?*' a brusque voice called. Sulat answered like she did with the barman. The voice asked the same follow-up question.

'*Mosier, sivupleh,*' Sulat said, exasperated. '*Parleh voo Viehlish?*'

The door swung open and a bent, paunchy, pouchy-faced man glared at them through watery eyes.

'What do you want?' he barked, wiping a bulbous and runny nose.

'*Mosier*, we need to discuss an urgent international--'

'*Kwa?*' the man interrupted, blinking at Sulat.

'My ship was attacked some days ago, by--'

'*Kwa?*' the man stepped out and pushed his face toward Sulat like an old turtle.

'MERFOLK!' Sulat roared, sliding her hands emphatically over her hips toward her feet. 'At Rhythlin Island. You.' She pointed at the mayor. 'Tell the king.' She pointed at her mouth and then in the direction of the capital city of Falez. 'To bomb the shit out of them!' She punched her fist repeatedly at the ocean. Alois ducked in time to avoid her swinging arms.

The mayor flapped a meaty hand at Sulat and went back inside his house, muttering something in which the word, 'Viehland,' was clearly audible, before slamming the door.

Sulat screamed, kicked the door, and stormed into the road.

'You're right, I had the Vurdence all wrong,' Alois said. 'What a helpful people they are.'

'Not the time, Alois,' Sulat snapped.

'So, what now?'

'We go to Falez. We'll force the king to listen to us.'

'Yeah, great plan. You know they're going to shoot us if we try to force it, right? We don't have a golden harp to buy our way in this time.'

'We're not nobodies, this time.' Sulat's voice had taken on the tone she used when a plan was forming.

'Very true. You're licensed to attack Vurdence ships and I'm Bertold's pet monkey.'

'What do you want to do?' Sulat rounded on him.

'I want to go home. Let's not bother with the Vurdence. Stay the night here, leave first thing in the morning.'

'Doesn't work like that,' Sulat said. 'You don't just climb on a ship and set sail. They have to unload, clean, reload, check everything, and then go. They might take passengers, but not for free, and loading and unloading cargo can take months. Plenty of these ships might not even be going out again until spring because fall and winter are stormy. Not to mention, they're probably all going through the Squalls, or taking weeks to avoid them. We might as well go to Falez, and at least do something while we're here.'

'*Spring*?' Alois asked, his blood rising. He'd told Johanne he'd be gone a few weeks. 'We come all the way back, book charter, and then what? Wait another six months?'

'Maybe.' Sulat shrugged. 'It takes as long as it takes. There's no way around it.'

'Sulat, don't you understand?' Alois' breath caught in his throat as panic climbed his spine. His tongue darted over the cold cut on his lip. 'I want to go home.'

Sulat's shoulders fell and she sighed. 'You might actually be safer on land.' *Maybe she does understand.* 'I suspect Breen will know as soon as you're on the water.'

'Maybe.' Alois balled his hand into a fist and hung his head. 'But I'd rather die trying to get back to Viehland, than live a long life cowering in Vurdia.'

'You might be able to convince Johanne to come here. Vurdence society is very fine.' Sulat attempted a reassuring smile.

'And Bertold?' Alois growled.

Sulat laughed. 'What can he do to you from Viehland?'

'Sulat.' Alois shook his head. *Don't get distracted.* 'Get me back to my family.'

Sulat paced in circles, exasperation etched all over her face.

'All right,' she said finally. 'We'll go back to the tavern. I'll see tomorrow if there are any ships leaving soon.'

Chapter Ten

Human

Okala tried to stand, and toppled over. The skin of his feet stung, his ankles crumbled under him, and he landed hard in the sand. A wide, blank silence filled him. He couldn't feel his family, the fish, anything. Little shapes moved about in the water, but whether they were seaweed, fish, or human trash, he couldn't tell. He was deaf, blind, numb. Alone.

I don't want this! I don't want it! He stood on tender feet and hobbled for the surf, stopping short. The memory of that searing, ripping agony throbbed everywhere, and he didn't have the strength to throw himself into it again. He glared at his legs, no longer pale bluish pink, but a light copper, and instead of scales, covered in fine black hair. He onto his side in the hot, dry, prickly sand and wept. His voice was thin and rough, his sobs coming in howls and gasps. Everything was wrong and harsh and scratchy.

He ached for the sea again. He wanted Marya to wrap her arms around him and tell him he was a foolish little guppy, that they'd put everything back right. To have his father be so disappointed but relieved that his son had come to his senses.

He had come to his senses, he truly had. He didn't want this heavy, clumsy, *itchy* body.

But it couldn't be undone.

He shielded his eyes against the sharp reflection of the sun on the water, which left streaks of colour across his vision. It may as well have been on fire, forbidden from him forever, lest he suffer that horrible pain again.

He lay there for what felt like hours, crying until he was weak, trying to comb his hair, and getting frustrated by the stiffness. But then his stomach rumbled and he sat up, longing for the surf. How easy it used to be to just reach out and grab a fish whenever he was hungry.

What do humans do for food? It was such a fundamental thing, he should have known. He should have asked.

He stood again, brushing the sand from his skin.

Maybe I can pretend to have lost my memory at sea and someone will take pity on me.

Stares followed him along the street when he finally reached the village, ignoring the aching in his skin and the sparks of pain that shot up his legs with every step. Men dragged boats up the beach, hauling out nets full of fish. His mouth watered at the flipping silvery things, and something else. A smell he'd never known before drifted over him on the breeze.

Food, every cell of his body moaned instinctively, and his stomach growled louder. *Human food.*

He couldn't stop the grin spreading across his face. How could he feel both of these things at once? How could he be so grief-stricken by losing one life, yet so excited about the new one?

A dark-skinned woman and tall man in a blue jacket came out of a tavern ahead of him. Could it really be them?

'Sulat!' he shouted, waving an arm and marvelling at the feel of the air all the way down between his fingers. The humans' mouths dropped open.

'Souls, man.' Alois pulled off his jacket as he rushed over. He pressed it against Okala's belly and pushed him backward into a space between buildings. Sulat followed close behind.

'What happened?' she hissed. 'I barely recognised you.' She pulled a green stone out of her pocket and held the hole in it up to her eye.

'And why are you naked?' Alois asked, averting his gaze.

'Sorry.' Okala was far too excited to be concerned about such a silly thing as nakedness. How could he be embarrassed about body parts he'd never had before, especially since he'd wanted them for so long?

He laughed at the shock on their faces. 'Breen made me human! I don't know anyone else up here, so I'm glad I found you.'

'I am, too.' Alois peeked around the corner of the building. 'But first thing is we need to cover you up. You're half a giant, you wouldn't fit in any of our breeches, even if we had any to spare.'

Both humans snickered.

Why should he hide his legs? Even Sulat didn't, even though most other females wore long fabric to cover theirs. 'I don't understand. You lot don't hide your legs. You just wrap them up.'

'No one's talking about your legs, son,' Alois said. 'Sulat, go see if the innkeeper or a patron has a spare pair we can buy. We don't have time to cut and sew a new set.'

'We don't have any Vurdence money, Alois,' Sulat hissed.

'There are different kinds of money?' Okala asked. *I'd never thought of that.*

'I have faith in you,' Alois said. Sulat huffed and stalked off, returning a moment later with a bundle in her arms. She pushed it into Alois' chest.

'Don't ask how I got these. You'll need to help him, he can't be much good at balancing on one foot.'

'Your feet are red and swollen, boy. What did you do to them?' Alois asked as Okala lifted one foot, holding onto Alois' shoulder.

'I don't know.' Okala said. 'It's possible I'm walking wrong. But I got here, so how bad can I be at it?'

'Well, a few things to remember, now you're human.' Alois did up the buttons, tightening the breeches around Okala's waist. 'You can't go about with no clothes on. You'll need shoes and a shirt. Also, you'll need to wash every once in a while.'

'Ahh, there's a problem,' Okala objected. 'I can't ever go back in the sea or I'll go back to the way I was. And it hurt, a *lot*.' A hard lump rose in his throat and his voice squeaked. *What was that?*

'Never?' Alois asked, eyes wide. 'Never *ever*?'

Okala shook his head, not sure if he could talk without crying.

'Well, that's shit.' Sulat said.

'But it's good, really!' Okala trembled all over and hugged his arms around himself. 'The merfolk always thought I was odd and I always wanted to be up here, anyway. I'm sure I'll make friends. I have you two. That's a start, isn't it?'

Okala followed Sulat and Alois back to the tavern where they'd spent most of their time. It was full of humans, hairy fishermen with smoking sticks in their mouths.

Excitement welled in him. He was still deeply sad, but the bubble of giddiness took up most his mind. A new adventure is the best medicine for sadness.

His human companions took him up the stairs of the wooden building to the chamber they shared. He tried to take in every detail along the way: the texture of the plaster, the ripples and bubbles in the glass windowpanes, the haziness of the air like water where a fish had disturbed the silty ocean floor.

The chamber opened behind a plank of wood and contained one large shelf-like structure with a soft pad. That must be what they slept on. In the corner, under the window, stood a table with a ceramic bowl and pitcher, and a rectangle of polished silver.

Sulat slipped into the hallway toward the rows of other doors as Alois handed Okala the mirror.

'Look how different you are,' he said, angling the smooth surface toward Okala's face.

The prince leapt back in shock. His hair was no longer blue, but black like the hairs on his legs and badly tangled, his large orange eyes had turned dark brown like Sulat's, and his full pink lips and long nose stood out, unfamiliar, set in that light brown skin. He swivelled his head to the side to better examine his cheeks and jaw. Only the colours had changed, but colours were defining underwater. The shape of the features meant next to nothing.

'Are you all right?' Alois asked softly, putting a hand on Okala's back. 'Bit of a shock, I imagine.'

Okala nodded, hot tears stinging his eyes. They quivered there, itching like everything else. Even crying was different up here. He laughed in spite of himself and wiped them away, leaving wet patches on his cheeks.

'Colours are everything in my kingdom. All of King Clyr's children have blue skin.' He held out his tan hands and flipped them over. 'I'm not his son anymore.'

A fresh wave of tears overcame him and he bent under the weight of the emotion. Alois pulled him into a hug and rubbed his back.

'You'll always be his son,' he said, his voice rumbling through his chest into Okala's head. 'I'm a father myself, and I can tell you that there's nothing my daughter could do, including turning into a mermaid, that would make her any less my daughter. And in a way, this is a good thing. You'll fit in better. We're not used to blue people up here.'

Okala coughed a wet laugh. 'That's true. I have to blend if I want a truly human life.' He held up the mirror again, but still flinched at the swollen red face that gulped back at him.

The door behind them opened and Sulat came in with a

sack.

'What happened?' she asked, her brown eyes flicking between him and Alois.

'Identity crisis,' Alois said softly.

'Ahh. This should help.' She tossed the bag on the table and unpacked a white shirt, two stockings, and scuffed buckled black shoes. 'It should be enough to take attention off you until we can get proper clothes. And you'll look more like the rest of us.'

The three went downstairs to where the other patrons sat clustered around tables. The scratchy fabric between Okala's legs distracted him awfully, but he fought the urge to tug at it. One or two men glanced his way, but no one stared like they had on the beach.

His heart tingled as he sat next to Sulat. *They've accepted me!*

He started to sing, as he always did when he was happy. He couldn't remember when he was last happy enough to sing properly.

His voice cracked and the tone wobbled uncontrollably. Several alarmed faces turned to him. He cleared his throat and tried again.

'Probably not the best time for that,' Alois said, leaning in and lowering his voice. Sulat glared at the other patrons, who turned back to their business.

'I used to have a beautiful voice,' Okala said, his throat tightening. 'I've lost my voice. I can't ever sing again.' He swallowed hard. 'Being human is...' He waved his hand in silence.

'Complicated?' Sulat asked.

Okala nodded. 'I wanted it so badly.' His voice squeaked. He screwed his eyes up, squeezing out fresh fat tears as he laid his head on his arm.

'There are some pleasures to being human,' Alois said. 'I don't imagine you've ever had wine.'

'Don't...' Sulat groaned.

'What? The boy's lost his people.' Alois stood from the

table. 'He's lost and confused and he wants to sing. Plus, he's with us in Vurdia. What better time to learn to drink?'

Sulat pursed her lips as Alois swaggered to the bar.

Alois and the barman exchanged words Okala didn't recognise, and Alois returned a minute later with a tray laden with bizarre treasures.

'He said you should try to speak the language,' Sulat said as he sat and ripped off a hunk of bread.

Alois snickered. 'Not likely. There you go. Eat and drink like a Vurdenceman.' He dug in the top of a tall green bottle with a curly bit of metal and pulled out a stick of spongy wood. He took a swig and set the bottle in the middle of the table.

Sulat pulled a short knife from her belt and cut into a waxy white lump on the tray. Okala gasped when thick yellowish goo flowed out. She spread some of it on a piece of bread with a piece of salt cod from one bowl, and a bit of strong smelling yellow paste from another.

Okala watched them eat in fascination.

'Bread. Cheese.' Sulat pointed with her knife. 'There are different kinds, I forget what this one's called.' She looked up at Alois, but he shrugged.

'Vurdence cheese.'

Sulat scowled. 'Anyway, it's made from cow milk. You know fish. The bottle is wine, made from grapes. The Vurdence eat a lot of all of this stuff. Lots of cheese, garlic, and wine. Fish, when they're on the coast like now.

'You've got human digestion, now,' she continued. 'You can still eat fish forever, but you've got to cook it.'

'Then we can move up to real food and alcohol,' Alois slurred around the mouthful of mush. 'Pies and potatoes. Raisin pudding.'

Okala nodded, understanding nothing that Alois had said. 'Can we get that today?'

Alois barked a laugh. 'Slowly, lad! You'll make yourself sick. This stuff here is pretty strong. Let's see how it sets first. Then we can get you some good roast beef when we get back to

Viehland.'

'*If* we get back to Viehland,' Sulat muttered.

Okala picked up the bowl of paste and sniffed it. It was what he had smelled, coming into town. 'What is that?'

'Garlic,' Sulat said. 'It's a plant. They mash it up with eggs and oil.'

'Breen said Vurdencemen taste like this, and I do smell it on them.'

Sulat's and Alois' faces twisted in disgust.

'I'm not going to eat you,' Okala said hastily. 'I was just wondering what the smell was.'

'I wonder what I smell like,' Alois said, taking a swig of wine.

'Unwashed man,' Sulat shot back.

Alois lowered the bottle and raised his eyebrows. 'You don't exactly smell like the waters of heaven yourself, princess. And I meant my, you know, my *meat*. I wonder what I would taste like to a mermaid.'

'Probably brandy,' Sulat said. 'And tobacco. Oh no,' she considered him for a moment. 'You eat better now, don't you? I don't imagine Johanne lets you put your boots on the dining room table. So, probably syllabub and sugar dolphins.'

Alois choked on his wine and buried his face in his elbow.

'Sugar dolphins,' he croaked, coughing as tears streamed down his red face. 'What would you be? Brandy and tobacco, as well. And what do you eat on that ship? Hard tack and pea soup.'

Sulat smirked. 'Like as not.'

'What does garlic taste like?' Okala asked, trying to steer the conversation away from eating people.

'It's pretty...' Sulat began.

'Pungent,' Alois finished and Sulat nodded.

Okala thought he'd watched them do it enough that he was ready to try. He'd never drizzled a liquid onto food before. When he'd pried a bottle open before, the liquid flowed out and permeated the water around him. It took him weeks to get the residue out of his cave and his scales were dull for days. He had never been sicker in his life. But here, the wine sat neatly in the bottle and cups. Everything was so much heavier on land.

Still, one thing at a time. Alois watched as he put the bread up to his nose. The sauce dripped off the bread and onto his hand, but he let it. The smell was strong, musty like mold, but stringent, and a bit smoky. Humans ate weird things. But Alois had already had a lot. People all around the room were eating the same thing with gusto as they chatted animatedly. And wasn't he human now? Surely this wasn't bad for him. He closed his eyes and took a bite.

Raw fish was soft, squeaky sometimes, clean, and a little salty. This was chewy and dense and sucked at his tongue like a sponge. The cheese was a slick, gummy lump, the sauce extremely acidic and tasted even stronger than it smelled. He coughed as it burned his mouth.

Alois laughed and Sulat pounded on his back.

'Not all human food is that strong, lad, I promise,' Alois said, pouring wine into a cup and pushing it close. Okala chewed and swallowed, his eyes watering, as he reached for the cup.

But that burned worse than the sauce! He coughed and sputtered and nearly dropped the cup, but Sulat caught it before much spilled. He pounded on his chest and tried to breathe through his mouth but the lump of bread stuck in his throat. He choked and gagged.

No gills! Swallow, Okala, swallow!

'Swallow it down, lad,' Alois' voice said. Okala steeled his resolved and gulped.

A muscle behind his ribs jumped and he sucked in a load of air with a loud *hic*!

Even Sulat laughed that time. 'Chew slower, boy. Take smaller bites. That's called hiccoughs. You just have to wait for them to go away.'

'Although they say dragging a sharp blade across the throat will get rid of them,' Alois offered, pulling out his own knife.

'A sharp blade across the throat will cure most things,'

Sulat cocked an eyebrow.

'But mostly, they just go away.'

Hic!

'You know, eventually.'

They were on Sulat's second bottle of brandy, Alois' sixth bottle of wine, and Okala's third pot of tea. He had been shocked when he burnt his tongue on the hot liquid, but Sulat reminded Alois that merfolk wouldn't have had hot foods. They convinced the boy that, unlike wine, tea would cool and stop burning, and when it did, he found that he quite liked the warm soothing drink, especially with sugar. He still wasn't sure about cream.

'What we need,' Sulat said, resting her bottle against her forehead, 'is money. I can keep picking pockets for food and lodging, but booking passage is expensive.'

'Can you buy a ship?' Okala asked.

'That's even more expensive,' Alois said. 'Technically, Sulat was gifted the first one.'

'And it can take months.' Sulat said. 'You have to find a captain who's selling, pay it off in chunks, assemble a crew if you don't already have one, then...' Her eyes slid out of focus, darting back and forth. 'Or we could steal one.'

'What?' Alois asked. Surely, he'd misheard her.

'We could steal one,' she said clearer. 'That's what we do best, Alois. We're thieves.'

The familiar fluttering came over him, the old thirst for adventure, the tingling in his restless legs. Could they do it? Could they steal a whole ship?

'Where are we going to hide it? It's not like I can shove it down the front of my breeches like with most things.'

Sulat shot him a withering look. 'No, you dolt, we'll stow away and then stage a mutiny and take over. Sail back to Viehland, get something together, come back to Rhythlin, take out Kellac, and --

'Wait, wait, wait. I see several flaws with this plan,' Alois interrupted. His mind was slow from drink, but even that didn't make her plan any more sensible. 'Stowing away-- doesn't that justify immediate throwing overboard?'

Okala gasped. Sulat smirked.

'Not with your shoulders. No ship has enough crew that they can waste a man your size. Okala is safe, too, and he's even more valuable if they find out who he is.'

'Fair enough. But what about you?' Alois pressed. 'A tiny woman like you.'

'You have so little faith in me.'

'I have endless faith in you, it's your plan I doubt.'

'Let me hammer out the kinks,' Sulat said. 'My plans usually work, as long as you don't balls them up.'

Sulat stayed up all night. The brandy worked its way through her system and her mind raced, jotting ideas on paper with a graphite stick. Okala and Alois both snored in the four-poster bed that dominated the room. There was enough space on the bed for her between the two men, but she'd get no sleep that night. She didn't sleep well on land, and she didn't have her sleeping powder with her.

It never occurred to her that merfolk snored. Or perhaps they didn't and the boy wasn't used to breathing without gills. There was a lot about merfolk that she'd never given thought to. She pushed her musings aside and forged ahead with the plan.

In the morning, Alois was the first to rise and he stomped to the tavern without a word to her and brought back a ceramic coffee pot and three heavy mugs. He slammed the mugs down and poured three measures of strong black coffee, and shuffled to the bed to rouse Okala with a foot to the back. Sulat sipped the bitter black sludge gratefully and watched the boy wake up. He floundered for a moment, pushing his dark hair out of his face, blinking at the light streaming in through the grimy window.

'It wasn't a bad dream,' he said thickly, his round features puffy from sleep.

'I thought you wanted to be one of us,' Sulat said.

'This is it.' Alois swung his arms wide, his loose shirt sleeves fluttering. 'In all its stinking, filthy, crusty-eyed glory.'

Okala moaned and buried his face in his pillow.

Alois laughed. 'It gets better. Wait til you meet the women.'

'Women,' Okala groaned, blinking up at Alois, his eyes flicking to Sulat.

'Men?' Alois asked, shrugging at Sulat. She shrugged back. It wouldn't be that weird to her. Okala snorted and flopped back onto his pillow. 'Here.' Alois handed Okala the cup of coffee. 'Don't spill. Things stain up here.'

Okala sat up and took the cup from Alois, hissing at the hot ceramic. He tipped the liquid gingerly into his mouth and winced.

'Why is human food so painful?'

'Ahh, but coffee gives life,' Alois said. 'Granted, I like it strong. Johanne doesn't like it at all.'

'Who's Johanne? You said that name before, on Decombre Island.'

'Here we go.' Sulat rolled her eyes and Alois pulled a face at her.

'She's my wife. You'll meet her one day. She'd love you.'

'*She's perfect, she's a goddess*,' Sulat mocked. 'And her daughter is an angel.'

Alois grinned into his mug of coffee and Okala squinted in confusion.

'But listen, now,' Sulat snapped the men's attention to her. 'I have a plan.'

Chapter Eleven
Le Capitan Amical

'So, let me get this straight: we're going to stow away on a Vurdence ship, then hijack it.'

'Yes.'

Alois ran his fingers through his stiff, greasy curls while Sulat sipped her brandy. 'Then we're going to sneak back past the island with the murderous mermaids, or else barrel through the big storms that kill people, with a foreign vessel and potentially murderous crew.'

'Yes. I can handle the crew.'

'Course you can.' Alois nodded. 'Go back to Viehland to meet the king, who told you not to come back until the pirates were gone.'

'Yes.'

'And then the king, King Bertold, the king who kicked his crown all around the throne room when the queen took up with a courtier--'

'King Bertold, yes. Move along.'

'--That his den of pirates is actually a colony of angry

merfolk against whom our gunships are useless, we've annoyed a Vurdence mayor, and by commandeering a Vurdence ship and imprisoning its captain we may have started a war.'

'And that since my ship was lost during a mission he sent me on, he owes me a new one, yes.' Sulat pulled a pipe and tinderbox from her pocket.

Alois whistled. 'Souls, Sulat. I don't how I'm going to ruin that carefully balanced plan you've made.' He finished the rest of his drink in one long swallow. 'All I wanted was to make Johanne happy. All those years ago, she was so sad...'

'Imagine how happy she'll be when you're a war hero,' Sulat mumbled around the pipe as she lit it.

Alois scowled at her. 'I *am* a war hero, firstly. And secondly, you don't really expect us to survive. Even if we do defeat this madman-- which we won't because we can't fight him. Even if, by some stroke of luck or Divine Intervention, or a comet lands on him and boils the sea, we'll be hanged. We'll either be shipped back here to Vurdia so they can hang us for mutiny and international embarrassment or something like that; or we'll be hanged by our own king as spies to salve Ranwar's wounds. And then Johanne and her family will be ruined and Rosabel will never be married.'

'What happened to "Oh no, we've never been in trouble with the law before?"'

'I have something to lose now,' Alois said darkly.

'It'll work,' Sulat said.

The next morning, the three of them stole from their beds, leaving the key on the counter, and slipped into the fog. The docks already teemed with men, hauling crates and sacks off and onto the ships, shouting orders, or pushing small boats into the dark water to bring in the day's catch.

Alois, Sulat, and Okala crept from building to alley, stack

of crates to waggons, avoiding the pools of light spilling from the hanging iron lanterns.

'We need a big one,' Sulat whispered. 'A ship the size of mine wouldn't have much room for us to hide without being noticed or needing someone to smuggle us in.'

'Have experience with smuggling stowaways, do you, Captain?' Alois asked, but Sulat didn't answer. Her dark eyes trained on something, like a cat who'd spotted a mouse. Alois followed her gaze. 'What are you looking at?'

'Change of plan.' She straightened and strode out with the confidence of a sea captain, without any trace of the stowaway.

Alois and Okala followed. Sulat walked straight up to one of the biggest ships in the yard, the one with a gap between two masts like a missing tooth, and only when they were directly under her, did the name painted on her hull come into view.

Martinette.

Sulat cupped both hands around her mouth and shouted, 'Ahoy, *Martinette*!'

One head and then another popped over the rail and split into surprised grins.

'Sulat!' One man waved his hat over his head.

'Permission to come aboard,' Sulat called back.

'Who's with you?' shouted the other man.

'Friends,' she said with significant weight.

The man disappeared and held a conversation Alois couldn't make out, then returned.

'Come aboard!'

Sulat stepped onto the plank that served as a ramp from the dock to the ship's deck.

'This is the ship I trained on, where I got most of my crew,' she said to Alois. There was a hardness under her words, but she didn't indulge her grief. 'Captain will help us.'

Martinette was massive, easily twice the size of *Meltythia*. From the dock, Alois had counted twenty iron cannon muzzles under hinged wooden flaps on one side alone, at least one deck more than Meltythia had, and a grand chamber at the back encased in glass windows, which he imagined to be far finer captain's quarters than Sulat's little closet. The main deck was much wider and lacked the two little buildings that *Meltythia* had, those functions presumably being given adequate space in the lower decks. She had three huge masts, with a larger space in the middle for a fourth, which lay in sections on the main deck. Alois understood now the sacrifices made on *Meltythia* for speed over space and defence. *Martinette felt* heavier, and all of those guns were no doubt a cheerful weight investment for so slow-moving and irresistible a target.

At the top of the plank, six men grinned excitedly as Alois, Sulat, and Okala hopped onto the deck. They offered rough handshakes all around.

'This is Alois, Lord Brynglas, my partner,' Sulat said. 'And Prince Okala of the Sandy Shore Merfolk.'

There followed a murmuring of 'my lords' and 'Your Highness' and uneasy bowing.

'And while we're on the subject of titles, I'm a "Captain," now,' Sulat said.

One man chuckled. 'Fermin's handing over command?'

'Of course not.' Sulat shook her head. 'I have papers of my own.'

Eyebrows raised at her words.

'So, that's where Wese went!' the man who had greeted them at the rail said. 'How is the old Lobster?'

Sulat clenched her jaw. 'Why are you in Pischum? You lot put in at Dunothe. This place isn't much of a market for Viehlish wool and slate.'

The crew exchanged uneasy glances. 'We lost Osid. We patched her up as best we could, but without a carpenter..?'

'In the Squalls?'

'In a way. He got sick before and couldn't get well. Finally passed in the Squalls, then we lost the mainmast, too. It crippled us as much as losing another hand would. We only just got started on repairs, now we're in smoother waters.' The sailor gestured at the sections of mast.

'So you're here for repairs.'

'And to get a new carpenter. What brought you to Pischum, of all places?'

'Long story.' A shadow passed over Sulat's face and Okala swallowed hard. 'I need to speak to the Captain. It's urgent.'

'Cap'n's in his quarters. Wait here while I wake him?'

'Of course.' Sulat waved Alois and Okala to the rail as the sailor strode off to the back of the ship.

'This is the ship you trained on, eh?' Alois asked. 'It's nice. A lot bigger than Meltythia.'

'A lot slower, too,' Sulat said, a weight settling onto her shoulders and around her chest.

She felt his huge eyes on her, and she folded her arms before he could reach out for her hand.

'They made a choice, Sulat. You didn't pressgang them, they chose to come with you.'

She had nothing to say, and anything said in guilt and shame, he'd counter with logic and his insufferable need to comfort.

Voluntary or not, they were still dead and the fact that it wasn't her fault wouldn't bring them back, wouldn't provide for the ones they left behind.

She wanted to lash out, to shoot something, to spar with a tree the way they used to. But damaging someone else's ship wasn't going to solve anything, and she needed Fermin on her side.

She rubbed her face. *Come back to the present, Sulat. Stay in the moment.*

'Have you thought about what you're going to say to him? It'll be tricky asking his men to sail directly into danger,' Alois said.

'He's reasonable. I just have to approach it properly.'

Alois tapped on the rail, and she knew what he was thinking. Diplomacy wasn't Sulat's strong suit.

But persistence is.

Otto, the quartermaster, coughed behind them, and knuckled his brow. 'Cap'n's ready for you.'

'Thank you for seeing me, Captain Fermin.' Sulat doffed her hat and bowed.

Captain Gidie Fermin sat at the head of his grand dining table, under a lit chandelier, with a pen and ledger at his elbow. He was as highborn a Vurdenceman as anyone was likely to encounter on the sea. His shiny black curls were tied in a queue, but that was the only concession he'd made for an early morning meeting. The night's stubble darkened his tan jaw, and he wore a blue silk robe loosely over his elaborately ruffled white nightshirt.

He inclined his head at her introduction. 'I remember you. You served briefly with me last year. You were Dilys' boy.'

'I was.'

'She was sad when you left. What can I do for you?' He folded his long hands on the table. He may have been asleep minutes ago, but he was listening now.

'I've come to ask for your help. I was in command of my own ship, a gift from my king. He tasked me to investigate the attacks on merchant ships going past Rhythlin Island. I did so, and found that it wasn't pirates, as he expected, but merfolk. They attacked us and destroyed my ship. I and Lord Brynlas were the only survivors.'

'I imagine, thanks to that young merman out there. I've

heard of merfolk saving sailors from shipwrecks before.'

'He helped us get here to Vurdia, but I need safe passage back to Viehland. I need to tell the king what I found out. We sought assistance from the mayor here, but he refused to give us an audience.' She paused. Alois always said to flatter people if you want something from them, make them feel important. 'I was relieved when I spotted *Martinette* in the yard. It was like running into an old friend when I needed one most.'

Captain Fermin smiled and flicked a speck of dust off of his brocade tablecloth.

'We've not finished repairs,' he said slowly, after a long pause. 'That gives me time to discuss the matter with my officers. I imagine Dilys will be in favour of helping you. But we still need to go to Dunothe to do business, which will take some time, as you know.'

'We don't have the time, Captain.' Sulat tried to convey urgency without raising her voice. 'We have to go back now. This is a matter of international trade, the safety of your countrymen, as well as mine. Your buyer may be put out but you'll be a hero of mankind. Wool and slate won't spoil.'

'The deal might.' Fermin said, straightening the pen and ledger.'The safest route to Viehland is to bypass Dunothe and skirt the Squalls to the east, which you know will add at least a week. It would be faster to go directly back, but it takes us past Rhythlin Island or through the Squalls, and you can sympathise with my hesitation, given this new information.'

'All the more reason to help me,' Sulat pressed. 'You've been warned. You know what's out there, you can't be caught unaware. Other captains,' she swallowed a sudden wave of bile and emotion. *Not now, you fool.* 'Other captains don't have the same warning.'

Fermin tapped the tabletop with his delicate fingers. 'But we are a merchant vessel. We are merchant sailors. We have only enough guns to protect us from other ships. And most of us, being Vurdence, have never seen battle even on land, let alone fighting foes on a different terrain in the water.'

Sulat leaned on his table. 'I have a solution to that, as well. My friend is a veteran of the Ettin Wars, an officer. And the boy is a merfolk prince. They can't train your men to the standard of the navy, but a bit of training and understanding is better than going in blind. It's better than what my crew had.'

She coughed to cover the emotion. He gave her a moment to compose herself.

'You have Letters of Marque?' he asked.

'I did.' Sulat ground her teeth.

'That makes you an agent of the Crown, yes?'

'Yes.'

'And, if I'm not mistaken, the wording of that license follows loosely that you are allowed to attack foreign vessels and take their ships, crew, and cargo.' Fermin picked up the pen and traced lazy circles over his table with the blunt end.

'Legally, yes.'

'So, legally speaking, my vessels could fall prey to you and your crew.'

'It's not much of a risk with my ship at the bottom of the sea.' She clenched her fist, her fingernails biting into her palm.

'No, but if I take you home, as you ask--as I would happily do for a friend--you could be given command of a new ship. You are in the employ of Viehland, in good standing, I imagine. What I'd like to know is if you still count us friends, *capitaine*?'

'I served under you, I know your crew, and you'll be doing me a significant favour. Not to mention a favour to a member of the gentry and a merfolk prince. And the kingdom of Viehland.'

'They're of no concern to me. If I do this for you, I want assurances that *you* will never attack this ship, any ship under my command, or any ship flying the colours of La Marchand des Coupevag.'

'Do you want that in writing?' Sulat straightened. *We're almost there.*

'I think that's the, uhh, proper way to do it.'

'Done.'

Sulat watched as he wrote out the terms of their arrangement in looping, elegant penmanship. They called in Alois and Otto long enough to witness their two signatures, before asking them to leave again.

Fermin held out a hand for her to shake. His skin was soft, more like a banker than a sailor.

'You've given me much to think about. As I say, we are still making repairs, so any decision I make is still a way off. I shall discuss the matter with my mates, and I will get back to you. Where are you staying?'

'We had lodging in town. We can get them again.'

'You are welcome to stay here on *Martinette*.' The captain bowed his head as Sulat headed for the door. 'Oh and *capitaine*,' Fermin said, straightening and lowering his voice as he stepped toward her. 'As a courtesy and uhh, comfort, you are welcome to share my cabin.'

Sulat appraised him; his fine clothes over a slender but sturdy frame, his smooth tan skin, and shining dark eyes and hair. He was a handsome man.

'That's courteous of you, Captain Fermin,' she said. 'But comfort is the last thing on my mind.'

In her cave, Breen sat on her rock with a large pearl, nearly the size of her head, and a beautiful stormy black. Glass and polished silver produced clearer images, but they required more upkeep.

Her assistant, Damla, stood by her side with a plate of dreamweed. The properties of the plant combined with using an outside tool rather than just her own mind allowed Breen to hold a connection with her catches deeper and for longer.

She popped a pinch of shredded weed into her mouth and chewed the stringy, bitter gob while she swept her arms over the pearl, trying to remember what the human looked like.

Tall, she remembered that, broad, but otherwise unremarkable in colouring or marking. She huffed.

'Do you need something else?' Damla's voice cut through her thoughts.

'No, thank you,' Breen snapped. She regretted it immediately, but the girl still didn't understand that magic was only partially about the tools and ingredients, and almost entirely about concentration.

Always wait until I ask, Breen had told her a hundred times. But a good assistant had to be a good servant, and good servants were trained to ask.

He's with a woman, she recalled, *in Vurdia*. The shadows on the surface of the pearl shifted as the room faded. Breen twisted her tail around her rock to steady herself. A shadow that might have been Damla moved about the room, but the only thing in focus was the black pearl in her hands.

She swirled her fingers lazily through her hair, concentrating on her catch.

Brown hair. He has a woman, but not the one he's with. Bertold's pet monkey. What's a monkey?

The shapes pulsed in and out of focus. A wide flat plane of dark grey under a slightly lighter grey. Other shapes moved around in the gloom. Shouts, the creaking of wood. *Is he on a ship? Is he leaving Vurdia?*

She sat a bit straighter and concentrated harder. Another man now, short and square. No, a woman, but dressed as a man. Short grey hair, but certainly a woman.

'You must be Alois,' she said, shaking hands with the catch. *That was his name!* Breen had heard it before. *Alois.*

'This is Okala, of the--'

OKALA! Breen squirmed with delight as her catch's gaze fell on the prince's human shape. *He found them, and he's now on a ship, no doubt heading for Ildecoke. What a delight! Imagine when Clyr finds out.*

Alois and the woman were talking now. He wanted to get home quickly, but avoid the Squalls and most importantly, Rhythlin Island.

Breen cackled. 'There's no way,' she whispered. 'The currents will force you to choose, and any sensible captain would choose the gamble of Rhythlin over the certainty of the Squalls.'

Breen settled onto her rock, in the cosy haze of dreamweed, to watch the conversations between her catch, human Okala, the new woman, joined eventually by the woman in the red headscarf she'd seen before-- the one from the ship the colony had taken.

They thought their fate was in their own hands, not knowing that it, like the black pearl, was in Breen's.

Sulat bowed and stepped out of the cabin onto the brightening deck. A familiar laugh met her ears and her spirits rose and cringed in equal measure. At the gangplank, Alois stood talking to a short, stocky woman with close-cut grey hair, who was laughing at something he'd said.

'So, this is Alois,' Dilys said, putting a square hand on his shoulder. 'You're right, he looks just like me.'

'I said he talks like you,' Sulat said. 'Incessantly.'

Dilys broke away to wrap her sturdy arms around Sulat. 'I heard what happened. I'm so sorry,' she whispered.

'You said I wasn't ready.' Sulat willed herself not to cry again. She was so exhausted of crying.

'We'll talk later,' Dilys said. 'I need to speak to the captain. You can show them to my cabin.' She strode off and Alois stepped up beside Sulat. 'So, a contract. That sounds like good news.'

'It's insurance. He hasn't decided yet.' Sulat rubbed the tattoo on the back on her neck. 'By the way, how would you feel about teaching the crew to fight? I volunteered you to be master-at-arms, if we need one.'

'Fine, yeah.' Alois nodded enthusiastically. 'Whatever you need.'

'And Okala, I need you to tell me everything you know about how your people do battle.'

The boy worried at a tangle in his hair, hunching his broad shoulders.

'What?'

'Well, Sandies and Rockies don't fight the same. We don't even have a standing force. When we do fight, we have very strict rules, meet on open planes, and that sort of thing. They, uhh, more prefer ambush.'

'That's valuable,' Alois said. 'Sulat and I know ambush tactics. I can work with that.'

Dilys entered her cabin about an hour later, leaving Alois and Okala to mill about, peering at the trappings of Second Mate, and Sulat explaining what all the different tools did.

'Sit, sit.' Dilys gestured at the chairs. 'My lord, are you a brandy or a port man?' Her hand hovered over the glass decanters that had been Sulat's primary domain when she had trained under her on *Martinette.*

'We're in port, aren't we?' he asked, grinning.

'Oh, very good.' Dilys chuckled at him and Sulat rolled her eyes as Dilys passed the glasses around. 'Your Highness, have you had the pleasure of fine spirits?' She held a glass of deep red liquid out to the mer prince.

He hesitated. 'Do you have tea?'

Dilys jerked her head at Sulat, who raised her eyebrows. 'Oh, that's right, you don't work for me anymore. I'll be back.' She backed out of the room and Alois snickered.

'I thought you were going to punch her. Is that what it was like when you were training?'

'Just like.' Sulat sipped her drink.

'That must have *killed* you.' Alois wheezed into his glass. 'Sulat is not made to serve,' he added to Okala.

'But I learned a lot,' Sulat conceded.

'So what did Fermin say?' Sulat asked, when Dilys returned with Okala's tea and settled herself in her chair.

'Oh, I imagine the same as he said to you. He wants to weigh the wasted time and money against the danger of sailing between the islands. Or cutting the difference by passing through the Squalls.'

'Is he seriously considering that?' Sulat asked incredulously.

'I doubt it,' Dilys grunted. 'We're between navigators again, as well.'

The navigator had been the soul they'd lost to the Squalls on Sulat's training voyage. She'd been replaced by an incompetent drunk, so Sulat and Dilys had had to act in his stead. He must have deserted. Ashryn, Sulat's navigator, had been mate and understudy to the first one, but now she was as dead as the other crew Sulat had poached from Fermin.

'So, we'll be making the charts, then.' Sulat said.

Alois, Sulat, and Okala were given cramped but comfortable cabins near the crew quarters. *Martinette* rarely took passengers, so the rooms were used as extra storage. Even with the sacks of grain, Alois was grateful for the full length bed.

Sulat, Dilys, and Fermin poured over charts for hours while Alois helped out with rebuilding the mast. Neither of them were much good at sitting and waiting patiently. Fermin still hadn't decided, but he wanted a solid plan and a sturdy mainmast before making his final ruling.

Okala sat in on the discussions, interjecting where he could. He strongly advised against threading between the islands, as that was where the Rocky Shore Merfolk were most likely to be, especially with Alois freshly Kissed, but to sail along the coast of Vurdia and then around the Squalls would waste valuable time, especially since *Martinette's* original port of call was on that route. Fermin couldn't abide passing Dunothe without stopping to conduct business, which could take months.

No one wanted to go through the Squalls, but autumn was coming quickly and the open sea to the west would be brewing storms of its own.

Fermin debated with his mates and eventually decided to acknowledge Okala's advice, but take safety over speed. They would just have to get past Rhythlin as quickly as they could.

Chapter Twelve
Siren Song

Passage between the tiny Lalarm Islands was agonisingly slow. *Martinette* was heavy with full crew and cargo. At top speed, it was less noticeable, but this tiptoeing sat her low in the water, groaning and bulging at every wave. The crew became restless, taking turns to stand at the rails for hours, watching the sea and exchanging nervous mutterings at every creak.

The news of the plan came as a shock to them. Most knew Sulat and sympathised with her loss, but that didn't make them any more eager to sail so close to creatures they feared.

'We're merchantmen!,' they said. 'We're not navy, how are we going to fight?'

'We're too slow with a hold full of cargo, how can we outrun them all the way back to Viehland?'

'Are we not to be paid for this voyage, then?'

Fermin used his customary blend of reassurance and authority to quiet the protests, and it was lucky for all of them that his reputation as a fair and steady captain was well-deserved, or else they might have faced mutiny.

Alois attempted to ease the tension by teaching the crew some basic fighting drills, should they need to draw weapons. Most of the men hesitated to spar with him, with the mark of his Kiss glowing clearly in the sunlight, so he enlisted Okala as his teaching partner. Okala, as Sandy Shore royalty, had even less fighting experience than even the Vurdence crew, most of whom had at least been in tavern brawls once or twice in their lives. He stood like a wooden statue and flinched wildly any time Alois got close with a fist or boot.

The theatrics did lighten the mood slightly, instilling in the men a confidence that at least they couldn't be worse than the prince, and they broke into pairs and groups to practice. Alois moved among them for a while, adjusting here and there before leaving them to it and joining Sulat at the rail.

Breen snickered in her cave at Okala, sabre in hand, lunging and parrying like a seagull with a broken wing.

'Is this where the humans are placing their hope?' she moaned, pitying. 'It's too easy, almost shameful.'

She cradled the pearl in one arm. By her side stood a rough stone sculpture depicting the peaks of the Lalarm Islands rising high above the scattered colonies nestled in valleys below. A plane of rippled glass hovered between like the surface of the sea, separating the two worlds. Chunks of wood moved slow as snails across the glass while brightly coloured grains of sand skittered across the bottom.

'You could have helped,' Alois said to the woman who was his partner.

'I didn't want to show you up, master-at-arms.'

'Show you up,' Breen whispered. 'Let's show her how you can fight.' She concentrated hard on her catch, his ship, and the water surrounding them. Her hand circled above the sculpture, searching for the telltale warm spot that would pinpoint which chunk of driftwood was his.

'Closer, closer, pet,' she whispered. 'There!' Her eyes fell on one pulling almost level with Decombre Island.

Damla rushed over with a bottle of wakejuice, the potion that cleared the body of all substances and unfogged the mind. Breen put her mouth over the opening of the bottle and sucked a bit of liquid through the soft sealed closure. Her veins tingled for a moment as the dreamweed dissipated.

The ship inched closer. Now was the time.

'Alert the king,' she said to her servant, as she steadied herself for what was to come.

She threw her head back, fixed in her mind the image of that tall broad man leaning on the rail of the ship with the wind blowing back his brown curls, and sang.

'Come to me, come to me now.'

Alois smirked, but his fingers drummed against the painted wooden rail, betraying his nerves. 'How long is this going to take?'

'I don't know,' Sulat said. 'I've never come this way back before.'

'I don't like it. I feel strange.'

Sulat's narrowed her eyes. 'What do you mean?'

He stretched his back and ran a hand through his stiff hair, shaking his head. 'I don't know. It's more than restlessness. It's like I want to jump in the water and swim. It's like that feeling you get just before a fight? Like I'm sizing everyone up, even the crew.' He shook out his hands and clenched and unclenched his fists. 'I don't know what it is. I just really want to be in the water.'

'Can you swim?' Sulat furrowed her brow. Even most sailors couldn't. She didn't know when he'd have learned, why he'd ever need to.

He shook his head. 'That's what's so strange. We'll get to Viehland faster on the ship, and I'd likely drown if I jumped.' His tongue flicked over the cut on his lip.

A chill washed over Sulat.

'Step back from the side.' Dilys came up beside them and pressed Alois back from the rail. 'Go sit.' She gestured at the cargo hatch, where several other sailors rested between shifts.

Alois strode dutifully away and Dilys leaned in to Sulat. 'He looks like a man about to do something desperate.'

'He wants to jump,' Sulat muttered back.

'Can he swim?'

Sulat shook her head.

'The sea can do strange things to heifers, even without the Kiss. I'll let the captain know, anyway.'

Alois watched Dilys go, bouncing one leg and rubbing his hands together.

'Am I your weathercock?' He grinned. 'Everyone's watching me more than the sails, now.'

'Can you blame them?' Sulat asked.

'Not really. I make myself nervous, if I'm honest.' He rubbed his mouth and leaned over his knees. 'What's happening to me?'

'Relax.' Sulat pursed her lips. 'When ships move slow, people get uneasy. We'll be fine once we're clear of the islands.'

'You don't think it has to do with...you know?' His tongue flicked over the cut on his lip again. 'You'd think more of these men would have been Kissed at some point.'

Not by someone like Breen.

'Lord Brynglass,' Fermin called from the door of his cabin before Sulat could answer. Dilys stood behind him, her arms stiff at her side. Alois jumped up. 'Come sit with me in my cabin,' the captain said. He spoke softer than he'd ever spoken to Sulat, and it worried her. *What does he suspect?*

Alois grimaced but joined the officers, and they shut the door behind him. Whispers flew at Sulat from the sitting crew and she shoved her hands into the pocket slits of her breeches.

It'll be fine once we pick up speed.

The wind brushed away the tiny curls that poked out under the back of her headscarf, but the unease remained. Hardly anyone spoke as *Martinette* weaved between swells, craggy shapes constantly looming in the haze, fencing them in. Faces jumped out at her from every rock formation, disappearing with the shift in angle. Fintips flipped in every wave, revealing themselves as rafts of seaweed. Every cry of a seagull sounded like the beginning of some hideous call, a song to pull the sailors toward the hidden rocks.

Sulat's senses reached out, searching for any sign, any hint of what lay ahead. Her ears reached. Her nerves crackled. Her eyes darted frantically from island to ocean. Cloud to horizon.

'Sulat.'

'Shit!' Sulat about jumped out of her skin. Okala stood behind her, palms up defensively. 'Shit, Okala.' She put a hand to her pounding heart and forced her breath back to normal. 'What?'

'We just passed Rhythlin Island,' he said.

How did I not notice?

Sulat wheeled around and, sure enough, there was the barren lump of scarred rock, hardly high enough out of the water to be visible as they slid past. There was nothing to show that anything had ever happened there. No planks of hull, no shreds of sail, no bloated purple corpses. It was just another unremarkable hunk of land, barely enough to warrant the distinction of 'island.'

A wave crashed on the rock shore and the foam pulled back from something red and sharp. Sulat's heart stopped, before realising that it was a bit of red seaweed that had flipped upright and dried.

Steady on, old girl. Don't lose your nerve.

'Turn around!' The door of the captain's cabin banged open and out burst Alois, Fermin and Dilys on his heels. 'Turn the ship around!'

'You don't give orders on my ship, my lord!' Fermin

shouted, fists clenched.

Dilys edged around Alois and pushed him back. 'Come on, my lord, let's get you settled and have some brandy.'

'Sulat, turn around, back to Rhythlin Island,' Alois shouted over Dilys' head.

'She also has no authority here.' Fermin threw an arm at Sulat. The crew stopped what they were doing to watch the altercation.

Alois broke free of Dilys, seized Sulat's shoulders, and shook her. 'By the souls, Sulat, *just do it*!'

His green eyes had gone bright, impossible blue.

'Oh, right, I see. Right away, of course.' Sulat dashed up the stairs to the helm and beckoned Fermin to follow. 'I think she's calling him.'

'So we should speed up, get out as quickly as we can,' Fermin hissed, waving an arm at the sea.

'*Capitan*!' a crewman shouted below. Three men piled on Alois, dragging him back from the rail.

Fermin muttered something in Vurdence before commanding his men. 'Restrain him. Take him to his cabin and make sure he stays there.'

A number of crewmen knuckled their brows and did as commanded, binding Alois' limbs, and wrestled him below-decks. Sulat cringed at the rough treatment, but she knew better than anyone what damage Alois' strength could do.

'He's not himself,' she said.

'It's the Kiss.' Fermin smoothed the front of his embroidered coat. 'I've seen it before. But I can't have him disturbing this ship. The crew are tense enough as it is. He won't be harmed.' He strode resolutely back to is cabin, a casual, 'As you were' to the helmsman as he passed.

Sulat made her way down to the cabins to check on Alois. She heard him before she ever made it close, shouting pleas and profanities, pounding on the door and walls.

'You took his weapons?' she asked the young seaman standing guard. The boy nodded, adjusting the gun belt at his hip. 'He headbutted Pid.' He gestured at a still figure lying prone on a cot nearby. 'Didn't want to see what he'd do with a sword.'

'Or guns,' Sulat agreed. The boy shook his head and pointed to a crate next to the door.

'His stuff's in there, in case he, you know.'

'Calms down?' Sulat offered. She knew Alois' temper. It flared quickly, burned hot for a while, then smoldered until something else distracted him.

'Dies,' the boy said.

'What?' Sulat froze.

The boy shifted uneasily. 'I never seen 'em calm down, cap'n,' he said. 'They just keep raving until they get away or, you know.'

'I *don't* know, seaman.' Sulat snapped. 'Until they *what*?'

'Well, the strain gets to be too much. They go mad or they just...they die.'

Sulat stomped past the boy, shouting for Okala.

'You didn't tell me he could die,' she hissed, dragging him behind a water barrel.

'I, uhh, I thought you knew.' Okala's voice was weak and thready, his fingers clenched and white.

'I didn't know anything! Everything I know, I got from you! *Speak*!'

'It's a tactic they use. Not us, we don't do that.'

I don't care what you lot do. 'What is the goal here?'

'If she gets bored waiting, she could lift the Call. And he could, theoretically, live out the rest of his life normally. Or she could continue calling him until he, uhh, either returns to her somehow or...dies.'

An empty hollow filled Sulat's chest as she released Okala's shoulder.

'Is there an alternative?'

Okala twisted his fingers together.

'Out with it!' Sulat barked.

'If she were to die,' Okala said in a jumble, 'he would be released.'

'Forever?'

'Yes, mostly.'

'Okala...'

'Well, her Kiss would still be upon him, so he wouldn't ever be totally free, but she'd never be able to call him again and he would still bear her protection from other merfolk.'

'So, that's it, general paranoia?' *Hell, I have that, and I live with it.*

'Yeah.' Okala twisted the fabric of his shirt.

'What aren't you telling me?'

'Well, it won't be easy, just like that. Breen is powerful, she's on her own terrain. You've only just discovered merfolk, you don't have experience fighting us.'

'Luckily for us,' Sulat growled, 'we have you.'

Sulat marched Okala to Captain Fermin's cabin and knocked.

Fermin's young cabin boy answered and let Sulat in. Dilys and First Mate Pers were there, also. Captain Fermin stood and doffed his hat, bowing to Okala. 'What can I do for you, Your Royal Highness?'

'I think we should make for land, Captain.' Okala tugged on his shirt, but his voice was strong.

'With all due respect, Your Highness, the faster we make port in Viehland, the faster we can have done with this whole business. I see no benefit to making land sooner than that. We have no advantage out here.'

'Captain, I believe Breen the Sea Witch means to kill His Lordship, and that the only real chance we have of saving his life is to confront her, and hopefully,' his voice cracked and Sulat groaned internally. He cleared his throat. 'Hopefully, break her power over him. I advised against going between the islands for precisely this reason.'

Captain Fermin laid his hand flat on the table. 'I acknowledge that I went against your advice, but it was the only course of action for me to take, therefore whatever consequences arise must be deemed unavoidable. If I must make the choice between him and my crew, he must be an unfortunate casualty, like so many before him at sea.'

'Captain, I believe we can achieve two things here,' Sulat cut in. 'We need him for this mission's success, as he is much more in favour at court than I am and he can convince the king of things that I can't.' *And if he dies, I'll have lost the last thing I care about. I'll have nothing left.* She swallowed hard, but pressed on. 'And if we can handle Breen now, we won't have her to contend with later. Removing her could create enough confusion to let us get home before they can regroup.'

'Kill her.' Fermin translated.

'Yes.'

Fermin stood up. 'The Sea Witch. You think we, a bunch of merchant sailors, scrabbling over uneven, slimy rock, will be able to find the Sea Witch, alone, and kill her?'

'I think we can lure her onto land, get her on her own, ambush her, and overpower her-- yes.'

'What about her magic?'

'Her magic only works in water,' Okala said. All faces in the room snapped to him. 'Did you not know that?' he asked. 'Her power is drawn from the sea. It's how the witches adapted, all those years ago.'

The Viehlish in the cabin shifted uncomfortably.

'So, if we get her onto land, she's powerless,' Dilys said.

'Essentially, yes. But she has to agree to go.'

'Why?' Fermin asked.

'She can't walk on her tail,' Sulat said quietly.

Okala nodded. 'So we have to somehow get Alois to the centre of the island and away from the holes.'

'What about mundane weapons?' Sulat asked. 'We take away her powers, then what? What other non-magic abilities does she have?'

'Well, I've never heard of her being a warrior,' Okala said. 'Though, they could have kept that secret. We don't exactly get along, Rocky Shore and Sandy Shore Merfolk.'

'So we have to assume that she can fight,' Sulat said.

'Her weapons would be things we get down there, like imitations of human weapons, but adapted. We don't use much metal, mostly fish bone, glass, stone, some rope.'

'Rudimentary and crude,' Fermin said.

Okala shrugged. 'Don't assume just because it's simple that it's not deadly. Your men don't wear armour, ours do.'

Fermin didn't answer for a minute. 'Pers, Dilys,' he barked and they rushed over. He turned his back on Sulat and held a hasty and mumbled conversation with his two mates while Sulat waited, impatient. Finally, he addressed her again. 'We will send a small landing party with you. I will not risk my entire crew. And if it looks like my men will not be enough to fight, you will retreat. Do we have an understanding?'

Sulat chewed her tongue. She didn't like that agreement at all. But arguing the terms could force Fermin to sail past the islands entirely, and who knew how far Breen's influence reached. At least this way, she had her landing party. Alois was still banging on the walls below, and she didn't see any alternative.

Grudgingly, she held out a hand, and Fermin shook it.

Dilys managed to find an ancient map of Rhythlin Island somewhere in the stacks, and unfurled it across the table in the chart room. With any luck, the topography of the island hadn't changed much since it was drawn, assuming it was ever accurate. The island was riddled with holes and caves, but the dead centre looked to be as flat and solid as they could hope for.

Martinette circled Grocachee Island, pointed her nose toward Viehland, and dropped anchor. Sulat's skin prickled as she climbed into the boat, expecting Breen to leap out of the water at any moment and seize Alois before they made land. But eventually, they bumped into the shore and climbed onto the rocks.

A crewman cut the ropes around Alois' legs so that he

could walk, leaving his hands and arms tightly bound.

Sulat splashed onto the shore with Dilys. He shot her a nasty glower.

'Why are you doing this?' he asked, dolefully.

'This is for your own good,' she reminded him. 'For all our good. King and kingdom and all that.'

'Since when do you care about king and kingdom?'

'I don't, but you do. And I want revenge.' *No sense denying it.*

'This plan won't work, you know that,' he muttered.

'It's the only one we've got.'

The wind picked up suddenly and blew hard against the little trail of people.

'You should go back, Sulat,' Alois said. 'Just let her take me. That's all she wants.'

'Horseshit,' Sulat retorted. 'And imagine what trouble Johanne would give me if I let another woman have you.'

'Johanne.' Alois shrugged. 'Johanne doesn't matter.'

Sulat scoffed. *Clumsy.* The sea witch had failed the test. It was clear now that Alois wasn't in control of his speech any more than he was of his will.

'Come and get him, Breen,' Sulat whispered as they neared the centre of the island.

'Oh, I have,' Alois said in unison with a voice behind them. Sulat spun around as the naked scaly torso of a yellow and grey woman with long blonde hair rose out of the sea.

'Come to me, my pet,' she purred, and her voice cut through Sulat, vibrating her bones and setting her teeth on edge.

Boom!

A dozen guns went off and a dozen bullets flew at the mermaid, but she didn't budge. She hovered motionless in the water, staring ahead, the smile widening on her lips. Sulat made to defend Alois just as two big mermen charged across the stone on crab legs, wrenched Alois away from his captors, and dove into Breen's pool. It happened so fast that Sulat had no time to react. She raised her blunderbuss on Breen.

'Thank you for returning him,' Breen said as she flipped her large striped fin and dove backward into the sea.

Sulat's finger tightened over the trigger and the shot landed uselessly with a *plunk* in the ocean.

Sulat stumbled over the jagged rocks to the pool where the mermen had taken Alois. She splashed through the pool and dove in, but Dilys pulled her back. *What have I done? What have I done?* she screamed in her head over and over. *He's gone. He's really gone now. What will I do?*

'You can't swim!' Dilys yelled. 'Sulat, you can't swim!'

Sulat swung to throw Dilys off, but teetered and fell on her knees on the sharp icy rocks, hot blood staining her tan breeches.

What am I going to do?

Two strong arms lifted her up.

'Come along now, come on,' a voice said from a great distance away. 'Come along now, we need to think of a plan.'

Her mind raced. Her mouth tasted like bitter metal. *Dive in the water, get him back. They can't have gotten far. Of course they can, they have fins.* She couldn't swim. *Ships are faster. Ships can't dive. No way, no way.*

Nothing she could do.

Stick to the plan.

The shards of her broken mind inched back together.

'No, you're right.' Sulat brushed off the heavy gnarled and rough hands. 'Back to the boats. We've got to push through to Viehland.'

'What? Just like that?' Dilys shouted. 'You want to leave?'

'What should I do? What can any of us do?' Sulat screamed. *Of course I want to get him back! Of course I want to dive down there and pull him back from her!*

She rubbed her face. Every inch of her body tingled, hummed like a harp string pulled too tight, ready to snap.

She wanted to scream, to pull her hair out, run in circles, shoot something. She threw her eyes to sea, expecting Alois' head to poke above the waves, having overcome his captors and fought his way back. But the sea was as remorseless as the panic rising in her.

This is your fault. You did this. You took him to Rhythlin, where he got Kissed. You pushed for this idiotic plan, and now he's gone. He's really gone, there's nothing you can do to get him back. And it's your fault. He could be safe with Johanne right now if you hadn't obeyed Renir like a lapdog.

The emotion bubbled over her and spilled out of her eyes. She heaved a heavy sob and fell to her bleeding and tender knees in the saltwater that stung almost too much to bear. But she did bear it, relishing the pain as it stabbed through her. She sobbed hard and loud, falling forward onto her hands which stung even more than her knees. Physical pain mixed with heartbreak ripping through her, threatening to tear her apart. Her ship, her crew, and now Alois. She wanted to fall into the water, to drown, to be taken by one of Breen's men. That would be poetic, to join Alois and her crew in their fate, for which she was responsible.

Dilys put both hands on her shoulders. Sulat's mind slammed back into reality, the icy howl of the wind, the salty sting everywhere, the bruises blooming under her skin, and the rage that had been fermenting under the grief.

'Let's get back to the ship,' the mate's voice said, loud and clear as a ship's bell. 'We can't follow him, and we have to get back to Viehland. The navy is the only hope he has now.'

Chapter Thirteen
Leverage

Hazy and jumbled thoughts chased each other in Alois' mind, fading like smoke whenever he tried to hold one. He needed Breen, needed to be near her. It was wrong, dangerous, but worth the risk. Other women hovered at the edge of his memory, Sulat and...a blonde woman. Who was that? And what was he planning before? Something about the king?

None of it mattered. He was going to be with Breen, she had come for him.

Water bubbled up around Alois and he went under, held fast by two powerful arms, realising too late that he hadn't taken a breath. The spell broke as his lungs strained, fighting to conserve the air he had.

Breen appeared in front of him, holding a shimmering ball. She pushed it at his head and he became aware of his wet hair sticking to his forehead. The bubble stayed where she'd put it.

'You can breathe now, human.' The mermaid's voice reverberated through his skull.

'You're not going to eat me?' Alois asked, salt water burning his throat. Breen smirked, baring jagged teeth.

'Not yet.' She swam on, her powerful tail sending ripples into his face as the mermen dragged him forward.

The island was made up of a collection of rocks with holes and furrows bored through it like worm-eaten bread. What appeared on the surface to be a shallow pool might be a hole into open water. The underside of the island was eerie, pockmarked and rugged, and instead of being carpeted in moss and slime, was strewn with straggly curtains of seaweed.

The mermen wound in and out of the weeds, around steep stalactites of rock, down through hidden tunnels and through winding cave complexes, following the sea witch.

The bubble around Alois' head wobbled and threatened go burst every time a strong current came through or the mermen bumped his head against a dagger of rock. He breathed in a lungful of air, held it as long as he could, then exhaled quickly and dragged in another.

Finally, the terrain cleared, the rough seafloor populated by a mass of shifting shapes. They separated into distinct slivers of darkness, each wiggling independently. A few came toward him and their outlines sharpened: more merfolk.

Some of them had the lower halves of long sleek fish like Breen, some were long and flat like eels, or shelled and scaled like turtles. Some with the round shells and ruffled feet of snails inched over the rocky sea bottom, some undulated with the tentacles of jellyfish and squids, or fluttered by with the rippling wings and spiney tails of rays. All had the naked torsos of humans in muted colours ranging from light grey or tan, to spinach green and brick red, to coal black. Many had tattoos and many were draped in woven seaweed or strings of pearls and shiny stones and shells. One or two of them had gold and silver adornments, or jewelry fashioned from human detritus. Alois spotted a fork twisted into an elaborate comb in the matted blond hair of one walrus-bodied merman with thick black lines painted on his walnut-brown skin.

The merfolk approached curiously, but no one said anything or impeded the progress of Breen and her prisoner.

A clam shell opened up and a woman with pink hair and skin poked her head out, lifted two sticks of coral, and banged them together. The ripple rattled Alois' teeth. Breen shot a wicked grin over her shoulder as the goons on either side of Alois held him tighter.

The procession stopped beside a large pillar of craggy rock. Breen's tail quivered as she held her arms wide. Everyone stayed still, save the flicking of fins or the billowing of tentacles. Even Alois hung limp between his captors, at once terrified and resigned to what was about to happen.

Something moved in the darkness, a shadow sliding down the jagged rock face. Two spots of pink light sparkled and expanded into circles that glowed through the rippling bubble, followed by the orange-and-white speckled head and torso of a man, joined to the emerald green armoured body of a shrimp with a dozen spindly scarlet legs. Just under his normal human-like arms, he had a second pair with huge round ends like balled fists. Around his neck, on a gold chain, hung the Day Star.

Alois would have recognised that jewel anywhere. It had belonged to Princess Dahna of Inchiajua, and had been worn by her impostor, Ydrae, at the Royal Wedding, last year. When Ydrae threw herself from the palace balcony into the sea, the Day Star went with her, presumed lost, a fact Dahna had never adjusted to. Now, here it was, sparkling around the mottled neck of an undersea nightmare.

'What is this commotion?' The creature asked, in a high thin voice that nevertheless reverberated through Alois' bones. 'What have you brought me, Breen?' He wrung his speckled hands, his pink eyes swivelling in their overlarge sockets.

'I've brought you the human,' Breen said, projecting her voice, and gesturing grandly behind her, sliding to the side. The mermen holding Alois moved forward and hoisted him up by the armpits. He could do nothing. He was outnumbered, unarmed, lost, and had only a tiny bubble of air to keep him from drowning before he reached the surface.

All he could do was stare back at the creature in front of him and brandish his very last weapon: defiance.

'If you're going to kiss me, you should know I'm with her.'

Each of the king's eyes moved independently of the other, as he inspected Alois.

'Not to worry, my friend, not to worry. I bow to Breen for her undeniable taste.' The king over-enunciated every word, and spread his second pairs of arms wide, but did not bend his torso. 'You are quite the catch, my good man, quite the catch.' He skittered up to Alois until they were almost touching noses.

Alois pulled himself together and laughed. 'The irony-- a human quite the catch for a fish.'

A hum circulated through the assembled merfolk, but the king put up a hand.

'Be not alarmed by this topsider's rudeness. He is ignorant because his people are arrogant and yet so--very--delicate.' He poked the bubble with the last three words. 'It's true that you are Breen's catch, but that's not as inconvenient as you might think. You see, she has control over you, but I have her loyalty. Don't worry, nothing will happen to you while you are my guest. You are much too important for that.'

He lifted a mottled hand and rubbed one of his eyeballs. Alois shuddered.

'If you're not going to eat me, then what other use am I to you?'

'Oh, now you want to talk properly. What a treat!' the king wrung his hands together. 'I'm sure we'll have some very enlightening conversations while you're with us. Comecome-comecome.' He beckoned to the mermen holding Alois. 'Let's build you a little, what's the word, aquarium?' He gave a high-pitched giggle. 'Because normally, you confine pet fish to a little bowl of water on land. But we're imprisoning a landman in a little bubble of air underwater. Same word, opposite meaning.'

Alois' head spun. *He's making word jokes. How mad is he? How can all of these people follow a man who is so clearly insane? Even Breen-- she has to see it.*

The king stopped on the other side of the collection of rocks that made up his castle, and raised both arms above his head. Breen swam up beside him and did the same. Bubbles erupted from all four hands, combined, and grew. Breen edged around the bottom, pulling the giant bubble to the sand.

'Oh, but, my friend, you are still bound. Did your people do that, I wonder? They didn't trust you much, eh?' King Kellac smiled at Breen. 'Never fear, I think you can be trusted here.'

Panic rose in Alois as Kellac edged out of sight behind him, but a moment later, his wrists floated apart, rope burns stinging in the salt water.

Alois' heart leapt into a gallop and he weighed the chances of escape.

No chance, at all.

The mermen holding Alois pressed him against the bubble. They pushed slowly but firmly, mashing Alois' face against the warm, leathery surface until it gave way and he fell onto his knees with a squelch in the wet sand, his clothes sticking to him and dripping in little plops onto the sand.

Alois scrambled to his feet, pushing his hair back, and faced the merfolk circling his bubble as though he were a fish in a bowl. The shapes fluctuated on the other side of the barrier, some of them only vague patches of colour against the grey blue water. Yellow-grey Breen barely stood out among her murky kin hovering close to the bubble.

'What are you going to do with me?' Alois asked Kellac, glaring up in his unnerving face. It was unusual for Alois to ever find someone much taller than himself, but the king's many legs gave him a couple of extra feet that Alois hadn't noticed when everyone was floating in the water.

'Why, you are our guest, Mr--uhh, what is your name, actually? Alois, was it?' The king paused and swivelled his eyestalks at Breen.

'Lord Brynglass,' Alois answered, pulling his shoulders back.

The king wiggled his fingers excitedly. 'A lord, eh? You must be very important.' The merfolk hummed again, some flashing their tails excitedly. 'Quite the catch *indeed*, Breen. Well, my lord, I'm afraid we can't offer you the comfort to which you are accustomed, but you can rest assured you will have all of the courtesy one of your, uhh, class deserves.'

Some of the other merfolk inched closer and he could make out their grinning faces now. Some had very long, very sharp teeth.

'You can't keep me here forever. I have friends up top and they will come for me.'

'Oh, of course they will, my lord,' the king said. 'Why, as I said, you're an important person.'

The merfolk taunted Alois mercilessly while he was in the bubble. They'd tap on the skin of it, making the whole structure pound like a drum. The loud vibrations made his eardrums pound and the bones of his skull ache. He'd cringe and cover his ears and they would laugh and swim or scuttle away. Occasionally, Breen would come and watch him. Alois had the distinct impression that she was reminding him that he was her pet, hers to do with as she pleased the moment the king allowed it.

The closest thing he had to an ally was a surly crab-bodied merman with armoured red skin and huge clawed hands. He squeezed himself through the bubble with a bivalve shell full of raw seafood and piles of seaweed. He tipped out the excess water and thrust the shell at Alois.

'Doesn't it bother you to bring me dead...crab?' Alois asked, peeking at the pink claws inside the shell.

The merman shrugged. 'I eat crab.'

That was fair enough, Alois supposed.

'I eat human, too,' the crab-man growled. A chill ran up Alois' spine, but he had his one weapon, still.

'Can't have me.' He grinned, licking the cut on his lip. 'By the way, can I get some water?' His saliva was thick and his tongue kept sticking to the roof of his mouth.

The merman blinked at him. 'There's a whole ocean out there. Just stick your head through the bubble.'

'I actually need fresh water.' Alois knew it was a gamble asking, but King Kellac wanted him alive for some reason, and he couldn't drink saltwater.

The merman scowled, pushing a couple of skinny pink feet through the bubble. 'I'll ask Breen about it.' And he was gone, leaving Alois with a handful of raw fish meat.

The translucent flesh wasn't as unpleasant as Alois would have expected. He felt a deepened kinship with Okala, now understanding what the boy had known before being thrust into the astringent world of Vurdence cuisine. The fish was wet and very salty, but it had a sweetness to it and didn't actually smell that fishy. It made him nostalgic for the days he and Sulat used to catch fish in springs and rivers for their dinners after a long day of walking. Nothing quite beat a bit of fresh trout cooked over and open fire.

Alois reclined on a cold rock and reminisced, sucking a gritty snail out of its shell. He had little else to do but eat and explore his memories, as all of his plans for escape ended in getting past the bubble and either being put back in or drowning. He waved cheerily at a spiny orange and white striped mermaid, and picked a bit of shell out of his teeth.

No doubt, they thought they'd broken him, but really, he was waiting.

Sulat will come for me. There'll be a scuffle, some opportunity for daring and heroics, then I'll go home to Parry House and my family.

He pulled out the painted miniature of Johanne that he

always kept in his pocket. It was oil paint and varnish, so thankfully, the water hadn't destroyed it, and her placid smile soothed his frazzled nerves.

The fight about chewing felt so distant, so insignificant, now. Of course, it mattered, Rosabel needed good manners to succeed in society. But, it was never about that. It was about the tension, the disappointment, the pressure. He just needed a break, some distance from it and change of perspective.

He gazed up through the dome of the bubble to the grey ocean beyond, and snorted.

Well, I got that, didn't I?

Miniature Johanne continued to smile as he rubbed a thumb over her face.

'If we have more children, I'll be happy. But if not, well, it was really only you and Rosabel that I wanted, anyway.'

He laid the miniature face down on his chest, folded his arms behind his head and closed his eyes.

Thumm--thumm. His teeth chattered and the vein in his temple twitched as pain throbbed through his head.

Damn bastards...oh.

Breen hovered outside the bubble, her fin waving lazily, and held up a pea green seaweed bladder the size of her head. She thrust her tan arm through the bubble, water running along her skin and down the inside of the barrier, pooling and darkening the now-white sand. Alois, pocketed Johanne's portrait, set down his shell, and sauntered to her. Her hands and arms were covered in thin delicate scales like Okala's, but her fingernails were murderously long and pointed.

'Be careful,' her voice hummed. 'If you set it down wrong, it'll spill. And it's not easy to make.'

'Sorry to inconvenience you.' Alois took the slick bladder around the neck, his hand brushing hers. She shuddered and pulled her arm away, wiping her hand on her back.

You're the one who's slimy. He might be dirty, but it was her fault, dragging him through the sea.

'The king wants you healthy. We can't have you drying

out, can we?' Her face twisted in disgust as she rubbed her hand where he had touched her. 'Anything else I can fetch you, while I have free time?'

'Got anything to read?'

Breen smirked and backed away from the bubble. Alois took a deep swig of the water. It was indeed fresh, and tasted sweet as sconch to his parched and salt-lined mouth. He wanted to drink the whole thing in one, but thought it would be best to only drink half, so he dug a hollow in the sand and set the bladder carefully in it. He settled himself against his rock again to finish his lunch.

Thumm-thumm.

By the souls. Alois woke, grinding his teeth. *What now?*

King Kellac wrung his long fingers and paced back and forth. Alois rolled onto his feet and ambled to the bubble skin, sweeping up his water bladder as he went. He made a show of bowing dramatically.

'A royal visit. Lucky me.'

The king chuckled. 'Mm, indeed. You are lucky. I hope you're comfortable. I hear Breen made you a special treat.'

'I'm sure it sounds strange to you folk down here, but we land creatures have to drink water every so often. I suppose it's like the whales who must come up for air.'

'Yes, it's a weakness,' King Kellac agreed. 'You're a puzzle, Lord Brynglass.' He knitted his fingers. 'Here you are, in our little bubble, but you seem perfectly at ease. What terrors you must have seen.'

'You have no idea,' Alois said. 'I'm just waiting to find out why I'm here.'

'And I'm here to tell you, at last. You have the ear of your king. You have standing at court, greater even than your friend, we heard as much from her own lips.'

'Oh, Your Highness...' Alois tilted his head back, finally understanding and seeing the future laid out before him. *They're not going to kill me, they think I'm going to negotiate.* A giddiness threatened to overcome him. He saw the path before him and he was as good as free. 'Oh, your Highness, you got the wrong one.'

'The wrong what? What do you mean?' Kellac asked, his voice betraying something sharper than curiosity.

'The wrong human. I'm soft. If you'd taken her, I'd roll over, give you anything you asked for; but you took me. You want to know why I'm not afraid of you? I've seen a lot of scary things, but nothing half as scary as Sulat when she's angry. She is fierce, she is ruthless, and right now, I guarantee, she is angry. You took a lot from her before, but now you've got me, and she'll cut a bloody swath through your people to get me back. It might be better to just let me go and make your peace with Bertold.'

Alois had won, he knew it. The king might be bitter to the point of madness, but he was no fool.

'She cares that much for you?' Kellac asked, his voice barely audible through the bubble.

'Yes, she does.'

'Then it looks like I have just the one I want, an excellent bargaining piece.' A grin spread across the king's thin blue lips, displaying four rows of translucent teeth. 'Breen, make some more fresh water.'

Chapter Fourteen
Emotions

Sulat still couldn't bring herself to believe what had happened. Every time her thoughts turned to Alois, as they did every few seconds, she only saw him disappearing into the surf. That was always where it ended, over and over. She couldn't picture anything that happened after; her imagination simply wouldn't go.

Was he drowned, held choking underwater by those webbed hands? Was he eaten, ripped apart by hundreds of jagged teeth? Was he taken somewhere and held captive, in a cave with a trapped pocket of sour air?

Her mind simply wouldn't accept that he was gone, that she couldn't leave her cabin right then and find him on deck, joking with the crew or trying to find work to do. Part of her wanted to look, to prove to herself that he was there, that he was fine. It had all been a dream, a hallucination, that she hadn't seen what she was sure she had seen. It wouldn't be the first time her mind had played tricks on her.

Her hands balled into fists and she banged them on her

knees. This was stupid...she couldn't doubt herself now. She couldn't lose control. He wasn't there, he was gone. There was no sense in giving herself hope.

He was taken, and it was her fault.

She should have protected him, shouldn't have tried to outsmart Breen.

You always think you're so damn clever, don't you? 'So damn clever.' She sneered.

Maybe there was a reason he was taken, a reason he was Kissed, *chosen* by Breen. Maybe he wasn't simply the first one to come upon her singing on the island, but that she singled him out. If Sulat could figure out what she wanted, maybe she could exchange it for Alois' life. There wasn't much she wouldn't readily give. She didn't have much left anyway. She just wanted him back.

No, it's useless.

She sank inside herself. The bottom of whatever kept her upright crumbled and she fell, tumbling into the despair and hopelessness that had gnawed at her in the days before she met him, when she was all rage and recklessness. Nothing mattered then, and now that he was gone, she had nothing again.

It was her fault. He was likely dead by this time, beyond her saving. Kellac would probably force her to do something demeaning, tease her with the possibility of saving Alois, and then reveal that he was dead the whole time, just to destroy her.

Sulat didn't bother with the glass, and tipped a mouthful of brandy bottle over her lips.

What was the point in any of it? What was the point in going on? She had only felt alive when she was with him, until she got her ship. Now it was gone, he was gone. She wasn't Captain Sulat anymore, not even part of a crew. She was just a broken woman on someone else's ship.

Another gulp.

There's no one. There's nothing. I might as well go back to the convent and live out the rest of my life with my mother.

Another gulp. Something twanged inside her.

Not that, I'd rather die. I'd rather be eaten or drowned.

Her spine tingled a little.

That's true. I'd rather be eaten alive by merfolk or drowned than go back to that place.

She sat up straighter. She had something to stand on. *I have that, he didn't give me that. I had it before.*

She lifted her head and took another gulp of brandy. The floor of the cabin was solid under her now, and she stood up.

'I am not defeated.'

She pulled her coat on and stomped out onto the deck.

'Okala!' she shouted, and the boy came running. 'How do I contact King Kellac?'

Okala hesitated. 'What are you thinking?'

'Why would Breen call Alois? Of all the men she's Kissed, why call one particular man, if she just meant to eat him?'

Okala pulled back. 'You think he's part of a plan?'

'How does the Call work?

'We can use it to entrance a large group of people a little bit, or one person completely.'

'But why? Why do you use it?'

'Well, they use it to crash ships when they're hungry. We usually use it to distract people so we can come and go unnoticed.'

'Would they call one single person just to eat them?'

'That is...unlikely.'

'So there's a purpose for wanting him specifically.'

'Well...sometimes,' Okala twisted a lock of hair.

'What?' *I've about had it with this boy not telling me everything.*

'A mermaid can sometimes call a specific man if she's fallen in love with him. That has happened.'

Sulat rolled her eyes hard. *ALOIS AND HIS WOME-- wait.*

'Breen's not the type to fall for a human, is she?'

'Admittedly, no...' Okala said slowly.

'So there's probably a bigger reason.'

'It...does look that way, now.' Okala conceded.

'How do I call them, then?'

'I don't know,' Okala groaned. 'If you had the Kiss, there could be a way, but you don't.'

Clarity broke through the clouds of despair and brandy in Sulat. 'I won't need to. If this is a plot, they'll come to me. Stop the ship!' Sulat shouted. 'Lift the sails, hold here!'

Sulat banged on Fermin's door and he was there before she could shout again. 'Captain, stop the ship.'

'Are you Kissed, too?'

'This was strategic,' Sulat said. 'Breen took Alois because she wants to barter him, they've taken him as a hostage. Why else would she have called him? She had a craving for a man who happens to be gentry, happens to be in a position to negotiate on Ildecoke Island?'

Fermin's shoulders relaxed as Sulat spoke. 'Why would Breen want his lordship?' he asked Okala.

'I know she and King Kellac had plans to get Ildecoke Island back, that's why she wanted me out of the way.' He swept a hand over his human body. 'But I didn't know they were already acting.'

'How long do you want to stay stopped here, *Capitaine*?' Fermin asked.

'Less than a day, if I'm right.'

Fermin whistled and ran a hand over his face. 'We were making with all possible haste back to Viehland.'

'That was before. If they want to negotiate, they need to be able to catch us, and preferably as far from Ildecoke as we can be.'

At the words, 'catch us,' everyone within earshot tensed, including Fermin and his officers.

'Do we want them to catch us?' he asked, his voice a little higher than normal. He didn't mention Sulat's ship-- he didn't need to.

'Every step is a gamble, Captain,' Sulat said. 'Even Okala is at risk, now.' *Flatter him.* 'Imagine the songs and stories of how you stared down the merfolk king on open water in defence of

Viehland.'

'Stories and songs concern me far less than actually sailing away afterward, especially Viehlish ones. How can I be sure that we won't end up their next meal?'

'Because they're not animals,' Okala said. 'Breen and Kellac are cunning. They must have chosen him, specifically him, for a reason. Breen wants a war, but Kellac wants to negotiate first. In that context, it makes sense that they took a lord. Attacking the ship that is headed to Ildecoke and carries someone who can bargain,' he waved a hand at Sulat, 'doesn't make any sense. You have to stop thinking about merfolk as mindless fish, but as humans who adapted to a different environment. Because that is what we are. *They* are.' He swallowed hard.

Fermin listened silently as Okala spoke, then took a deep breath.

'Raise the sails, lower the anchor. We will wait here until nightfall.'

Breen tipped the glass bottle of filtered freshwater into a seaweed bladder. It felt like menial kitchen work, like she was a servant with nothing better to do than cook their prisoner his special meals. But it had to be her. Damla had never mastered the art of collecting bubbles from the gas spring that was so vital to the process.

How badly Breen longed to just eat him; but he was important, and important people had to be kept healthy. Funny how even land animals got too dry.

'Breen!' Damla called from the big cave. 'Something's wrong with your map. One of the ships has stopped moving.'

That's odd. Breen pinched her eyebrows together. 'Which one, Damla?'

There was a pause, then, '*Martinette.*'

That's the ship my man was on, and his woman, too. And

Okala.

Breen sealed the bladder tightly, removing it from the glass bottle, and gave it a little shake to mix the sedative she'd added. She hurried into the chamber, thrust the bladder into Damla's hands and leaned over her map of the islands and driftwood. It was true, the one marked *Martinette* was holding stationary as the waves and other bits of wood moved around it.

'Is there something wrong with the magic?' Damla asked. 'Oh, but isn't that the ship our human came from?' She leaned next to Breen and squinted at the anomaly. She poked it with her finger, but it bounced back to the same spot and held still. 'What are they waiting for?'

Waiting, that's it. That's what they're doing. Breen grinned at her assistant. *That makes things a bit easier.*

'Us.'

No one spoke, only the creaking of the wood and the ropes broke the silence. Fermin positioned himself at the wheel, the place of best visibility on the ship. Sulat stood behind him, drumming her fingers on the polished wood of the staircase railing. Dilys was beside her, stiff and anxious, and mercifully silent.

A great roar thundered toward them and it took a moment before anyone noticed the bubbles that heralded something big coming from deep water.

The sea rose like an island before breaking over the backs of a dozen creatures in dull, muddy colours, framing the monster in the middle.

Sulat knew him immediately. He had haunted her every thought for nearly a week.

Panic rose in her and she gripped the rail, resisting the urge to take cover, to find a sturdy shield, her heart beating so fast it made her dizzy. *All of these people are going to die.*

She gulped for air and something touched her. She jumped violently, but it was only Dilys, squeezing her shoulder.

'Touch your boot, girl,' Dilys said in her ear, low enough for only Sulat to hear. Sulat bent and ran fingers over the tooling on her tall leather boots.

The tension eased and the world righted again. That's when she noticed the wet brown and blue bundle at Kellac's scarlet front feet.

He's alive! They've brought him here to bargain!

'I recognise you, human!' King Kellac shouted, his voice piercing the air like an icy wind. Sulat winced. 'And I imagine you recognise me, though you came back with a different ship. Come and treat with me. I think I can find terms we would both find agreeable.' He wrung his hands together, the Day Star sparkling on his chest.

'The only term I will agree to is the immediate end to the attacks on our ships.' Sulat shouted back.

'You don't do this much, do you? Don't you want to hear what I want?' Kellac grabbed a handful of brown hair from the lump at his feet and shook it.

'Is he alive?' Sulat asked.

'Come and see,' the king said with a grin, dropping the body back at his feet. Sulat quivered with rage as she gripped the hilt of her sword.

'Tell me first. If he's alive, I'll treat with you. If he's dead, I'll kill every last thing with fins I can find.'

'Ooh, your fishermen won't like that,' the king chided.

'You can't expect me to negotiate over a corpse.'

The king smirked and kicked Alois with one of his many thin red legs and Alois flinched. He groaned and rolled slowly over. A heavy weight lifted from Sulat's shoulders. *There's hope, after all.*

'Prove Breen isn't controlling him.'

King Kellac huffed and hoisted Alois up. 'Say something only she would know.'

Alois' lips parted weakly and he mumbled something too

faint for Sulat to hear. Kellac bent his bald head over Alois and then straightened.

'He said, "bloodworm." Does that have any significance to you?'

Sulat almost laughed. *Ass. He would use that memory. Well, if he still has his stupid sense of humour, he might be all right.*

'Good, send him over,' she shouted.

The king giggled, high and manic. 'And relinquish my best leverage? I think not, Captain. I think not.'

Sulat turned to Captain Fermin. 'I want to invite him onboard.'

'On my ship?' Fermin choked, his fingers closing white around the rail.

'I can't go to the water.' Sulat tried not to move her lips much. 'He has legs, he can come aboard, and he'd have to leave Breen where she is.'

'What's to stop him breaking my ship like he did yours?' Fermin hissed.

'What's stopping him anyway?' Sulat asked. 'If he was going to eat us, he'd have broken your ship already.'

Fermin looked to his officers. Otto shook his sweaty bald head, but Dilys stayed still, watching Sulat.

'If there will be a fight, we will have a moment of advantage.' Sulat said. 'If we go to water, we'll start off behind. Let's try to end this without fighting.'

Fermin's lips parted with a dry smack. 'I don't need to remind you how many souls are onboard here. Are you confident enough in this wager to add them to the ones already weighing your heart?'

A hard lump choked Sulat, but she nodded. She wasn't, but boldness was the only plan that had a chance of working.

'Come aboard, Your Highness,' she called. 'We will extend you safe passage, or else continue shouting over the wind like this.'

Kellac grinned at her beneath those unnerving eyes for a moment before lifting Alois in his speckled arms, wading into the sea, and paddling through the water to the ship. He took hold of the steps jutting from the side and climbed, Alois hanging limply, and slipped onto the deck like a centipede. Sulat's stomach roiled at all of those legs, but clenched her jaw as Alois thudded wetly onto the deck and rolled onto his back with a groan.

Sulat stepped forward, extending a hand. 'Welcome aboard, King Kellac.'

Kellac's hand was hard and cold, jointed like a gauntlet, when he shook.

'What an honour,' he giggled, his eye stalks swivelling to look at each of the surrounding crewmen, who all shifted nervously.

'I am Captain Gidie Fermin,' Fermin said, stepping forward with his hand out. 'This is my ship, *Martinette*. Welcome aboard, Your Royal Highness.'

Kellac's eyes widened. 'Two captains? Oh, that's right,' he giggled, covering his mouth and patting Alois almost affectionately with one of his red legs. 'You haven't got a ship, Captain Sulat. Generous of Captain Fermin to let you borrow his, and all of these fine sailors, just to treat with me. And Prince Okala.' Kellac bowed deeply, grinning. 'Breen did a marvellous job on you. You must be so happy, in your truest form, where you belong.'

Okala didn't shrink from the taunt, but Dilys stepped closer to Sulat. She needn't have, Sulat was far too angry to rise to that kind of bait. She wasn't about to misstep, not with Alois right there.

'I understand that you are the representative of the Viehlish king,' King Kellac said.

'In a limited capacity,' Sulat agreed.

'But you can negotiate in his name.'

'To a point.'

'Oh, all I want is a meeting.' The king clasped both hands over where his heart would be on a human torso. 'And my demands are simple. I want my island and my palace back. Give us back what is ours and we will be your allies.'

'You're a murderer. How can we trust you to keep your word?'

'You forget!' the king screamed, wrenching Alois up by his hair again and extending a sharp claw under his jaw, 'what I have to trade. I want my island. Our island that was stolen from us when your murdering ancestors pushed us into the sea! You think you have the moral advantage here?'

Sulat resisted the urge to say, 'Not *my* ancestors.'

Alois' eyes rolled to Sulat's and she thought his head shook. Or was it the king shaking him around? *Keep it together, girl.*

'You're offering one man in exchange for the seat of power of my kingdom. I speak for the Crown. Do you think this man means more to the king than his capital?'

'And what does he mean to you?'

Sulat couldn't allow her true feelings to show, she had to maintain distance.

'A hell of a lot of trouble, truth be told.'

Something passed across Alois' face. Was it a smile? Was he fighting whatever was suppressing him? She was terrible at reading faces, but the rest of his body was so limp, she couldn't read it either.

'Well, allow me to relieve you of your burden.' Kellac poked his claw into the skin of Alois' neck. A spot of red beaded at the point. 'If he's no use to you, he's no use to me.'

He's bluffing. He can't kill Alois. Only Breen can kill him. Right? Sulat didn't dare look at Okala for confirmation. *Oh, souls, he'd better have his lore right.*

She forced herself to shrug.

'Oh, she's cold,' the king whispered into Alois' ear. Alois' huge green eyes rolled up into his head. 'He told us you would come for him. That you would cut a bloody swath through us to save him. How disappointed he must be.'

Sulat put on her best 'Sorry' face. 'What else do you have to trade?'

The king tossed Alois over the rail into the water. Breen rose up, two burly mermen behind her with Alois slung behind them.

'Kill him,' the king said dismissively.

'All right, all right,' Sulat said as blood smeared down Alois' neck. 'You've made your point. But whatever you do to him, I don't have the power to hand over the capital. All I can agree to is getting you a meeting with people more senior than me.'

'I agree to those terms.'

'Fine. Give me back Alois and I'll arrange the meeting.'

'I think we'll keep him for now. You've seen what I have, I want to see what you have.'

'They're all in the capital.'

'We can swim, Captain.' The king said, his tone one of talking to a child. 'I think you'll find we can swim rather quickly when there's reason for it.'

Sulat bowed as the king climbed back down to the water. She knew he couldn't hurt Alois, and she had to maintain the illusion of that ignorance. Hopefully there would be plenty of fish between Rhythlin Island and Ildecoke to keep Breen well fed.

Chapter Fifteen
Choosing A Side

'He can't kill him, right?' Sulat asked again. Her insides fluttered and twisted in a constant cycle. Even brandy soured her emotional stomach.

Okala pulled a chunk of hair down over his nose.

'*No*,' he whined. 'How many times, Sulat? Alois is bound to Breen. Only she can kill him. If she dies, he's free, but still protected. Those are the rules.'

'I'm just making sure,' Sulat said, pouring another drink and knocking it back. 'But Kellac can order her to kill him, still.'

'Yes,' Okala took the bottle and swigged from it. 'And you've "made sure" about eight times now. The rules are the same. For what it's worth, and I know her better than you do, she's crazy, but she's not stupid. She'll kill him eventually, if she gets the chance, but not until he has absolutely no use left. So, as long as you're alive and care about him, and have any tiny bit of power, she'll keep him alive to use as leverage against you.'

'Swell,' Sulat grumbled, taking the bottle back and passing it under her nose. Her stomach flinched. 'What I want to know is how Kellac got a hold of the Day Star.'

'The what?'

'The jewel around his neck.'

'Oh, Kyri gave it to him.' Okala rolled onto his elbows. 'She found it during her Breaching and took it to him. That's how she got an audience to begin with. Then she decided to stay. How did you recognise it?'

'It's famous, belonged to the princess. Princess Dahna, on land. I never forget a jewel.' She took a swig of brandy, ignoring the nausea. 'We were thieves, me and Alois, before I got my ship. He's always been a liability. That damn bloodworm should have been the final insult.'

'What are you talking about?' Okala flopped onto his side and groped for the bottle, tugging at the corner of his eye.

Sulat rolled the cool bottle at her temple before handing it over.

'That was the codeword he gave Kellac. Not long after we joined up, we were being tracked by a couple of thief takers. They'd tried to sneak up on us while we slept, but we heard them and got away. We didn't have time to get dressed and ended up naked in a pond.' Sulat laughed at the memory. 'His face was so red, I thought he would explode. When we were sure the takers had gone, he told me that a bloodworm had crawled up his ass and latched on.' She fanned her warming face. She'd been so angry at the time, but the story was funny now. 'I had to dig it out with my *fingers*. Hold that image close, if you ever imagine that our life on the road was glamorous. I don't know why I did it, back then. It was much more like me to let it drain him dry. I should have.'

'You don't mean that,' Okala said. He laughed all through the story, but now he was very serious, laying heavily on his arm. 'You love him, really.'

'All right, you're done.' Sulat stood and reached out. 'Give me the bottle. Go to bed.'

'But I'm not sleepy,' Okala moaned as the bottle slipped out of his hand.

'Up you get.' Sulat steadied herself and hoisted the boy under his arms. He was considerably taller and broader than she was, but she'd done it before with Alois. Okala took his own weight, but stumbled on wobbly legs, no aid from the rocking ship or the brandy, to the door.

'You feel guilty because you know he wouldn't have left you with Kellac. He would have died trying to free you.'

Sulat's guts writhed in her belly. 'Yeah, well he's an idiot. That's why it's lucky he was taken, and not me.'

Okala snickered and shuffled from the cabin.

'Hey! What are you doing here?'

Sulat leapt to her feet. Okala's voice sounded startled and her mind formed an image of Breen or worse, King Kellac, clicking around the deck of Martinette. She dashed outside and stopped cold.

Three women with brightly coloured hair stood on deck, naked from the waist down, bold as honesty in the moonlight. They carried spears and held the crew pressed against the rail. All three were athletically built and bore a striking resemblance to Okala before his transformation, with their blueish pink skin, large orange eyes, full features, and chest markings.

'Oh, hey, Sulat, these are my sisters,' Okala slurred. The nearest to him, with long green hair, darted to him. She seized him around his shoulders and dragged him to the edge. 'No, what are you doing?'

'All of you, stay where you are,' the blue-haired mermaid called, waving her spear, and following the other. 'Let us take our brother, and we'll give you no trouble.'

'What's going on?' Sulat shouted.

The third sister advanced on her, brandishing her spear, matted blonde braids and woven seaweed drapes swinging around her. 'We want no quarrel with you, human, so let us take our brother, and we'll leave you in peace.'

'Take me?' Okala whimpered, struggling. 'You don't understand-- I want to be here! I can't go back. Neri, I can't!' His voice cracked in panic and he clawed at his sister's arm.

'What's going on?' Fermin burst from his cabin, pulling his dressing gown around himself. 'More mermaids?'

'Stay back, humans,' the blue one growled, helping her sister with the wriggling Okala.

'I can't go back in the water!' Okala screamed. 'I can't, please. It'll kill me! Breen cursed me!'

Neri paused.

'Breen gave me legs. But if I touch sea water again, the spell will kill me,' he panted, pushing at the hands binding him.

'What are you talking about?' the blue-haired woman asked, lowering her spear. The jellyfish on her shoulders writhed, the only motion in the shocked scene.

Fermin made a gesture, but Sulat waved him down. 'I think these mermaids are friends,' she whispered. 'Despite what it looks like.'

'Let me go,' Okala whispered. 'I'll tell you everything.'

The mermaid's yellow-finned arm slipped from him and the other two closed around him, whispering. After a moment, he pushed them apart and addressed the crew and captains.

'These are my sisters: Vila, Ytaso, and Neri.' He gestured at the women, who made no attempt at covering their bodies despite the humans staring at them. 'These are my friends, Captains Sulat and Fermin, and the crew of *Martinette*.'

Vila tossed her blue hair, Ytaso set her hands on her hips, and Neri planted her spear on its end on the deck and squared her shoulders.

Crewmen whispered all around Sulat.

'Let's go somewhere private to discuss this,' she said, finding her voice.

'That's a good idea,' Captain Fermin said, pushing in front of Sulat. 'Won't Your Royal Highnesses come into my cabin?'

They ushered the three mermaids and Okala into the captain's darkened quarters. Sulat cast a cautionary glare around the crewmen, placing a pointed hand on the butt of her blunderbuss. The men shuffled back to their work.

'Here,' Sulat tossed a blanket to Vila as all three sisters sat in a line on the bed and Fermin set to work lighting candelabras. 'That's more skin than most people on this ship see in a year. So, you know.' She flapped her hands at the sisters and they spread the blanket over their laps, grimacing at the roughness of the fabric.

'How are you on this ship?' Sulat asked, leaning against the table. 'How did you get legs?'

'It's the Breaching potion,' Ytaso answered. 'When we turn fifteen, we drink it and we can go to the surface for a day. Our sea wizard taught me how to make it.'

'She's his apprentice,' Okala muttered to Sulat.

'But Okala, what's this about a curse?' Ytaso asked. Okala pulled on his bottom lip.

'It's not a potion, Breen made me human. Permanently.'

All three mermaids gasped in unison. It was as if he had announced that he was already dead. Vila covered her face and sobbed, Neri closed her eyes and bit her lip. Ytaso just stared. Okala shifted in his chair and picked at the fabric of his breeches.

'So...that's why I can't come with you. If I touch the sea, I'll be a merman again.'

Neri's face snapped around and Vila stopped crying.

'You said it would kill you,' she sniffed.

'Well, maybe not literally. But the spell hurt more than you can imagine. I was ripped apart.' He spread his legs as if to illustrate and Neri covered her mouth. 'I can't go through that again.'

'But you can come back,' Ytaso said, still staring.

'I'm not coming back,' Okala said. His voice was stern, strong.

'Okala, don't be a fool.' Vila shouted and jumped to her feet, the blanket slipping from her lap. Sulat and Fermin looked hastily away as the mermaid stamped a foot and advanced on her brother. 'You are a merman, you are prince of the Sandy Shore Merfolk. You will rejoin your people, this instant. That is where you belong, not up here, fighting some war you don't even understand.'

'And if you must fight,' Neri stood, too, 'you'll fight for your people. That's where you belong. With us.'

'*Oh yeah*!' Okala shouted back, throwing an arm wide. 'Sixth in line, the freak of the family, the merman who would rather be a human. *Split-fin*. Don't think I don't know what you all call me.' He pointed at each of them.

'You're still our brother,' Ytaso said. 'If there is to be a war, we should all be together.'

'No!'

'You know, it doesn't matter.' Vila put up her hands. 'This curse is reversible as soon as you're in the water. The course is clear. You're coming with us.' She hooked an arm around him and Ytaso followed.

Sulat and Fermin pushed off the table as one. Sulat pulled Okala out of Vila's hands and pushed him behind her. Fermin placed himself in the doorway and crossed his arms.

'I'm sorry, Your Highnesses, but on this ship, I am the law,' Fermin said quietly. 'This man is a part of my crew, now, and I cannot allow you to take him, if he does not wish to go.'

'The Sandy Shore Merfolk are not enemies of humans,' Vila said, raising her chin and her spear. 'We only want our brother.'

'But your brother has chosen his side. I'm afraid I'll have to ask you to leave my ship.'

'Don't be fools, you're outnumbered,' Okala said softly.

Vila inched her spear higher, but Ytaso tugged on her. Neri joined in and the two coaxed their sister onto the deck. The crewmen paused their work to watch as the girls climbed back down into the water. Under the waves, their legs fused into long colourful tails and they hovered until the ship passed them. Then they flipped into the water and were gone.

'Thank you for standing up for me,' Okala said quietly. Fermin inclined his head.

'Part of the crew.' Sulat stalked past him and into the stairwell. 'Now go to bed.'

'Heave to!' Someone shouted on deck.

'Heaving to!' Came the response from the crew, and *Martinette* slowed to a stop.

'What now?' Sulat and Fermin roared in unison, storming onto the deck from different directions. Fermin was dressed now, no doubt sensing that the mermaid princesses wouldn't be the last weirdness of the evening.

'We're supposed to be at full sail!' He shouted. 'What is the meaning...'

Just off the bow, a collection of bubbles formed and broke over a fiery red head, crowned in crimson coral. A bare-chested man with a green tail and huge sceptre made of polished coral and gold rose from the water, pointing at Sulat.

'Are you Captain Sulat?' he asked, his voice vibrating through Sulat's bones.

'I am,' she said, raising her voice over the waves slapping the side of the ship.

'I am Captain Fermin,' Fermin pushed forward. 'I am in command on *Martinette*.'

'I am King Clyr,' the merman said, holding his arms wide. *Obviously*. 'You have my son prisoner.'

Sulat opened her mouth to answer, but Okala charged the rail.

'I'm not a prisoner, father!' he bellowed at the assembled merfolk. 'Breen came to me and offered me her spell.'

King Clyr jerked back at the sight of his son, and the whole group gasped.

'Breen!' a scraggly-haired and heavily scarred merman

hissed behind the king.

'I accepted,' Okala continued, 'and then I came to find Captain Sulat, to warn her. It was my choice. You won't do anything about king Kellac, and you know he's mad, so I will.'

'Okala, you are my son,' King Clyr growled. 'You are a prince of merfolk. You will return to your people.'

Okala set his jaw. 'No.'

'This is not our fight, Okala. This has nothing to do with the Sandy Shore Merfolk. This is between the Rocky Shore and the humans. Both sides can fight their own battle.'

'You really think they'll stop there?' Okala leaned over the side. 'You think once they've knocked down the king *on land* that they won't come after us, after Open Water Merfolk, after the Arctics, and the Deep Seas, all the other merfolk in the water? He wants the capital back so that he can unite the merfolk again, rejoin the undersea empire.'

Several of the people in the water whispered to each other. The king didn't take his attention off his son.

'That is not for you to say. And it is not your place to get involved.'

'Which is it?' Okala bawled. 'Do I stand with my people because they need me, or do I stay out of it because it's none of my business? Look at the books, Father. Ask Adeto. Find one instance of a time when the undersea empire wasn't at its own throat, tearing itself apart. You would yield to that madman just because he has the audacity to try to bring an empire back together that didn't work?

'Everyone is so enamoured with the legends of when we were a mighty people, before the humans took it away from us. But it was never true; we were weak, we were starving. We got pushed into the sea because we couldn't fight. And then in the water, we couldn't live together. We're better off now.' He barked a laugh and gestured around. 'Look how wealthy we are. You are wearing gold. Gold you got from human merchants. We are thriving.'

'The Rocky Shore Merfolk are not thriving,' the king

shouted back. 'You always say that you cannot begrudge a creature fighting to survive.'

'The Rocky Shore Merfolk are monsters!' Okala screamed. 'They attack people when they're hungry. They think they're too good to eat fish, like the rest of us.'

'That is their choice!' the king roared, slapping the water.

'No, Father, it's our choice! If we unite with them, they'll be making the laws because they started the war. Do you want to eat humans? I don't.'

The merfolk whispered amongst themselves again. The king waited for the commotion to quiet before addressing his son again.

'Come back, Okala. Let's talk this through somewhere else. We shouldn't discuss eating humans in front of them.'

'I'm fine,' Sulat called, crossing her arms. 'It's not the first time someone's debated eating me.'

King Clyr scowled at her and lifted an arm. 'Okala, come away, now. End this.'

Okala straightened, squared his shoulders, and shook his head. 'No, Father. The time for talking is over. King Kellac and Breen aren't talking anymore. You do what you think is right for our people, and I'll do what I think is right. I love you.' His voice cracked as he stepped away from the side of the ship.

'*OKALA!*' the king roared.

'Okala,' another voice joined in-- softer, a deep female voice. A blue-haired mermaid with a crown of golden coral spikes rose out of the water, clad in deep purple shells. Okala paused. His shoulders tensed and a vein pulsed in his neck. He shook his head again and stomped downstairs.

'He's gone, my lady,' Sulat called over the side. Whoever this mermaid was, she clearly meant something to Okala, but even she couldn't shake his resolve.

The mermaid sat taller in the water. 'Then he has chosen you over us, Captain. I hope you look after him as well as we would have. He's not as strong as he thinks he is.'

'I think he's stronger than you lot give him credit for.'

The merfolk sank quietly back below the water. Sulat waited and watched, but they didn't return.

'All right,' she said to Fermin. 'I think we're done.'

'Open the sails,' Fermin called to his crew. Most hopped back to work, but a few hesitated. 'Did that go well?' He muttered to Sulat. 'I can't tell.'

'You heard them. This isn't their fight.'

Okala sat on his hammock, his face twisted and puffy, tears flowing freely over his cheeks. Sulat leaned on a post and pulled a handkerchief from her cuff.

'Need a minute?'

Okala jumped and wiped his wet face, sniffing hard.

'I'm sorry for crying all the time,' he said, his voice thick. He coughed. 'How do you get the--?' he gestured at his throat and pounded on his chest.

'You don't get mucus and congestion underwater?' Sulat asked, cocking an eyebrow. 'Must be nice. Get used to it, fish boy. One of the joys of dry land.'

He coughed again and pounded his chest. 'Sorry,' he mumbled. 'Sorry you had to see that. It's hard to argue like a man when everyone still sees you as a child.'

Sulat snorted. 'It's hard to fight like a man when all people see is a woman. But that's an advantage, it gives you the element of surprise. They expect to be able to command you like a child, but when that fails, they'll have to look at your arguments through their own adult eyes. And they'll understand. They might not always agree, but they'll see that you came to your decision by a man's reason. Speaking of, who was that last mermaid?'

Okala swallowed hard. 'She's my oldest sister, Marya. She's the queen.'

'Your father is the king and your sister is the queen?' *Gross.*

Okala laughed wetly and blew his nose. 'It's not like that. She rules beside my father, but they're not married. When my mother died, Marya was old enough to rule and, you know, she's been trained since she was born to be queen, so it was natural that she ascend. My mother died a few days after I was born, so Marya has always been like my mother. And the queen.' He laughed again.

'She's wise and strong and everyone loves her, but...' He pulled his shoulders up to his ears. 'She's like him. She loves all the songs and stories and she knows they're all made up. *She knows*.' His face reddened and his hands balling into fists.

'So, I had an audience with the whole court,' Sulat mused.

'Lucky you,' Okala grumbled. 'Fun, aren't they?'

'Your father looks reasonable.'

Okala laughed and threw his arm out. 'You heard him! "None of our business"'. That's reasonable to you?'

Traditionally, yes.

'So, I've met you father and your four sisters.' Sulat whistled.

'Four *of my* sisters,' Okala corrected. 'There's still Kyri, but she's with Kellac. Oh, and you met Adeto, though not formally. He was the old wizard behind my father. He agrees with me, but he's from the old ways. His loyalty is to the king, right or wrong. He's the stupid kind of loyal. The kind that follows blindly, the kind that isn't actually looking for the best way.' Okala sniffed hard.

'Right,' Sulat stood. He was a sweet boy, but she could only handle so much crying. Usually none, but he managed to find her soft spot. 'Well, we're going to do what we can. I'm going to get Alois back, if they haven't broken his fool neck by now, and hopefully we can do something about Kellac before it gets too far out of hand.'

'Oh, and Sulat,' Okala called as Sulat reached the door. 'Don't call me, "fish boy". It's just as bad as Split-Fin.'

Sulat nodded and made her way to her cabin. A few crewmen threw her nervous glances but she stared them down and slammed the door. Okala reminded her of herself sometimes. Her own mother had known that one day she would run away, but Sulat doubted she ever expected her to actually do it. She still occasionally got emotional remembering her mother's warm hands, her soothing voice, her face.

No. Sulat set her jaw. *She had a choice, too. She could have left. There were other options. She chose to stay, she chose to let the nuns...*

Don't go there, Sulat. He's dead, it's done. And you met Alois and things have been tough, but you've been free.

Tears welled in her own eyes and she squeezed them out with her fists. *Damn Okala, making me so...like this.* Family wasn't all it was cut out to be. What mattered was personal strength, fortitude, survival. Okala would learn that soon enough.

Good for him, cutting ties, doing what he wanted, what he felt was right. To hell with other people. And good for him for standing up to her and demanding to be addressed with respect. The Okala who found them in Pischum wouldn't have had the bravery.

Sulat sniffed hard and stood up, smoothing her skin-tight breeches. *Enough.* She cleared her throat, wiped her face, and got into bed.

Chapter Sixteen

Split-Fin

King Kellac took his lunch in his new favourite spot, beside the bubble at the base of his palace. His human prisoner was much better company than he'd expected, being both witty and extraordinarily cocky for a man in his position.

He must either be very brave, or a fool. Though, it is possible to be both at once.

'Breen's going to get jealous if she finds out we're spending so much time together,' Lord Brynglass said, as Kellac approached with his servant, carrying his basket of limpets.

'Oh no, I don't think so.' The king settled in the coarse sand. 'After all, you are a gift for me. A generous gift.'

Another merman appeared out of the gloom, bowing as he approached.

'An emissary from the Open Sea Merfolk, Your Highness,' he croaked. 'And, uhh, Queen Vor.' The merman's black-and-white striped tail twitched nervously.

'Vor? In person?' Kellac stood on all of his legs, his insides quivering. Deep Sea Merfolk rarely ventured this high except on very rare, very special occasions.

'Yes, Your Highness. She's waiting in your throne room.'

'Another time, my lord,' Kellac waved at his captive and sped off, a call of 'I won't wait around forever,' following him on the current.

Whispers and hums hovered in the water as Kellac raced back to his limestone formation. He skimmed up the outside wall and directly into his largest chamber.

Queen Vor was a horrifying thing to behold. She was a wriggling mass of tan and purple organs pulsing under glass-clear skin, with glowing white eyes, and deep red talons. A protective bubble full of cloudy black water hid the worst parts of her body, while also shielding her from the dangers of the terrain.

'Kellac,' she screeched in greeting. 'The prince of stone. The broken carapace, the blue star, the scream in the dark.'

'Uhh,' Kellac hesitated. He'd been warned that Deep Sea Merfolk had developed their own sort of dialect that took some getting used to. 'It's an honour to finally meet, Queen Vor.'

Beside her, hovered a young merman with brown skin and a smooth, scaleless grey tail. He edged a little away from the Deep Sea queen.

'And you are from the Open Sea,' Kellac offered a hand, and the young merman shook.

'From King Deldra, Your Highness.'

'Deldra?' Kellac raised his eyebrows. 'Really?'

The merman nodded, casting a nervous glance at Queen Vor. 'He wanted me particularly to impress upon you than he is not committing to anything, but he is willing to listen to your ideas.'

'Well, that's a start,' Kellac said. 'And don't worry, I don't think she'll bite.'

'The moon does not shine on underwater lakes,' Vor growled, smiling.

I think that's a smile. Unless it's a threat and she's baring her teeth...

'What does that mean?' Deldra's emissary whispered.

Kellac cleared his throat. 'It means that, uhh, despite our adaptations to different environments, we are all one,' Kellac bluffed. Vor's smile widened and she pointed a cracked claw at him. He relaxed. 'Very good. Oh!' He beckoned to his servant. 'After this meeting, remind me that I need to speak with Princess Kyri. If this goes well, I may have a little job for her.'

'A pearl is brightest after the shell is broken,' Queen Vor said.

Only by leaving what is comfortable, can our strengths truly be found. Is it a good or a bad thing that she's starting to make sense to me?

The crew huddled in groups in the galley, whispering amongst themselves and casting dark looks around. Okala collected his food, bumping square into one of the riggers.

'Watch your step, Split-fin,' the man sneered.

Okala went cold. 'What did you say?'

'Isn't that what those girls called you?' Another crewman joined the first, towering over Okala.

'How did you know that?'

'They listened at the door,' Sulat growled.

'Three mermaids flop on deck? Yeah, we listened.' The second man took a step toward Sulat, but she didn't react. 'Is it true? You're the one who got us wrapped up in this war?'

'What do we have to do with that?' another crewman shouted. 'I say we toss the boy over the side, let them have him back if they want him so bad, if it'll keep us out of it.' A grumble of approval met his words.

'No!' Okala shouted, shrinking toward Sulat.

'It's because of me,' Sulat said. 'And it's too late. We're already involved, from the boy up to the captain. You might as well mutiny.'

Silence fell instantly and the crew exchanged uneasy expressions.

'That's what I thought,' Sulat dropped her voice. 'Throwing him back won't save us, his people aren't our enemies. He's our only chance of success, because he's giving us merfolk secrets. So sit, eat your food, and keep your nerve.'

The men dispersed, still glowering at Okala over their mugs of beer. He sat with Sulat, and tried to eat the extremely salty food, but found he had lost his appetite. Unbidden, the craving for fish made his stomach growl.

'You need to keep your strength up,' Sulat said, jabbing her spoon at his bowl. 'The only way to get respect on a ship is by working as hard as everyone else.'

The hand holding her spoon was rough and calloused. His hands were smooth and pink, his legs long and lean, his back not strong enough for hauling ropes. The other men around them were built more like Alois, broad and muscled.

He pushed his bowl away. 'I'll never be able to do that.'

Sulat huffed. 'It takes training and consistency to get there. And you don't need to do the same that they do, just do the best you can. Be seen working, and find what you're useful for. Or else, stay out of the way and don't let them upset you until we make land.'

'And then what? Will it be like this everywhere?' Okala folded his arms on the table and laid his head down. 'Where will I go when we get to land? Where will I live?'

'You're royal, so you'd be like an ambassador. You could apply to live at the palace.'

'Roddlemere Palace?' Okala's breath caught in his throat. The ancestral home. He'd be the first merman in generations to step foot back in the palace his people had built.

Sulat must have noticed the crack in his voice because she nudged his shoulder. 'Not a bad prospect, eh?'

But I'd be living as a guest of the king. Indignation twisted his stomach. *A guest in my people's house.*

Okala wouldn't have said he was anything like Kellac, but even he had to admit that the prospect tasted rotten.

'But then what? Will I live like everyone else, or will I be a curiosity? The merman with legs?'

Sulat snorted into her beer. 'Welcome to life topside, Your Highness. That's my struggle every day. A woman in breeches, an Ebian who is servant to no one. People don't know how to even speak to me. I have to fight for respect every damn day.'

Okala watched her for a long time. Could he face a life like that?

You must be so happy, Kellac had said. *In your truest form, where you belong.*

He knew he shouldn't let Kellac get to him, but the Rockie king had pinpointed immediately what bothered him the most. He'd wanted to be human for so long, to walk among them, one of them, but would he ever be? Or would he always be Prince Okala, even on land?

'I'm going to go to bed,' he said heavily.

'Anything worth having is worth fighting for,' Sulat said. Okala nodded and took his bowl back to the cook.

One of the riggers held up two fingers as he passed. Okala pulled his jacket a little tighter and stepped outside onto the deck.

The salt spray and rain felt familiar, almost comforting on his skin, and he angled his face up into the wind. He missed Marya terribly. He knew she'd tell him to come home, to remember these days fondly, but to recognise that his place was with his people. That if he was restless and unfulfilled, she'd find a position suited to him, give him something important to do.

Useless platitudes. Angry tears ran down his face, hidden by the rain.

No one thinks I'm any use at anything. Only Sulat and Alois give me any credit, and I can't help them because I'm the wrong kind of merman.

His cheeks flamed. He wanted to dive over the edge, find his cave, and hide forever. The last thing he wanted was to cross the deck full of working crew, go to his dry cabin, and sleep under his scratchy blankets. He missed his rock, the slick woven seaweed blanket, the smoothness of life underwater. Here, everything was so rough, so hard, so heavy. He felt out of place, the delicate boy who didn't know how to do anything. They even had to teach him to eat and dress and walk properly. He leaned on the rail and gazed out to sea.

'Will I ever feel like everyone else?'

He knew the answer; he never had, and he never would. If he stayed on land, he would always be a man who used to be merman. If he went back to the sea, he'd always be the merman who wanted to be human.

Not one of us. Split-fin. Fish boy.

He wiped tears from his eyes and crossed the deck with his head down, ignoring the shouts of the crew. The likelihood that any of them were talking to or about him was slim, but he'd rather not hear it, all the same.

His cabin was dry and clean, just as he'd left it, and he sat on his bed. The wool blanket made his skin prickle, but the warmth comforted him as he snuggled down, imagining the arms of his sister rocking him to sleep.

Pers called shift change and Okala made himself useful to a rigger, ladling water from the barrel into the man's filthy cupped hands. As he returned the ladle to the bucket a shape caught his eye. A cloud of purple strands and a face.

Marya.

He leapt backwards so violently, he fell off the bench and landed hard on the deck. A few crewmen looked at him in alarm. He giggled nervously and got to his feet, adjusting his clothes.

'It's nothing, I lost my balance.'

He had to get out of there, take a walk, clear his head. He made his way to the rail and steadied himself. It wasn't as relaxing a thing as he wanted it to be, staring at the home he could never return to. But at least, Marya wasn't there.

He leaned his back against the wood. A swabbie scrubbed the beck nearby. He knocked the bucket and it slid toward Okala. Marya's round orange eyes peered at him under the slopping soap bubbles.

'What do you want?' he hissed.

'Who are you talking to?' the craggy-faced man asked, eyes narrowed.

'No one. It was just...nothing.' Okala hurried away, across the deck as quickly as he could without causing protests. Rain water from the night before puddled against the rail, and Marya's face followed him along the length of the ship. He picked up his pace and dashed for Sulat's cabin. He wrenched the door open and threw himself onto her cot, pulling his knees up to his chest.

'Sulat, I'm going mad.'

Sulat sighed. *She's losing patience with me.*

'Okala, sometimes sailors are rough.'

Okala stopped her. 'I'm seeing things.'

She frowned. 'What kind of things?'

'My sister, Marya. I saw her in the water barrel, and then a swabbie's bucket, and then she followed me in a puddle all the way here.'

Sulat picked up a glass of water from the floor and handed it to him.

'No.' He pushed it away.

'Just look. Is she still there?'

Okala snuck a peak, and sure enough, there was Marya, purple haired and crowned, exasperation and concern on her face. Okala swallowed hard and nodded.

'Talk to her,' Sulat said.

Okala hesitated.

'It could be important.'

'You believe me?'

'I've heard voices no one else did. I can't explain it, but I'm sure I didn't imagine it.'

Okala stared at Sulat a moment longer, surprised at the gentleness in her face. He took the glass and gazed down into the water.

'Hello, Marya.'

'Okala,' his sister said in her measured voice, tinged with the tone she used in her duties as queen. 'This has gone on far enough. We need you home.'

Okala's eyes flicked from his sister's face to Sulat's. 'Can you see her? Can you hear her?'

Sulat shook her head, but she didn't seem concerned that his hallucination was talking to him.

'Are you real?' he whispered into the cup, feeling foolish.

Marya clucked her tongue. 'She can't hear or see me. Adeto cast a spell so that I could talk to you. Now, listen to me: our sisters have told us about what you discussed on the ship. We're all sincerely sorry that we hurt your feelings. We didn't realise that you took it so personally.

'But things are happening now. We need you here with us. Kyri is back and she's told us of Kellac's plan. If she understands it properly, Kellac is planning a massive invasion of Ildecoke. You are in danger if you remain with them.'

'Is that what he told her to say?'

'Okala!' Marya shouted. 'Will you stop or not?'

'I don't trust her, Marya. She's working with him.'

'She's back with us, as you should be.'

'If the humans really are in danger, and Kellac has lied to her, which I believe he has, they need me.'

'How? What can you do?'

'I can tell them things. About merfolk tactics.'

Marya fell silent and a sternness shadowed her face

'You would betray us.' She paused and her voice dropped very low and soft. 'Okala, don't make me Kiss you.'

Okala's blood ran cold.

'You wouldn't.'

'To save you?' Her golden eyes met his. 'To protect our

people?'

'Marya...'

'You're human now. It would work.' She frowned, more sad than angry. 'I don't want to, don't make me.'

Okala dumped the water on the floor. Sulat hissed through her teeth.

'I'll clean it up,' he said, kicking the puddle into a hundred disconnected droplets, pulling off his shirt and mopping up the puddle.

Sulat crossed her arms. 'What'd she say?'

'She threatened to Kiss me.'

Sulat's eyebrows shot up. 'They say I'm cold.'

'What do I do?'

Sulat didn't answer, but continued to watch him.

'Sulat, *what do I do?*'

'I can't tell you.' Sulat shook her head. 'I know what it's like to be different, I know how it feels to want to be anywhere but where you are. Some of us will never fit in, no matter where we go. Alois was the closest I ever found to home, but the time came when I had to leave him, too. I found this ship, full of people driven to wander, like me...then I left them. I lost my own ship and crew, I lost Alois again. Some of us are destined to walk alone.'

Tears welled up in Okala's eyes. He knew what he had to do, but the memory of the pain was still fresh, and he shook at the thought of bringing it back voluntarily.

Sulat sat next to him. 'If you choose to stay, I'll protect you. And if you need to go, I won't stop you.'

The next morning, Okala steeled himself and ordered a fishing net to be brought to Sulat's cabin. He sat on her bed and stared at it for as long as he could, his stomach flipping like a fish stuck on the beach. Sulat just sat in silence with him the whole time. Her presence made him feel stronger, but he was glad of her silence. If she had spoken, he might have lost his nerve.

'I'm ready,' he said, at last. She nodded and carried the net out to the deck.

The crew were quiet as they tied the net into the crane arm. Okala removed his clothes and lay down in the centre. The crew pressed in, Sulat and Captain Fermin at the front.

The captain extended a hand and shook with Okala. 'We are in your debt, Your Highness.'

Okala nodded at the quartermaster, who winched up the net, swung it over the side into steel-blue nothingness, and dropped the net and the prince into the water.

Okala screamed at the icy water and the fire on his skin. Pain rippled across him as tiny scales slashed their way to the surface. Deep gashes opened on the sides of his neck. Molten pain ran down his spine as his dorsal nerve forced its way between his human bones. His legs snapped together, bound tighter than any rope could, numb from constricted blood vessels and nerves, pain ripping up him from ankle to groin as the flesh melted and fused together. His feet flattened as if by a rolling pin, the tiny bones cracking and crumbling, until they were twice as long and thin as paper.

He breathed through the pain, the shock too sharp to scream, and when it was over he just lay there, gulping water and flopping as his nerves readjusted to his old body.

The faces of the crew above were masks of horror and fascination. They pushed each other about for a better view, though none of them seemed to enjoy what they saw. He raised a shaking arm to wave that he was all right. Scales sparkled in the morning sun and water dripped from the webbing between his fingers. It was familiar and yet wholly foreign.

'I'm all right,' he croaked. The crew jumped and some of them clapped their hands over their ears. He found the edge of the net and slipped over it into the open water. 'Thank you, Captain Fermin, for all of your help.' The captain waved back. 'And Sulat.' Okala's throat closed. He couldn't say it.

She grimaced a smile and waved. He took that as good enough, and dove under the waves.

Chapter Seventeen
The War Council

Martinette had been close to Viehland, and therefore close to the Sandy Shore Merfolk colony. Okala knew what was coming: the people would spot him and raise a cry, King Clyr and Marya would swarm him and lock him up until they knew what to do with him. The best way to avoid all of that was to sneak in, but he had no disguise to use, and the light was against him. So he'd have to rely on speed and boldness.

He paced himself until he got close, not wanting to tire himself out. As the great palace loomed ahead and he picked out individual shapes, he steeled himself for what he had to do.

He put on a burst of speed, sliding along the outskirts of town until he was directly in line with the entrance, then he raced straight through the crowd of people beginning their day. Heads turned as he passed and the predictable cries of, 'Prince Okala!' and 'He's not human!' followed him as he sped past.

Hurry, hurry, he begged his tail. *Please get me there quick enough to surprise them.*

He swam up the side of the palace, to the alcove that was his bedroom, and slipped inside. There was his smooth bedstone, and all of his things, where he'd left them. How badly he wanted to rest, but there was too much to do.

The palace was still and quiet, despite the rising din outside, so Okala took what was left of his chance.

He swam through the stiff sand formation until he reached his father's chambers, and stopped outside in front of the large, muscled guard. He dragged his fingers through his silky hair, his heart lightening at how much easier it was to comb again.

'An audience, please,' he panted to the guard. The merman's eyes bugged, but he bowed and parted the seaweed curtain to allow Okala to pass.

'Okala!' King Clyr rushed to his son from his balcony overlooking the village. 'I wondered what the commotion was.' He wrapped Okala in a tight hug, then pushed him back to check him over. 'You've really returned to us. Ytaso said you wouldn't, that you feared the pain of Breen's spell. Does this mean you're here to stay?'

'Yes, Father.' The words nearly choked him. 'But it is necessary. I have to tell you what I learned from the humans.'

'That's all over now,' Clyr said, his voice heavy with relief. 'You're back where you belong, and we can put all of that behind us. Get back to our normal life.'

Okala clenched his fists. 'Will you listen to me, for once?' he shouted, all peace gone.

Clyr gaped, shock all over his face. 'Why are you so upset?' He swept the hot, angry water away from Okala and put a heavy hand on his shoulder.

'There is a war coming, father.' Okala threw his father's hand away. 'A lot of people and merfolk are going to die. This is important.'

'It is not our fight, Okala. It is between the humans and the Rocky Shore Merfolk. I've said as much to Kyri, too.'

'It *is* our fight!' Okala shouted back. 'You want to distance us from the Rocky Shore, we the peaceful colonies, we with ambitions of trade treaties with humans? If they're to be our allies one day, let's support them now.'

'And turn against the Rocky Shore?' King Clyr shouted. 'They are at least merfolk like us. The humans don't know us apart!'

'Then we must show them! I met humans who understand, and they have the ear of the king. We can begin a new day for merfolk.'

'And what do you propose we do about the Rocky Shore? What if they win this war?'

'We're not against all of them, not even against all Rocky Shore, just Kellac's colony.'

'What is going on in here?' Marya swept into the room, concern creased between her brows. 'Okala! You've returned!' She rushed at him and hugged him tight, then put a hand to his face. 'Ytaso said coming back would kill you.'

In a way, it has.

'No, only hurt a lot.'

'Well, thank the tides for that,' Marya said, her eyes full of sympathy. 'What are you two talking about?'

Okala shouted, 'Father wants to hide from the truth!' at the same time King Clyr yelled, 'Okala wants to go to war!'

Marya's eyes flicked between the two of them, and she sat on a round stone.

'Tell me,' she said, softly.

Clyr waved an arm at Okala, who launched into his account of what happened to him. When he got to the part about finding Kyri at King Kellac's palace, Marya stopped him. She whispered to the servant to fetch Adeto, and they three sat in silence until the mage arrived. Adeto wanted to hear the whole story directly from Okala, beginning with the night Kyri disappeared.

'I heard that he'd changed, but no one knows much beyond that, and with you and Princess Kyri gone, and the debate of whether or not to get involved unresolved, I haven't been able to get more information.'

Okala told his story again, hastily skimming the details up to that point.

'He's changed colours?' Adeto asked, listening intently. The hard lines of his face deepened and he looked afraid. 'That...that sounds like a kingmaking spell.'

'What does that mean, Adeto?' Marya asked. 'He was already a king.'

'Legally and politically, yes.' Adeto spoke slowly, as though trying to remember something long forgotten and teach it at the same time. 'Anyone can be born anyone's son, but that doesn't necessarily make them a good leader. A successful kingmaker spell essentially makes someone the most concentrated version of themselves, removing the insecurity and doubt that gives most of us humility.'

'But he was so dull and timid before,' Clyr scoffed. 'Concentrating that should have turned him into stone.'

'Perhaps she botched it.' Adeto shrugged. 'Perhaps she tried to make him into what she wanted him to be. She can't have had much practice. That sort of spell is used once in a dozen generations. It's too volatile.'

Anyone can be born anyone's son, but that doesn't make them a leader. The spell makes them the most concentrated version of themselves. Makes them stronger.

Okala's heart fluttered. What if the spell's success with Kellac gave Breen the confidence to try again? What if she'd cast it twice?

'Continue, Okala,' Marya said.

Okala raced through the attack on *Meltythia*, the rescue of Sulat and Alois, his brief return to the colony, and Breen's arrangement with him.

'What did she use?' Adeto asked.

'A spell,' Okala said, staring at Adeto, willing the old wizard to read his suspicions. 'I went on the beach and she said a spell and I turned human.'

'And it hurt?' Marya asked, her eyes round.

'Well, yeah.' Okala forced himself to remember both of his transformations as coldly and impersonally as he could. He didn't need to relive the pain and cry like a child while arguing that they join the humans in war. 'But it gave me the ability to walk on land, to see how they live, to board a boat and watch how they negotiate.' Adeto stared back, his expression cloudy as though he were starting to catch on to what Okala was trying to tell him.

But that was something they'd have to discuss later. The main focus of this discussion was still active.

'They have no hatred of us anymore,' Okala directed back at his father. 'Most of them don't even believe we exist.'

'They will hate us again,' Clyr said heavily. 'When they find out about us, they will fear us, and that fear will lead to hatred.'

'Not if they learn about us as allies,' Okala pressed.

Marya and Adeto watched him, brows furrowed, inscrutable thoughts passing behind their eyes.

Okala pressed on, recounting his time in Vurdia, his experiences on *Martinette*, how the captain listened to him, how affected Alois was by the Kiss. That interested all of the merfolk in the room. Adeto knew of only a few accounts of how humans lived with the Kiss, all of them parts of legends.

'And it was Breen who Kissed him?' Adeto asked.

'Yes.'

The mage nodded silently.

'What are you thinking, Adeto?' Marya asked.

Adeto shook his head. 'I don't know yet, but there may be something we can do, if this human man connects Breen with King Bertold through the human woman. There may be some advantage to that.'

'It's an intellectual puzzle only,' King Clyr said dismissively. 'Because it doesn't affect us. He connects the humans to Breen and the Rocky Shore Merfolk, not us. If we take Okala out of the equation, nothing changes. We have no link here. It doesn't concern us.'

'But Father, consider what Okala is saying.' Marya sat straighter and folded her hands in her lap. The tip of her golden coral crown nearly reached the king's eye level. 'In a few days, the humans will know about us again, whether we help or not. If we don't help, they won't know that there are different colonies, they'll think us all the same. We live closest to their kingdoms-- if humans seek revenge, it will be *our* people who suffer, even if we stayed out of it. It is as much a defence for us as for the humans. We'd be getting ahead of the tide.'

'How are they going to get to us underwater, Marya? That was the whole point of leaving,' Clyr said. 'And if it does come to that, we can enforce stronger rules about Breaching, we can build defences. We can move, if we need to.'

'Or we can negotiate treaties,' Marya countered.

'And what of the army?' Clyr hissed. Marya had always been against having a standing army, as Sandy Shore Merfolk were staunchly peaceful. 'Will you call for soldiers? Will you lead them into battle?'

Marya set her orange eyes on him, and the water around her stood still. 'If that is what must be done.'

Clyr huffed and threw his hands up. 'I can't believe the three of you--warmongers! Peace First Marya, Always Another Solution Adeto, and Okala...who loves humans *so much*.'

'Say it,' Okala growled. Clyr set his jaw, unwilling to use the word that caused such a rift in their family.

'Can you stand to be up there, on the surface, watching them die?' Clyr asked.

'I can stand to be by their side, helping, defending them.'

'Oh! Another thing!' Clyr threw up a hand. 'Defending them--*their* island, that they stole from us! You want to help them keep it!'

Marya and Adeto looked to Okala for a rebuttal.

'Ildecoke Island in human hands is better than in Kellac's,' he said, steadily. 'If Kellac wins the island back for us--*if*, because there are more of them and we'll be fighting on their terrain, which we haven't set foot on in centuries--*if* Kellac wins, he'll name himself King of All Merfolk. Can you bow to him?'

Clyr scoffed. 'He may be king on land, but we in the sea colonies will remain independent.'

'You think so?' Okala asked. 'You think that others won't be impressed, won't rally behind him for what he was able to do? And when he amasses that support, you think he won't move to unite the colonies into one kingdom? Can you serve Kellac, Father? That is the question.'

Marya shuddered.

The motion was not lost on anyone in the room. Clyr was not a young merman, Marya would be the next leader. His decision now would affect her rule. Could he stand by and allow Kellac to establish an empire that would eventually force her to submit? Or force her to fight a war for independence, a war she'd have to fight without him by her side?

Clyr's eyes rested on Marya for a long time before looking to Adeto standing silently, and Okala watching everyone.

'I will meet with Kellac and hear what he has to say.'

It was nighttime when Okala finally arrived at his own little chamber. He had spent most of the day in his cave, tidying his treasures. It wasn't damaged as he'd feared because someone, probably Marya, had set a guard to watch it and make sure no one disturbed it. Still, some little fish had gotten in and tried to make the items into homes to hide from bigger fish. Okala didn't begrudge them wanting somewhere safe to live, but he was back now, and they needed to move on and find somewhere else. He ushered them gently out, and set about removing the piles of sand or mucus bubbles they'd created, and straightened the items on the shelves.

He flopped onto his bedstone and rubbed his fins, imagining that he could still feel the tiny bones in the meaty stubby feet he'd briefly had.

'Okala,' a voice whispered. It was Vila, at the mouth of his chamber.

'Come in.'

She entered, followed by Ytaso and Neri.

'We brought you some things we found,' Neri said. She held a dented pewter mug, Vila held out an iron nail, and Ytaso gave him a chunk of brass the size of his palm, embossed with the letters, 'TYTHIA.'

He swallowed hard. They were from the wreck of Sulat's ship. All those lives lost, so much anguish. He accepted the gifts with good grace. His sisters didn't know the significance.

'Thank you, I love them.'

'Is it true that King Kellac wants to go to war with the humans?' Neri asked, sitting beside him.

'Technically, he wants to negotiate,' Okala said heavily. 'But I don't think he really believes that he'll get anywhere with it. So, in effect, yes.'

His sisters exchanged worried looks. 'And you want...us...to join in?' Neri asked.

'On the side of the humans?' Ytaso looked at him like he'd lost his mind.

Vila reached out and held his hand. She had always been the sweetest, but he could tell by her face that she thought he must be very sick.

'I made friends when I was with them. They're not bad,' he said, fully aware of how childish he sounded. 'They're more like us than not. They can listen, they can be reasoned with. We can have friendship between humans and merfolk.'

'But they tried to kill us,' Neri said.

'*Centuries* ago,' Okala moaned. 'They're not like that now. We can make peace that is good for everyone. They were afraid of us once, but if we can meet again on sane terms...' Okala scratched his scalp. It was frustrating arguing peace to pacifists. This conflict was coming anyway, they couldn't avoid it. Wasn't it better to get ahead of it and be on the right side when the tide went out?

'We can't go to war,' Vila said. The other sisters shook their heads.

'Why not?'

'They still have Kyri,' Ytaso said.

'I thought she came home.'

'She did,' Neri said slowly, 'but we think that there's something she's not telling us.'

Okala almost laughed. 'Well, then. I'm not the only one who's invested in this. If Kyri is with them, she's voting to go to war, too.'

'We can't fight against her,' Vila said.

'So, what then? She's going to fight, and the humans are going to fight. Put the issue of who is right aside. Don't you want to be there to protect her? You lot were very insistent that you come rescue me--why not rescue her?'

His sisters stared at him a minute, blank shock on their faces. As one, they straightened and left.

'So that's seven for war, and only Father against.' He sighed and lay down on his rock. 'I hope he'll have a chance to see Alois.'

Chapter Eighteen

A Change In The Tide

King Kellac lounged in his throne room, listening to Breen bark orders at the servants. He recalled with difficulty the days when he had been meek and quiet, and shuddered at the hazy memory. It hadn't been long that he'd been on this path, but it felt like centuries.

'I'm hungry,' Breen whined, throwing herself onto a stone beside Kellac. 'I know you have your reasons for not eating my human, but there's so much meat on him. Surely we can take a little without diminishing his worth.' She gazed out of the alcove toward the shimmering bubble.

'He is more than a mouthful,' Kellac chuckled. 'But I don't trust the captain.'

'She looked sincere to me,' Breen said. 'She yielded quickly when you threw him to me.'

'Oh, aye, she cares for him, that I believe. But I suspect she will attempt some trickery. He assured me that she would wreak bloody vengeance, but she didn't. Does he not know her as well as he thinks, or is she sticking to a bigger plan? Best to keep our biggest piece big. We can still use him to control her, and to gain some ground with the impostor king.'

The allied merfolk forces agreed to meet here at Rhythlin Island and go together, so Kellac had to stay, no matter how anxious the waiting made him. Breen had Damla tracking *Martinette*, they would know when the humans landed on the capital.

A great commotion of bubbles and vibrations rose up from the seafloor and Kellac hurried to the mouth of his chamber. People stood motionless in the town square, whispering to each other, as a richly dressed procession wound their way through the water.

The merman at the front was tall, with long red hair flowing out behind him, the mermaid at his side small, and brown-haired, with a distinctive pink tail.

Kellac writhed with pleasure.

It worked. She brought him. I never doubted her.

King Clyr, Princess Kyri, and the rest of the delegation rose through the water to hover at eye level with King Kellac, who raised his head in greeting.

'King Clyr, it has been too long since we met.'

'I hardly recognise you, King Kellac,' the Sandy Shore king said, his deep voice hitting Kellac in the gut like a punch.

Kellac chuckled. 'I had some improvements done to my image. I hear some members of your family have also made some changes.'

Titters shook the water around them as the Rocky Shore Merfolk enjoyed the jibe about Prince Okala. Kyri pursed her lips and blushed, but the king showed no reaction.

'My daughter tells me that you are planning an offencive to reclaim Ildecoke Island from the humans.' Clyr swept a thick arm toward his youngest daughter. 'I have come to hear you.'

'Very good, your Grace, very good.' It was all Kellac could do to keep from rubbing his hands together in glee. *King Clyr, of all people! King Clyr, of the We Like Humans So Much One of Us Ran Away to Be One Merfolk! What a treat!* 'I have some ideas that may interest you, if you've finally seen the wisdom and necessity of our cause.'

'I am here to listen.' Clyr held up a broad hand. 'Listen only, Kellac. I have no intention to make any alliances today.'

'Of course not, Your Highness. Of course not.' Kellac nodded fervently. *Flatter him. Make him feel the higher ground. But win him, whatever you do.* 'Listen first. Then think, discuss it with you advisers, your queen, you historians. Then decide.'

Clyr nodded slowly, his face unreadable. Kellac took that for encouragement. He invited the whole bunch of them inside and offered around juice weed sacs.

His insides fluttered in excitement. Out of all the planning and scheming he'd done, this was his big moment. He had to sell it.

'You know the stories,' Kellac said, pacing. 'Back in the days when Ildecoke used to be uninhabitable, shipping was impossible and fishing was even more dangerous than it is now. It is said that the Squalls takes one human life for every voyage through--back then, it was worse. Every voyage risked a whole crew.

'Talented men and women along the coasts made a living offering talismans and spells to protect the fishermen and sailors. But as boats and navigation improved, these people were deemed less essential. Unease crept in. If they protected, did they also attack? Could they call storms to drown their enemies? Could they shrink whole shoals of fish? Was their power the cause of the Squalls to begin with?' Kellac wrung his hands together. He had the room's attention.

'People today fear their power being discovered, but that fear is nothing compared to the terror and paranoia then. At its peak, people in coastal towns were rounded up and taken to Ildecoke Island. Treeless, the people couldn't build boats to cross the strong currents that cut the island off from the mainland at high tide, and archers took up position at low tide to shoot anyone attempting to cross on foot. The people on Ildecoke had to learn to survive on their own.

'Their powers protected them, and they adapted to an amphibious life, half on land, half in the water. They learned to swim fast, to catch fish with their bare hands, to eat sealife and seaweed raw. They dressed themselves in the things that washed on shore from shipwrecks, adorning themselves with shells, strings of pearls, shiny stones, and braided rope. They chose a leader from among them, and he founded the first line of kings to rule from Ildecoke.' Perhaps it was too much detail to lay on an old and well-known story, but Kellac couldn't resist a bit of drama.

'The Island had no trees, but it was abundant in stones. It took years, decades, but through persistence and their enhanced abilities, much stronger then, less diluted by mundane human blood as it is now, they eventually built Roddlemere Palace, and made it the home of their beloved king. Impressed with what they saw from the mainland, humans swarmed across the straight with their armies and families, to claim Ildecoke.

'The people fought, of course they did, but contrary to what humans had believed, these people were not able to do much damage, especially malnourished and hardscrabble as they had become. The humans drove them straight into the sea with nothing but what they wore on their bodies. Humans claimed the island as their own, and haven't left since.' The tension in the room spiked, the resentment of centuries vibrating the water.

'For a generation, the people of Ildecoke wandered, searching for a place to stay, but every island that looked promising was soon discovered, and they were chased away again. The only place left to them was under the waves. So, they dove, and there they stayed.

'Eventually, cracks appeared within the community, and the people of Ildecoke parted ways. The outcasts even among these outcasts made their way to the deepest trenches of the sea, to practice their shadowy ways; the resentful ones who wanted total isolation travelled north to the places where no human could survive; the ones who just wanted to live and be left alone set out for open sea, happy to drift among the seaweed and dive with whales. Some of them,' Kellac gestured at King Clyr, 'hovered as close to humans as they could, collecting what humans threw away, and waiting for their chance to come back. And some of them,' he put a hand to his own heart, 'full of rage and pain, hid in rocky caves, using their voices to lure ships to the rocks, or else take cover and wait for their chance to strike.'

'I know the stories,' Clyr said, solemnly. Kyri's eyes shone with anticipation.

'Your people have done well, Clyr,' Kellac said, waving a pink hand at the Sandy Shore king's jewel-encrusted chestpiece of intricately twisted netting. 'Picking up what falls off ships, or bits of shine that are dropped in at the outskirts of your colonies. You're doing very well, very well, indeed. It's no wonder you want peace. You'll only prosper more than you do already, if all goes well.'

'You don't hide your own wealth.' Cly pointed at the blue jewel on Kellac's chest.

'Hard won!' Kellac snapped. 'We work for our trinkets. We sing, we scavenge. We hunt. Not all of us sit with our hands out, waiting for gems to fall into them. But.' At a glance from Breen, he composed himself. *Stay in control, Kellac. Win him.* 'It's not our fault. It's *their* fault. If we can come together again, we can have our island back. I'm not talking about killing the humans.' Kellac put his hands together. 'I'm not like them. I just want my-- *our*--island. They can have the mainland. Like they intended from the start.'

'I've been listening to this for years, Kellac.' Clyr pressed his lips together. 'Not from you, but from others. Every few years, someone has this ambition, and the same concerns come up every time. But that was years ago, magic was stronger in us. We could adapt from land to water, we can't do that anymore. And secondly, we have adapted to different environments. How are you going to pull Deep Sea Merfolk from the depths? The thinness of the water up here alone would kill them, not to mention the light. And the Arctics? They want nothing to do with integration. The Open Sea Merfolk are staunchly apolitical. Your only hope is my people, but as you say, we prosper from life as it is right now. Why would we want to change that?'

Clyr's face took on a tone of sympathy, as though he were apologising for winning his argument.

Not so fast. Kellac let a moment of silence stretch between them before asking softly, 'How is Prince Okala?'

'He has returned to us.' Clyr's voice was steely and the gentle smile faded from his face.

Breen twitched beside him. *Tread carefully.*

'I imagine he had an interesting story to tell,' Kellac said softly.

Clyr nodded, his orange eyes sliding to Breen, who held her head straighter.

'Quite an adventure, he had,' Kellac continued. 'He was, what was it?' He looked to Breen. 'Four days topside? Nearly a week? Hardly worth what he endured, but still. Quite an adventure.'

'It was a valuable learning experience,' Clyr said delicately.

'Oh, no doubt. No doubt he learned how disorganised humans are, how they fear us, how they still mistrust people with powers. But also,' he held up a long finger, 'how easy it is to make the transition from water to land.'

He allowed a moment for the idea to sink in.

'Your wizard has a potion that allows your people a short time on land. My witch has a spell which allows permanent transition. I'm sure there's a way to--' he pulled his palms together to meet in front of him. '--come together.'

Clyr didn't answer, but Kyri's eyes widened, impressed. *I may rely on you after all, my pet.*

'And it's kind of you to worry about the other kings,' Kellac went on, addressing Clyr's other reservation. 'But you needn't be concerned. Queen Vor, in particular, has shown some interest.'

Clyr's eyebrows shot up. *That got him.* 'I would advise you to be cautious, Kellac. Vor can be...unpredictable.'

'So can I.' Kellac swept up into Clyr's face, nearly nose-to-nose. The king didn't flinch, but his guards snapped to his defence, and his daughter yelped and backed away. 'That's what makes this all so fun. Those humans don't have any idea of what we're capable. Don't you have that itch,' he dropped his voice to a whisper, 'that ancient yearning in the pit of your being?' He tapped Clyr's abdomen and the water around the guards hummed in warning. 'That longing to be who you once were? To stop picking up rubbish, stop trying to repair a damaged reputation, stop hiding? You're a king! By the shoals, don't you want to walk in the sun with your head held high? Don't you want to walk the halls of a real palace and not just that sand castle you live in?'

'There's more of them. And some of them have magic, too.'

'Come see what we have,' Kellac raised his voice and stepped back. 'I think you'll be impressed. Yes, very impressed.'

King Kellac led the Sandy Shore king out of the palace and down to the bubble where the human prisoner was held. 'The female Okala befriended has the power to negotiate with Ildecoke, and this male is her mate.'

'Ehh,' Lord Brynglass cringed. 'I'm not her *mate*, in that sense.'

Breen flicked the bubble and the human grimaced, putting his hands over his ears. 'You will hold your tongue.'

'You are Alois?' Clyr directed at the human.

The man nodded. 'I don't think I've had the pleasure.' He approached the skin of the bubble and looked Clyr up and down.

'I am King Clyr, of the Sandy Shore Merfolk. You were kind to my son.'

The human's eyes widened, and he bowed deeply. 'Your Grace.' He bowed again to the princess. 'You must be Princess Kyri. You look like Okala.'

'You dare address me, human,' Kyri hissed in disgust.

Kellac smirked. Kyri understood, even if her father didn't.

'How is Okala?' Lord Brynglass asked Clyr. Breen thumped

the bubble again and the human winced.

'He has returned to us,' Clyr said.

'No!' the human shouted, visibly upset. 'What do you mean, he returned?' His eyes snapped to Breen. 'He said your spell would kill him if he touched water again.'

'Oh no, only that he'd wish it would.' Breen smiled slyly.

'So, you see, Lord Brynglass,' Kellac said, excitement rising in him. 'I have you, but your people have, well, no one. Who are they going to bargain with? I admit, I felt like I had the weaker piece, with only a lord while they had a prince. But now, I feel much better.'

'How nice for you,' Lord Brynglass sneered.

Clyr eyed the human strangely, like he saw something Kellac didn't.

'Does this colour things for you, Clyr?' Kellac gestured for them to go back to the palace. The human hovered by the skin of the bubble as they let him be swallowed by the murk.

'It does, somewhat,' Clyr said slowly. 'So you plan to negotiate?'

Kyri's face lit up. *Her daddy is going to yield.*

'I intend *to be seen* to negotiate.'

'Why not do it in earnest?' Clyr asked. Kellac tried not to groan. *Ever the peace-maker.* 'Why not bargain for a region of Ildecoke where we can cohabitate peacefully? Or perhaps a different island we can have to ourselves?'

Breen thrashed her tail.

'Because Ildecoke is ours,' Kellac said, putting up a hand to still her. 'They gave it to us. It should have been ours forever.'

'That was a long time ago.' Clyr shook his head, still not convinced.

'It is time,' Breen said, finally unable to keep her silence. 'I had a vision, I delivered a prophecy. The time is upon on us. There will be a war, King Clyr. There will be bloodshed. Will it be your people bleeding and dying, turning the foam red? Or will you storm the beach with us, and reclaim your birthright?'

Kyri's face shone with hope, and King Clyr recoiled. 'This

is madness.'

'There doesn't need to be blood,' Kellac said soothingly. Breen's expression turned angry; she was sure there would be. 'We have the human. His female will negotiate for us, for his safe return.' The tip of Breen's tail snapped through the water, and warmth radiated from her. 'We can --' he locked eyes with her, '-- *turn the humans against each other.* Put these two between us and Viehland.'

'Two humans against an entire country while we try to seize the capital?' Clyr's face was all shock and confusion.

'Two *important* humans,' Kellac corrected. 'And speaking of influence, did I mention that Deldra is with me?'

Clyr's face slackened and Kyri broke into a grin. Deldra, King of the Open Sea Merfolk, was Clyr's closest ally.

'He wants control of the shipping lanes,' Kellac said lazily, inspecting the tip of one of his swimmerets.

'I will agree to this exercise on one condition,' Clyr said. Kellac nodded to indicate that he was listening. 'I want the human.'

'Under no account,' Kellac said. *My greatest asset, you must be joking!* Breen's anger flared again.

Clyr slumped in on himself and held out a meaty hand.

Triumph exploded inside Kellac as he extended one of his own to seal the deal.

'This is the cresting of a glorious new age, Clyr. We're leading our people home.'

Clyr nodded sadly, and led his delegation to the mouth of the cave.

'And Clyr,' Kellac called, unable to resist himself a little power move to establish who was in charge of the revolution. 'Kyri stays with me.'

Kyri squealed and joined him as her father silently swam away into open water.

'How did it go?' Marya asked, rushing to King Clyr as the group returned from the Rocky Shore colony. 'Where's Kyri?'

'He insisted on keeping her,' Clyr said.

'Well, we knew he would, if you took her,' Marya sighed.

'He likes to collect his bargaining pieces. That human he has looks to be in good condition, and he sees Kyri as an ally. She's safer with him. Where's Okala?'

'Here, father.' Okala approached, wringing his hands.

'Do you think you can find the human ship you were on? That woman friend of yours would probably be interested to hear what I've found out.'

Chapter Nineteen

Homecoming

Martinette slid into her berth at Ildecoke Harbour. Captain Fermin bounced on the balls of his feet near Sulat, his fingers clenched around the rail. *Martinette* had returned far too early to have unloaded and loaded in Dunothe. How long would it be before his employers recognised her rigging and figurehead? What would he tell them when they asked?

'Leave it to me, Captain,' Pers said quietly as the gangplank lowered to the jetty.

Fermin nodded curtly. 'How long do you think you'll be?' he asked Sulat.

'I can't say. I don't know when I'll get an audience.'

She stepped onto the gangplank, pulling her hair back and twisting her scarf around it. The sun was bright in her eyes and she sorely missed her hat.

She missed a lot of things.

Stop it.

Across the dock yard, where the inns and taverns and

bawdy houses vied for the attention of the sailors, Sulat spotted a carriage discharging its passenger.

'Captain!' a voice shrieked.

Sulat started, then scolded herself. *Who would call you that? They're all dead.*

The voice shouted again, and Sulat pushed on through the crowd toward the carriages.

A hand yanked her back by the shoulder. Ire flared in her and she threw the person off, spinning around on her heel.

Ashryn.

Sulat blinked into the girl's round bespectacled face. Her mind exploded into a tangle of possibilities and impossibilities.

The ship went down. It was in splinters. Only Alois and I survived. That's what Okala said.

She put out a hand and felt the fabric of Ashryn's shirt. It felt like linen, rough spun and warm. Other people on the dock moved around both of them, no one avoiding Sulat like she was talking to herself.

'You were lost,' she said, at last, her voice tight and hoarse, muffled as though she were hearing herself from a long distance away.

Ashryn smiled and shook her head. 'There were two boats still intact. Wese, Eaton, and Darib were in one. They pulled me up. Garad, Pirin, Foth, Arin, and Itai were in another. But we couldn't find your friend.' Her shoulders fell.

Sulat's grip on Ashryn's shirt tightened. *Nine crewmen survived. NINE!* A giddy bubble rose in her belly, but she fought it down.

'How did you get back?'

'We went from island to island. My boat was in front, naturally, as I'm Navigator. Eaton and Darib rowed for days. Wese kept everyone's spirits up.' Ashryn put her hand over Sulat's. It was warm and soft. Some of the fog cleared. 'Eaton was sure you'd survived. He was determined to get home and send out search parties.'

'Did you tell anyone what happened?' Sulat croaked.

Ashryn nodded and pushed her glasses back up. 'In the end, we yielded to Foth, who insisted on having the ship registered as Lost at Sea, and you and His Lordship and everyone else declared dead. We didn't want to, Eaton is still angry, but who would take his word that you survived?'

'They won't have to,' Sulat said, gesturing at herself. 'Are the rest of the crew here? Gather everyone up and come to my house. We'll go to the palace together.'

Sulat left Ashryn, changing course and heading home rather than to the palace.

The path to her little house in the cramped dockyards felt like walking through a dream, hazy and lightheaded. Heat spread throughout her body and her skin tingled.

They're alive, some of them made it.

'Tansy!' she called, her voice high and tight from elation when she walked in her front door. *Damn it, pull yourself together, woman.*

A cry echoed from the kitchen and even the twinge of old annoyance couldn't dampen Sulat's mood.

'Captain!' the middle-aged blonde maid squeaked, hurrying into the hall, her face pale. 'You were gone ever so long and they said you was dead, I wondered what to do for the best. Your bills--' she gestured to a messy stack of envelopes on the table.

Sulat waved her away. 'Never mind that now, I'm into something important. I'm going to change my clothes, and some sailors are going to arrive. Please put some food together and bring the brandy up from the cellar.'

'The--the good brandy?' Tansy hesitated.

'Souls, no, the cheap stuff. But lots of it.' Sulat scooped up the bills and skipped up the stairs to her room. Her head swam and she leaned against the door frame to calm the spinning.

Easy, girl, easy. Get a hold of yourself.
They survived.
Pull yourself together, you have to see the king.

The sparse and simple furniture throughout her house

could have come from a single room at any inn, spread out over three floors, the majority of it in her bedroom. The bed was large enough for three, but she slept in it alone, most of the time. The porcelain chamberpot and solid wooden chest underneath, and the heavy dresser and wash table by the window gave the master bedroom the distinct appearance of a room that was seldom occupied, and therefore not in need of any sort of personality.

She flung back the doors of the dresser and rummaged through the jackets, breeches, and shirts to find something suitable for a royal audience, or, more likely, the Lord of Shadows. The one dress she owned, the one she'd worn to Alois' wedding, was crammed in a corner, wrapped in oilskin to keep the insects off, but otherwise kept away from any viable options.

Stripping off the stiff and stinking clothes she'd been wearing since the shipwreck, she pulled out a blue jacket Alois had bought her, a pair of brown breeches, and a fresh, crisp, white shirt, along with smart shiny black boots. She had so many shoes, it was difficult to choose. Alois loved to tease her about it, calling it her one concession to womanhood. He commented that she had more shoes than Johanne did, and that was probably true.

I'll be getting him back soon, too.

Her hand hovered over the fur lined slippers she'd kept all these years since leaving the convent, but no. Just change into normal clothes and head to the palace.

She poured water from the porcelain pitcher into the bowl. Tansy may have worried that she was never coming back, but to her credit, at least she kept the washing water clean. The little lump of white soap and soft sponge on the table were welcome luxuries after so long away.

Sulat took a moment to revel in the simple pleasure of dipping the sponge in the water, lathering it up with scented soap, and running it over her filthy body, watching the grey water run off and puddle on the floor, leaving behind clean, delicately-perfumed skin. She considered quickly lathering up her hair and rinsing it in the bowl, but no. That would be a whole process. Better to ask Tansy for hot water tonight after the meeting. Just wash enough to not offend the nobility, and change into clean clothes. That would be enough.

She tossed the sponge onto the surface of the water and leapt back, nearly slipping in the puddle and toppling over.

Okala's face hovered beneath the surface. Sulat ripped the sheet from the rung under the table and wrapped it around herself, peering into the bowl. Perhaps she'd imagined it.

No, there he was, smiling at her.

'You chose my washbowl?' Sulat whispered to him, his features rippling under grey water, soap bubbles floating on top.

'I don't choose the water, any will do. It's just what you happen to be nearest when I call.'

'What do you want?' Sulat dipped down to dry herself and the puddle on the floor.

'My father had an audience with King Kellac, he knows the plan.'

'What is it?'

'Meet with Bertold and make his demands. And if that doesn't work, attempt an invasion that will probably fail and make life a lot more difficult for all of us for a long time.'

'Well, that's what we expected, isn't it?'

'It is. Where are you? I don't recognise the cabin.'

'I'm at my house on Ildecoke.'

'You're on land?' Okala's voice sharpened.

'Yes, I'm going to see the king, to tell him what happened, to warn him.'

'Good.' Okala's shoulders relaxed. 'I'm relieved you made it home safely. Now, we just need to get Alois out alive.'

A nerve in Sulat's back tingled. *Don't think about it, focus on the steps ahead of you.* 'I'm working on it,' she muttered. 'Is there a way I can take you with me to the palace? Maybe in a glass bottle?'

'It doesn't work that way. I can only appear to people I have a personal connection with. I'm not actually physically in your home. So you can see me, but they wouldn't be able to. And you'd look mad talking to water. Better to tell them what I've told you. You could bring them down to the water, but travelling that fast is painful for me, and it's unwise for the king to be close to the sea right now.'

'No,' Sulat agreed. Her face split into a wide grin. 'But Okala...my crew survived. They're here.'

Okala opened and closed his mouth silently a few times. 'They can't have. I was there. I saw...*things*.'

'Not all of them,' Sulat waved hastily. 'But some of them.'

'How?'

'They found a couple of boats.'

Okala fell silent for a moment. 'Sulat, I'm so sorry.'

Sulat laughed. 'For what?'

'I--I only saw you and Alois. After everything happened, I only saw you two. I looked for others--'

'It's not your fault,' Sulat said. 'Given everything, you did more than anyone asked of you already, and you have my gratitude.'

'Well, I hope they help you with the king.'

The front door opened and shut, so Sulat sent Okala back to his business, put on her clean clothes with shaking hands, and headed downstairs.

Tears leapt to her eyes and she angrily wiped them away as eight men and Ashryn stood. They all rushed her, crying, 'Captain!' and 'I don't believe it!'

Even Eaton cracked a smile and it looked so uncomfortable on him, Sulat almost felt guilty for making him happy. They all had something in the way they stood, the way their clothes hung on them that had changed.

What had they seen out there? What had they been through together?

'At ease, sailors,' she croaked, pushing them away. 'Are you the only ones?'

Their shoulders slumped and they nodded. Foth hung back, fiddling with his waistcoat.

'We looked for more,' Wese said, taking off his hat and squinting at her, even in the dim indoor light. 'We docked at the little islands and kept going back to look, but didn't see nobody. We're right sorry about your friend, His Lordship.'

Sulat shook her head. 'He's fine, I think. It's a long story. Sit.'

She got them caught up on all that had happened to her as they ate cheese and ham with bread and butter. They gasped and shook their heads and groaned all throughout her story.

'So we need to speak to the king now,' Sulat said, finishing her story and her brandy. Nods circulated the room, and a few stood to leave that minute.

Souls, it's good to have them back.

They all folded together into two carriages and made their way up the cramped and winding roads to the palace.

Sulat gathered Eaton, Wese, Ashryn, and Darib around her in her carriage, to tell them more that she'd remembered. And she wanted to do it without Foth hearing.

'He's different now, Cap'n,' Wese said in a soft voice. 'He's one of us, proper. Don't think he'll be givin' you any more trouble, now on.'

'What does that mean?'

'A week on the sea in a rowboat with nought but eight others what hates you changes a man. Shared adversity can be a marvellous thing. He learned a lot about trust and leaning on each other and not making assumptions. He sees things a bit more our way now.'

'We can trust him, Captain,' Eaton said. His deep slow voice instantly soothed her.

'And also that breeding and training doesn't matter a lick in an open boat,' Ashryn said. 'You find out what your real strengths are, and it's not always what you thought. Turns out he's a real charmer when he wants to be, and even more unscrupulous than we thought.'

'And you didn't tell Renir what happened?' Sulat asked.

Everyone looked uneasy.

'Not Renir, no,' Eaton said. 'With you and his lordship dead, we don't work for the Crown anymore, and it was all we could do to get back to Viehland alive. We didn't know any of this about the kings and the war, or any of it. We just knew we weren't the first crew to run afoul of creatures at sea, and we just wanted to have a bit of normal before figuring out how to go on with our lives.'

The carriage rolled to a stop outside the palace doors. Sulat hopped from the carriage and led the others up the steps.

'Captain Sulat,' she said to the palace guard. 'Elmor Foth, and extant crew of *Meltythia*.'

The guard nodded and allowed Sulat and her men to pass. A footman inside the gates bowed deeply.

'His Royal Highness the King is at his table at the moment and does not wish to be disturbed. Would you be content to wait, or else speak with Lord Renir?'

'How long is the wait?' Sulat asked, knowing the answer already.

'The king will not have unscheduled visitors until Public Hours, this evening.' At that time there would be dozens of other vying for his attention.

'Lord Renir, then.' Sulat gestured with her hat, and the man bowed and strode off. Sulat knew the way to Renir's office but these things must be done officially.

The crew muttered to each other and marvelled at the opulence of the palace as they passed through the halls to the receiving rooms.

'I'm glad you survived, Captain,' Foth said quietly, all air of the fussy courtier gone. 'We feared no one would believe our story.'

'I would have expected you to come to Renir immediately.'

'And tell him what? "Sorry the mission failed, we got attacked by mermaids and now everyone's dead?" I just...I lost my taste for nursemaiding out there, and I gained, I suppose, perspective. The laws of Viehland don't really apply once you leave the shore, and I'd rather get home alive than die with honour at sea.'

'Foth, I think you're finally a member of the crew,' Sulat laughed. 'You finally earned your Lobster properly.'

'A real Lobster, eh?' He tapped his tattoo. 'Makes you wonder what all the fuss over The Squalls is about.'

The footman stopped at the door of Renir's office and let them in.

'Captain Sulat and the crew of Meltythia,' he announced to the secretary. The wigged and bespectacled man jabbed a pen at a couple of chairs nearby. Sulat sat in one, and the men insisted that Ashryn take the other. The rest of the crewmen stood around them as though guarding them.

'What's he like?' Wese whispered, fidgeting.

'Mostly formal,' Sulat said. 'You've done nothing wrong, Wese. You don't have anything to be afraid of.'

'I've never been in the palace. Makes me worry I'll be arrested for not tying me scarf right.' He tugged at the fabric around his neck. The other crew fiddled with theirs, too.

'That's not a crime,' Sulat chuckled. 'You're here to report a threat to the kingdom. Calm down.'

The door of the office swung open and everyone but Sulat and Foth jumped.

'Come in,' Lord Renir said. He nodded politely at everyone who passed, and shut the door behind them. 'I expected you back long ago, Captain. And then I heard that *Meltythia* was lost.' He sat behind his desk, gesturing for the others to sit in the chairs circling the large table.

'It was,' Sulat said. 'It's not pirates, it's merfolk.'

The crew stiffened. Ashryn bowed her head. Renir scratched with his pen on a piece of paper.

'Merfolk don't attack ships that frequently.'

'King Kellac is making a bid for Ildecoke.'

Renir set his pen down. 'Really? One merfolk king against the whole of Viehland?'

'It's not just one colony.' Sulat recounted what she'd learned, as well as what Okala had told her.

'How did you come into contact with a merfolk prince?'

'He saved me and Lord Brynglas from the shipwreck.'

The crew fidgeted in their seats.

'He is sympathetic to humans and is the son of the king of the colony closest to us, who are also the last holdouts against King Kellac. I believe they will be our allies when Kellac arrives.'

'I don't think we can rely on any merfolk to side with us,' Renir said. 'They harbour deep resentments and they have long memories. More likely he's pretending to be our ally as he is pretending to be theirs. That's the trouble with double agents. Every side thinks they've got the advantage.'

'I trust Prince Okala. I don't trust easily.'

'And you may be right to. But I can't put the safety of the whole kingdom on your trust of a merfolk prince that you only knew for a few days. It's my job--my *duty*--to be suspicious.'

Sulat huffed. He had to assume Okala was a spy, but she couldn't let up, either.

'The agreement for getting Alois back was to negotiate with you,' she pressed on.

Renir blinked slowly at her. 'What did you agree to?'

'I agreed to open communications.'

Renir's shoulders relaxed. 'Then we may have a chance of saving him.'

The sailors tensed again, but Sulat didn't. She'd gotten herself and Alois out of sticky situations before.

'I can't promise we will be successful,' Renir said softly. 'Kellac sounds like a madman. Obviously, we won't budge on the Island, and that could bode ill for His Lordship.'

'If we get the king to the beach, I can get Alois back. But I think Kellac will attack anyway.'

'Leave that to me.' Renir stood and opened the door.

'Thank you for bringing this information to me. I will be in touch when you are needed. And keep away from the prince.'

Chapter Twenty

The Battle Of Ildecoke

Sulat sat in the dockyard tavern with her crew, and a mug of ale. Their nervous muttering mingled with the chatter of the other patrons frayed her nerves to shreds.

'I'm going out.' She scraped the chair back and stalked out into the sun. Sailors bustled around her, oblivious.

These poor fools. She dug her pipe out of her pocket and packed tobacco into it. *They have no idea. How am I going to keep them from losing their heads and killing the wrong merfolk? Assuming the right ones even come.*

Her stomach squirmed at the idea of someone shooting Okala.

Alois is better at this.

Her stomach flipped over. She couldn't stop the memory of him trussed up and bleeding.

She took a deep drag from the pipe and rubbed the fabric of her shirt hard between her fingers, focusing on the rough texture. *Focus on anything else. Anything else.*

'Captain!' Wese shouted behind her. He pointed at the

street where a black carriage discharged Lord Renir.

The Lord of Shadows strode purposefully toward Sulat, attracting stares from everyone he passed.

'Very subtle,' Sulat said.

'As intended,' Lord Renir agreed.

'So he is heading for the sandy cove?'

'Indeed. We can't meet here with--' Renir waved at all of the activity going on around them. 'Plus, the docks make things awkward. Much better to do everything in private.'

'You wouldn't want transparency in politics.'

Renir only smiled and invited her to the carriage. Sulat went with him, signalling to her men.

'You still think there will be a fight?' Renir asked, holding the door open.

Sulat scoffed, climbing into the carriage.

'What is the point of all of this hostage taking and posturing, if they're just going to attack anyway?' Renir followed her and shut the door. Sulat's crew loaded into another carriage nearby, pointing at the hers.

'Is the king going to relinquish the island?'

Renir snorted.

'A part of the island?'

'*His* island?'

'Any island.'

'The king doesn't like to be threatened. He's not the easiest to negotiate with.'

'Then, we'll fight.' Sulat said. 'As long as we get Alois back, I don't much care.'

'You forget yourself, *Captain*.' Renir put delicate emphasis on the last word. 'Don't forget how you came by your promotion, and what the terms are. You should care what happens, now that you're a loyal patriot and servant to the Crown. Remember that if this kingdom falls, you fall with it.'

'And the next one may be more sympathetic toward me. I know which stone sharpens my sword right now, but it's not the only one that can.'

'You think you're the only one of your kind who works for us? People like you aren't hard to replace.'

'Small sticks float, my lord. People like me know how to survive.'

Renir smiled in the dark of the carriage and smoothed the rich brocade at his knee. Despite his threats, he liked Sulat, and she knew it.

'You think Lord Brynglas is still alive?' he asked.

'Kellac is using him as bait.' Sulat clenched her fist. *He'd better still be alive.*

'And the young prince? Have we heard from him?'

The carriage curved around a cliff, onto a quiet stretch of empty shoreline. She pushed the door open and leapt out without answering. The other carriage pulled up behind as Renir followed her out. Wese and Eaton were by her side immediately as a third carriage arrived, painted solid black, with no adornment.

Only one passenger would be in a carriage so unremarkable.

Everyone bowed low as the footman opened the door. A jewelled shoe pointed out of the carriage, followed by the rest of the king, his eyes disappearing as he squinted at the glittering sea. Other ministers climbed out, followed lastly by the crown prince.

'Well, where *is* he, then?' King Bertold barked, his vast belly bouncing with every other word.

Sulat stood with her crew and the king and his court for the better part of an hour, ignoring the king's huffing and muttering. Eaton and Wese stood still as statues on either side of her; Darib, Ashryn, and the rest behind her in a quiet show of support.

If Kellac has any idea of his own safety, Alois will be alive.

Something bobbed up out of the water. Then another, and

a third. One by one, merfolk broke the surface and their bodies shimmered with scales and water droplets as they moved toward the beach. They were a horde of muted colour, a mix of all different kinds of sea life, each holding a weapon of some sort in their hands.

The guards around the king cocked their muskets loudly and pointed at the merfolk. Lord Renir steadied them with a gesture, but the king and prince didn't flinch, either by the display of strength from the merfolk or the response of their own men. Wese and Eaton did straighten a bit, tightening their grip around their own weapons. Darib moved closer to Sulat and she heard the glide of metal.

'Steady, men,' she said softly. 'I don't want any of you to be the first to act.'

The merfolk in front fanned out along the waterline where the waves lapped around their hips, just enough to show that they had half transformed and did have legs: intent to stay in the water, but prepared to go on land.

Not good.

More came, forming a line three rows deep, before Sulat spotted him. The mottled pink head of King Kellac, followed by golden-haired Breen, broke through the swells, and the rows of merfolk parted to allow them to pass. A merman with legs like a crab followed behind, dragging something bound in fishing net. As he stumbled closer, Sulat recognised the broad frame and shaggy brown hair.

Sulat's bones melted in relief. The men around her breathed out audibly.

'Steady,' she reminded them.

Alois lifted his dripping head and caught her eye. He winked, but he looked wrong, pale and droopy.

What did they do to him? Still, he's alive. That's all that matters.

King Bertold stepped ahead and King Kellac, on his many legs, stepped out of the surf. Breen stayed behind, draping a lazy arm around Alois' shoulders.

The human king and everyone on the beach bowed their heads to the king of the Rocky Shore Merfolk. Kellac grinned before also bowing his head around his eyestalks, which remained fixed on the humans. Bertold, tactfully, did not stare. It was probably a royal skill to remain professional in the face of the outlandish.

'Greetings, King Kellac,' King Bertold said. 'The Kingdom of Viehland welcomes negotiations with the kingdom of the Rocky Shore Merfolk.'

'Oh, but we're not a kingdom, Your Grace, not a *true* kingdom,' Kellac's voice boomed. Humans who hadn't spoken with merfolk before covered their ears and winced. 'We're a colony. We have a monarchical government, it's true, but we are still subjects of the kingdom of Viehland, in our hearts.' He placed two folded hands and two club-like limbs over his chest.

A few merfolk behind him scoffed, but he continued.

'And we are not just the Rocky Shore. We also represent the Open Sea, Deep Sea, and even--' he reached back and dragged a young pink mermaid with brown hair in front of him. 'Some Sandy Shore Merfolk. Give her a little bow. She's a royal, too.'

Renir's eyes snapped to Sulat as the humans all bowed. She shook her head.

This girl must be Princess Kyri.

'Perhaps you're looking for a wife, Your Highness,' Kellac said to Prince Bertold.

'A generous offer, Your Grace, but I'm already married,' the prince answered. 'To the woman who owns the jewel you wear.'

'Oh this?' Kellac ran his fingers over the star sapphire at his throat. 'No, Your Highness. Once it lands in the waters, it becomes ours. And under the water, he who finds a thing is he who owns it. Although, technically, she found it, so the offer stands.' Kellac shook the girl's arm. 'I understand you have another son, Your Grace.'

'I was under the impression you wanted to discuss territory, King Kellac, not marriage treaties,' King Bertold said.

'A marriage treaty would be a tidy way of achieving both

goals, don't you agree? But nevermind.' Kellac released the girl and folded his fingers. 'You see, my people were treated rather badly some time ago, and we'd like some justice.'

'What would be suitable justice for you?'

'Ildecoke Island.' Kellac's voice took an edge, strong and direct, his signature mania gone.

A few courtiers smirked and Prince Bertold coughed behind his hand.

'No.' King Bertold said steadily.

'Just like that?' Kellac hissed, taking a step closer. All armed men tensed, but Renir eased them back. 'Your people forced us onto this barren island and when we didn't die, you forced us into the sea and took the island as your capital. It was our sweat, our magic that made that rock habitable. You couldn't keep it up, which is why you've built your bridge to bring supplies in. If that bridge fails, you fail, you all die. You took everything from us and destroyed it!' He took a deep breath and ran his hands over his bald head. 'We do not ask to be allowed back among the people. All we want is our island back.'

'And what am I to tell the hundreds of people who live here now?' Bertold asked.

'The same thing you told us: get out.' Kellac glared hard at the human king. 'Use your guns, if they won't go peacefully. It worked before.'

Breen hissed her assent behind him, and such a hissing rose within the ranks of the merfolk that Bertold looked afraid for the first time.

Movement at the corner of Sulat's eye drew her attention. Several heads popped quietly through the water.

Sandy Shore Merfolk, they have to be!

'These are your demands?' Bertold asked.

'They are.' Kellac held his head high. Behind him, Breen squared her shoulders.

'And in exchange? What are you offering me to give over the seat of my kingdom and displace hundreds of my most loyal and powerful subjects, not to mention a lucrative and strategic port? I hope you're not hoping to bargain with one human.'

'He's mine.' Breen ran her hand along Alois' cheek.

'Lord Brynglass? Dear me, no. He was my agreement with her.' Kellac nodded his head at Sulat. 'To get her to arrange a meeting between us.'

'You have your audience. I want my partner,' Sulat said, the strength of her voice surprising her.

The men around her shifted as Kellac wheeled his eye-stalks on her. 'Give him back, Breen.'

The grin slid from Breen's face. 'Your Grace--'

'Give him back,' Kellac hissed. Breen hesitated a moment, then wrenched the rope out of the crab-man's claws and shoved Alois into the water in Sulat's direction, tossing the rope after him. He got clumsily to his feet and splashed between mermen up to Sulat, panting with the effort.

'Get behind me,' Sulat whispered and he obeyed. Someone moved behind her with the rattle of heavy wood and metal.

'Thanks,' Alois whispered to someone.

Breen stared at them, her chest heaving, her hands clenched into fists. She ran her tongue over her teeth-- she still owned him, even if she'd given him back.

Kellac directed his attention back to Bertold. 'What I have to bargain with is history. Your people have forgotten, but mine haven't. You'll be displacing hundreds, but giving thousands a home, their pride back. We are at war amongst ourselves constantly, you'll bring peace to us. Let me remind you, *again*, that we are your subjects. Peace for us is peace for you.

'What's more, we'll be a beacon for the others of your kind who are different, like us. They'll flock to us, so that those inland who are persecuted for their magic can find a home.'

'There is no magic in Viehland,' the king interjected. 'Humans don't have magic.'

'Where do you think we came from?' Kellac screamed, suddenly bursting into a rage. 'Do you think we sprang from fishes? Sprouted human faces because, what? You're all so handsome that we fish can't stand to look at each other without jawlines and arms? We were *humans*, driven from the kingdom and forced into the sea because we had magic!'

'We are very remorseful for the misdeeds of the past, but life has moved on. We are not the same people we were then. You won't find human society to be as it is in the stories.' Bertold said calmly, though his foot shifted in the sand.

'And what of now?' Kellac scuttled closer. Several guns raised, but he didn't flinch. 'How do you find our society, Your Grace? You thought your ships were being attacked by human pirates. Human pirates don't eat the fallen, do they? Our bellies have been full for months, we've never been stronger.' A great swell of hissing met these words. 'We are everywhere, the sea is teeming with us. Ahh, as if on cue, here come more! Our Sandy Shore brethren. Listen closely to them, your grace, their colony is just off your shores.'

Sulat groaned internally as Sandy Shore Merfolk rose fully out of the water and glided toward the two groups. The human ministers and courtiers stepped back, away from this second group, but Sulat and her crew, the soldiers and Renir, and the two Bertolds stood still.

A lot can be said about the king, but he's no coward. Sulat had to concede a twinge of respect for her king.

King Clyr led his envoy to the meeting with the other two kings. Behind him came the wizard, the mermaid princesses who had come on deck to retrieve Okala, and Okala himself. The queen and oldest sister, Marya, was not there.

Okala met Sulat's eyes and gave her a grim nod.

'King Kellac, King Bertold.' Clyr inclined his crowned head at the kings, who did the same.

'What the hell is going on?' Alois whispered behind Sulat.

'If you don't know, I don't. You saw them more recently,' Sulat muttered.

'Okala didn't tell you?'

'I'm not sure he knows.'

The Rocky Shore Merfolk look uncomfortable, and Breen and Adeto bristled at each other.

They don't know what's going on, either.

Sulat stepped her feet a little farther apart, sure that she could reach her weapons, if things went badly. Others behind her mirrored her movement.

'I make greeting to you. We are neighbours, though this is the first time in centuries that we have met,' Clyr said to King Bertold.

'You are welcome, King Clyr,' Bertold said, his shoulders tense.

'I hope that what is discussed here today will bring lasting peace between our people,' Clyr said. He also stepped fully onto the sand, though unlike King Kellac, with naked human legs. The Rocky Shore Merfolk scoffed at this display.

'You see, none of us want a war,' Kellac said, stamping a couple of his feet excitedly. 'This is no show of force, Your Grace, no threat. Just a little lesson that you are not alone out here. You may be numerous on this island, but we are numerous in the sea, and it takes no effort at all to come onto land.'

'You'll excuse me if that sounds like a threat to my ears,' King Bertold said.

'That's entirely your interpretation,' Kellac said smoothly. 'My allies and I only want what is owed us.'

Clyr's hand tightened around his trident.

Oh, he didn't like that.

'On the contrary,' Clyr said, and Kellac's eyestalks twisted. 'The Sandy Shore Merfolk seek no claim to Ildecoke Island.'

Bertold's eyebrows rose. The Rocky Shore Merfolk hummed and a few thrashed their tails. Behind the Shandy Shore king, Adeto reached into the pouch at his hip.

'The Sandy Shore Merfolk are among the most peaceful of the colonies, and our interest in this meeting is to ensure that no further subjugation will come to the people of the sea.'

'What are you doing?' Kellac whined. 'We had an agreement.'

'I agreed to consider what you said,' Clyr corrected him. The merfolk on both sides murmured louder. 'Our people have no love of war. We have made a good life, we are here to ensure that we may continue to prosper.'

'So you do not challenge human ownership of the island?' King Bertold asked.

'No,' Clyr said. 'If the humans wish to keep it, nothing changes for us. If the Rocky Shore and their allies gain control, it will mean widespread upheaval for all merfolk. My advisers and I believe that the King on Ildecoke will attempt to unite all merfolk colonies, and we have spent so long as distinct groups, that we do not believe that we could live together again, in much the same way that merfolk and humans will clash if forced to live together. King Kellac has painted a lovely picture for you of idyllic merfolk communities interacting in kinship and harmony, but the opposite is true.'

Kellac's skin reddened. 'You coward. You *traitor*! You--'

Breen shrieked and yanked something like a jellyfish out of the water, sparkling and fizzing in her hand. She hurled it at Adeto as merfolk on both sides ducked out of the way. It hit his shoulder and burst, bubbling over the brown skin. He howled in pain.

'Assassin!' she screamed, pointing at him. Purple spines shot from her wrist. Adeto threw up an arm, deflecting them.

He threw out his other arm and a great tangle of seaweed wrapped around Breen, pinning her arms against her body. She cast her face to the sky and storm clouds gathered overhead, opening a deluge upon the assembled delegations.

'This was a plot!' Kellac shouted at Clyr. 'You came to kill me and lay yourself before the humans! They tried to destroy us and you would bow to them!'

'The tide has turned, Kellac, can't you see that?' Clyr bellowed over the thunder. 'We need to move forward into this new world, not cling to the hurts of the past. They'll never heal. We can't undo what was done to us. Even if you won the island, would you feel better? Or would you push for the mainland where we came from originally? Would you seek to subdue the humans and exact revenge by killing them?'

'She knew,' Kellac said, backing away. 'She was right. We could never win peacefully. There are too many among us who are content to be treated like inferiors.'

He lunged for King Bertold, slamming his forearms together. The humans, Sulat included, toppled like skittles as the Rocky Shore Merfolk surged onto the beach and through the surf at the Sandy Shore party.

Alois scrambled to his feet and dashed across the dampening sand, reaching the king a second behind Kellac. The king swiped Bertold across the middle, opening a wide bloody gash in the king's round belly. Alois kicked Kellac hard, knocking him off his many legs long enough for the king's entourage to get to their feet.

'No!' Kellac shrieked. 'You will yield!'

'You don't command me,' Alois growled back, tripping over Bertold's swordbelt, which had slipped off by Kellac's strike. The guards bundled the king and prince into the carriage as Alois drew his own sword. 'You should have let her eat me.'

'I may yet, my lord,' Kellac giggled. 'I may yet. Alas, I can't touch you, myself. However,' he rubbed his hands together and shouted, 'Find the woman! Captain Sulat, bring her to me!'

'No! Sulat!' Alois bellowed, hoping she would hear him and save herself.

'Get cover!' Sulat shouted over the rain, pointing to a large driftwood tree trunk up the beach. So far, the merfolk were fighting each other, now that the royal carriage was speeding away. She had to protect her men. Alois was engaged with Kellac, but he was safe so long as Breen was distracted by Adeto. 'Let them tire themselves out and get away when you can.'

Thunder cracked overhead and lightning struck Breen, shattering the seaweed that bound her.

'Run!' Sulat screamed at her crew, struggling across the sand. They dove behind the driftwood, as the whole thing stood up on its brittle, twisted roots and walked down the beach toward the water.

Foth screamed and took cover behind Darib's large torso, while Eaton and Wese stared dumbfounded at the tree.

It staggered to Adeto. Beside him, Ytaso threw something from a sack at Breen, which landed and crawled all over her. Neri burst out of the water on yellow legs and charged up the beach, followed by a dozen mermen, straight for King Kellac.

Breen screamed and lifted her arms as though directing marionettes. As one, everyone on the beach-- Sulat and her crew, Alois, Kellac, and all of the merfolk-- lifted into the air.

Sulat twisted to tug off her sword belt. They wouldn't stay in the air forever, and she didn't want it under her when she fell.

A green and blue shape shot at her and tangled her up in strong arms.

'I have to Kiss you, Sulat,' Okala's voice said thickly.

'No!' Sulat kicked at him.

'Kellac wants you!' he whined.

Behind him, the horde of merfolk turned their eyes on her.

'Fine! Fine!' She pulled him tight to her by the shoulders.

He wrapped her in a tight hug and sank his teeth into her shoulder. An icy wave spread down her arm and over her whole body.

They landed together in a heavy thud, and blood sank into the sand as she struggled to stand back up.

'I'm so sorry, I'm so sorry.' Okala backed away and spit out a mouthful of blood.

A cry rose up as the advancing merfolk groaned at the bite on her shoulder, and Kellac screamed over the crowd. Sulat, full of rage and invincibility, drew her sword.

Alois watched her fall. He wanted to run to her, but humans began to appear on the far end of the beach, drawn, no doubt by the noise and sudden storm.

Behind him, more merfolk emerged from the foam; tall and lean, with brown and grey skin and meaty fins along their legs; followed by rolling black bubbles full of white and glowing creatures.

Shit!

He ran backward toward the humans. Sulat stood, Okala rolling off of her, blood streaming down her shoulder, and a cry of rage rose from the Rocky Shore Merfolk.

Yes!

The Kiss wasn't ideal, but at least she was safe. They'd have time to deal with it later.

Some of the new humans had gone back for weapons or backup, some charged in with what they had on them. With great cries and gusto, they waded into battle, swinging wildly at anyone in their path.

'Not the...the colourful ones!' Alois bellowed over the din, trying. 'Just the ones that look weird!'

Some heeded him and switched targets, some rebelliously engaged whoever was nearest, friend or foe.

The Open Sea Merfolk swung enormous bone clubs and swords lined with teeth. The Deep Sea merfolk lashed out with glowing tentacles and antennae, stunning or ensnaring human and merfolk alike.

'Sailors and fishermen. Souls, this is the last thing we need,' Sulat growled, appearing at his side.

'It could be good,' Alois said, but his voice betrayed his trepidation. 'How do you feel?'

He searched her face and found only anger there, which was as good as he could expect.

Wave after wave of seamen and dockworkers, not to mention fishwives and urchins, swarmed onto the beach, screaming and launching themselves at the merfolk. One managed to pierce a Deep Sea bubble, releasing a gush of thick black water and a writhing translucent monstrosity made of fangs and spines. It shrieked and wriggled before lying still, smoking at the edges.

'How are we going to control them all?' Sulat shouted, dragging her attention away from the horror. 'We have to get the Sandy Shore out of here.'

'No chance. They're in it, now,' Alois shouted back. 'We just need to find a way to spread the word.'

'Any suggestions?' Sulat asked, backing against him as another surge rushed past her.

A sound rose over the shouting. At first, it sounded like a bird; then like a shanty, like the men were rousing themselves to fight. But it had a tone, a piercing quality that irritated Sulat's ears.

More voices chimed in, different songs-- some lilting and ethereal, some dissonant screeches and clicks-- all with the same insistent quality.

Alois passed a hand over his face. 'Shit.'

'What?' Sulat grimaced at him.

'You don't recognise that?'

'No, should I?'

'It's...it's their song.'

Humans all around them dropped their arms, their faces slack. They moved as one, turning on their fellow humans.

'No!' Sulat bellowed. 'Shit! What do we do?'

'Luckily, this is easily solved.' Alois pulled back and punched the nearest man. The sailor reeled, then steadied himself, shook his head, and ran at a screaming mermaid.

'We can't punch all of them!'

'But they can be knocked out of it. It's not permanent like the Kiss. They just need a distraction.'

Some men weren't affected by the song. They watched Alois throw the punch and followed suit, throwing blows at random.

Sulat growled, breaking up a brawl erupting near her. 'Okala!' she shouted, as the boy reached them, still wiping blood from his chin. 'Is there a counterspell to the song? We can't have these assholes fighting each other and you lot!'

'Okala!' Vila called from far away. She crouched over a wounded sailor, brandishing a spear at three advancing Rocky Shore mermen. She chanted in a low voice, holding a hand over the human's deep cut.

'We're trying. There aren't enough of us. *NOW! WE NEED YOU NOW!*' he screamed at the other end of the beach.

The boy had lost it. Battle hysteria was a real thing, but this wasn't the time. Sulat slapped him hard across the face.

'What was that for?' he cried, putting a hand to his cheek.

'You can't lose your nerve. We need you.'

He pointed in the direction that he'd shouted. A number of people moved slowly across the sand, naked from the waist down, but heavily adorned up top. The woman in front was unmistakable, her dark purple hair standing out against the light sand and grey sky.

As they approached, they brought something else with them, a song of their own, sweet and lyrical. Light danced around them, from mirrors in their hands, flashing across the beach, scattering light and snippets of song. The notes landed like darts, waking humans from the siren song.

'Get her!' Breen screamed, throwing another jellyfish at Adeto, and missing. 'Kill the queen!'

A few Rocky Shore Merfolk and enchanted men broke away from the fight and charged the beach. But they were no match for the red streak that darted out of the sea and landed with a spray of sand in front of Marya. The procession stopped, but otherwise showed no sign of concern. Their defender, Princess Ytaso, threw a handful of sand into the air, coalescing and forming a hard crystal shell around the singing mermaids. The attacks bounced off the barrier, the spears and rocks landing harmlessly in the sand.

Okala dashed to the bubble, lending his own voice to his sisters, and standing behind Ytaso.

A bolt of lightning struck the barrier with a tremendous crack, leaving nothing but a black stain.

'Your quarrel is with me, Breen,' Adeto growled.

'My quarrel is with your entire cowardly kind,' Breen spat back.

Her shoulders slumped. The lightning bolt had cost her a great deal.

The wizard grinned, and his confidence buoyed Okala.

Adeto's smile widened and widened, elongating and sprouting sharp teeth. His arms also grew, stretching and splitting and curling, suckers popping up along the insides.

Transmutation, Ytaso had said, was a classic Sandy Shore scare tactic.

'Nice try, gentle Sandy,' Breen sneered. 'We have real monsters.'

She cast an arm out and a huge wave of water followed, knocking a group of humans off their feet and sweeping them, screaming, into the sea. Rocky Shore Merfolk swarmed them, pouncing on the bodies, the thrashing forming a red wall between her and Adeto.

Okala's stomach twisted and waves of nausea threatened to overpower him.

Tentacles whipped over the wall and in one swift motion, Adeto was on the other side, practically on top of Breen, snapping grotesque jaws.

Breen commanded the seaweed to bind him, as he had done to her, to drag him back and hold him still for another crack of lightning. It hit him square in the chest.

Adeto fell to his knees in the surf, shock on his shrinking face, gasping. He pitched forward and his tentacles twitched violently as they receded back into muscular arms. Breen approached slowly, savage triumph on her face.

It was all Okala could do to keep singing. If Marya's spell failed, the humans would turn, and all would be lost.

Adeto raised his face to the advancing sea witch, and pulled the netting away, exposing his chest to her.

'I can't defeat you,' he growled. 'Kill me now, and make me a martyr.'

'No!' King Clyr lunged toward the conflict, hurling his spear at Breen. She swung an arm, deflecting it easily, then froze, her golden eyes on the Sandy Shore king.

She twisted her hand in the air and the spear flew from her fingers at King Clyr. The world slowed as the king stumbled and fell backward in a slow arc, landing in a great splash of foamy surf.

Okala's voice failed. The barrier disappeared in a crackle of light as Ytaso tripped and skidded to the water. Okala landed on his knees in the sand and Marya put her hand on his shoulder. Her fingers trembled, but her song never faltered.

Breen hissed in satisfaction, turning back to the wizard. Adeto stared, wide-eyed at her.

A great shriek rose up all around them. Four mermaids screamed in unison and as one and rushed at Breen. Vila dipped down as she passed Adeto, ripping the glass dagger from his belt. They laid blow after blow on Breen, but she twisted her body this way and that, so that none of the blows landed. Kyri lunged at Vila and wrestled the dagger away from her.

'Whose side are you on?' Neri cried.

Kyri didn't answer, but twisted her face into a grotesque mask as she plunged the dagger into the sea witch's back. Breen's dorsal nerve glowed blue when Kyri ripped the dagger out. Kyri paused, then pulled Breen's head back by the hair and dragged the dagger across her throat. She tossed the body, gushing blood, face first into the surf.

Alois pitched forward, howling, a hand clapped over his mouth, his eyes screwed up in pain. He heaved and panted, on all fours in the sand, tears streaming down his face as he screamed at Breen's body, her coppery hair floating in the foam.

She's dead, she's gone. It's over.

'Get up, come on.' Sulat dragged him to his feet as the storm clouds dispersed and the rain stopped. He gasped and sputtered, leaning on her to remain upright.

Three of the mermaid princesses stared at their youngest sister, who panted above the body of the sea witch. She wiped her brow with her arm, streaking blood across her forehead, and slid the dagger into the belt at her waist

Another shriek pierced the quiet that followed Breen's death. Thunder crashed and bodies collapsed in a wide arc as King Kellac came screaming across the beach, banging his forearms together. He plunged into the surf and lifted Breen into his arms. He screamed again, cradling her greying body against his brilliant one, her graceful tail dangling limp over his hard carapace. Blood flowed over her, her eyelids hanging half open.

He charged at each of the sisters in turn, but his heart wasn't in it. He was a wounded animal, flailing in agony, and not capable of any of the fierceness in his breaking heart. Words spilled sharp and incoherent from his slackening mouth as he spun in circles, his pink eyestalks swinging.

Sulat drew her sword, but Alois put a hand on her shoulder.

'He's going to do it. I've seen this before.'

Kellac wailed at the sky as Breen's body slid from his arms

and crumpled awkwardly on the dry sand. He stepped over her and blundered in a swaying line up the beach. He dug in the sand for something. A moment later, he held it high over his head.

'Behold!' he screamed. 'Breen the sea witch is dead. Witness as our noble endeavour is killed in its infancy by the human king's very sword.'

The pulled the thing apart with a flash of silver, and swung the point of the sword beep into his chest.

'Souls,' Sulat whispered and Alois hung his head.

Silence fell as Kellac's body buckled on itself and toppled onto the sand. Gradually at first, then in a great wave, merfolk retreated to the sea like schools of fish leaping across the sand, dashing in every direction. Some straight back to the sea, some forward to seize a fallen body, some to latch onto a distracted combatant and drag then to the sea.

'No!' Alois and Sulat shouted in unison, diving forward to rescue what living humans they could.

'Leave the dead!' Sulat shouted to whoever could hear her. 'We can't save them all! Focus on the living!'

When the last of the Rocky Shore army retreated, barely a single corpse, not even King Kellac's or Breen's, remained on the beach. All that remained were some confused and frightened humans, and some very nervous and wary Sandy Shore Merfolk.

All five mermaid princesses and Adeto stood fierce guard over the body of King Clyr.

'I'm so sorry,' Okala said softly, stepping up beside Sulat. He prodded the spot where he'd bitten her, still tender.

'We'll talk about it later.' She brushed his hand aside.

'What do we do about all of them?' Alois asked Lord Renir, gesturing at the sailors who had come to the rescue. 'They'll want to know what happened.'

'Let me handle them,' Renir said, with barely a hint of agitation.

Chapter Twenty-One
Calm

The retreat left so few bodies on the beach that the cleanup of the battlefield lasted barely long enough to process what had happened. There would only be a handful of burials, and hundreds of tankards and glasses raised to men 'lost at sea'. That was what they told a widow when there was no body to bury. What else could be said about their deaths?

Sulat and Alois sat with the crew of *Meltythia*, hung low over their glasses of brandy, trying not to hear Wese's quiet sobs. Ashryn had no more tears left to cry, and Eaton busied himself with carving another figurine. This one had a thick curve like a fishhook where its legs should have been.

Did he get Kissed? Sulat would have to ask, eventually.

She cast her eyes out to sea. How many merfolk, friend or foe, hovered out of sight?

Ildecoke. Island of Shells, that's what it means. There were place names that sounded like they belonged to mermaids. It was all around them, stolen land.

Sulat rose, told her tablemates that she needed a smoke and stepped outside. She packed tobacco into her pipe and lit it, leaning against the wall.

Alois followed her out, and did the same.

'They were right,' she said. 'Breen and King Kellac.'

'What?' Alois sputtered. 'They were *right*? Invade Viehland and demand Ildecoke back. Wage war, unite the colonies, all of that? Eating people?'

'Yeah.' Sulat nodded, her eyes still on the sea, the sweet tobacco smoke enveloping her. 'Not eating people. But the rest of it.'

'How do you figure?'

'They didn't leave voluntarily, they were forced onto this island to die. And when they didn't, they were forced into the sea to die. Like Bogomil and Ingad, fleeing into the sky because humans were killing all giants, not just Ettins. Just killing a whole group of people, out of fear. And then, with the merfolk, we forgot. It became a myth for us, but they've been out there the whole time.

'When slavery ended, my people never got an apology, but at least it was acknowledged. At least we're here, in everyone's faces, fighting for ourselves. Merfolk were forgotten, they should get something. If not the island, then an apology or *something*.'

Alois laughed and shook his head.

Anger flared in Sulat. 'What's funny?'

'It's always me making this argument. "These people have suffered, it's unfair." And you'll be saying, "Life is harsh, no one is ever made a promise."' He shrugged dramatically.

'Maybe I'm closer to this than you are.'

'Well, let's tell the king that. If this happened once, it'll happen again. Kellac is dead, but he did pull a lot of Merfolk to him; a couple of other colonies, who're probably still angry. Perhaps even angrier, now. This would be a good time to negotiate, while we have the victory. Extend the hand of peace and give them something they want.'

'They want Ildecoke.'

'We know that won't happen. But there may be something else.'

If they were going to be summoned to the palace, which would likely happen any time, they needed to clean up. The carriage that took them to Alois' house on the Overlook stank of smoke, vomit, and all manner of humanity who had sat on its threadbare velvet seats.

'What happened to you down there?' Sulat asked over the rattling of the metal wheels against cobblestones. 'Now that we have a chance to talk.'

Alois wiped his palms on his stiff breeches. He didn't really want to talk about it, but he wouldn't have a choice, soon.

'You remember how you felt in the cage on the cloud, last year?'

It wasn't the first time they'd been locked up, but the combination of confinement, threats of being eaten, and a deep injury had produced one of the worst hallucinatory episodes Sulat had had in years. It was the closest thing Alois could think of to describe his experience in the bubble.

Sulat's face darkened and she nodded.

'It was like that, only their threats weren't empty, like Bogomil's were; they didn't lock me up for *their* protection. They taunted me constantly, didn't let me sleep much or eat much, I had to beg for water. The only thing I had for comfort was the idea that they wouldn't kill you. Thankfully, as mad as they are, they're more calculated than just voracious predators.'

A brown and cream carriage stood outside the narrow house when they arrived, and Alois groaned.

Johanne knows about the shipwreck. Why else would she be here, this close to autumn? The court season is weeks over.

He steeled himself and knocked on the door.

'Forgot your key?' Sulat asked.

'Left it at my other house.'

The brass handle turned and Rustiss, the butler, opened the door, shock etched on his face.

'M--my lord. We didn't expect you.'

'Nor did I. Is the lady in?' Alois asked, his stomach twisting with nerves and guilt.

Rustiss nodded grimly, stepping aside to admit Alois and Sulat. 'She's overseeing the move.'

Alois and Sulat pressed through into the sitting room just as Johanne came down the stairs, dressed in a simple black shift, an oval mourning brooch pinned where her chatelaine used to be.

When their eyes met, she wobbled and landed hard on the stairs. Alois rushed to her and she clutched his jacket, her eyes swinging between him and Sulat, gasping for air.

'They said...they told me...the ship...*sank*,' she said shakily.

Sulat stood still as stone behind him.

'It did.' Alois helped Johanne to her feet and guided her to the sofa under the single-paned window that looked out over the sea. He flicked his tongue over the cut on his lip that was still cold, despite Breen's death. 'We have a lot to talk about.'

Johanne put a hand to her stomach and nodded, tears leaving cloudy tracks down her powdered cheeks.

Sulat stood in the middle of the room, bouncing a fist against her thigh.

She doesn't know how to excuse herself.

'Sulat, you don't want to be here for this, do you?' he asked.

Sulat shook her head and backed away, relief on her face. Johanne leapt from her seat and rushed to Sulat, wrapping her arms tight around her shoulders.

Alois didn't hear what Johanne whispered, but when she pulled back, the women squeezed each other's fingers. Sulat shook when she nodded at Rustiss and stepped through the open door. He hailed a passing carriage and helped her in.

Johanne rejoined Alois on the sofa, her face pale. She threaded her fingers between his and stared hard into his eyes.

'Tell me everything.'

The carriage arrived at Sulat's house as the lamplighters made their way across the docklands. Only one light glowed from the house, and when Sulat walked in, Tansy jumped up from a seat at the dining table.

'Captain,' she said groggily, 'I didn't know when you'd be coming home.'

'It's fine, Tansy. Please heat me some water for a bath and bring some food up to my room.'

Sulat tossed her hat onto the peg by the door, hung up her coat, kicked off her boots, and stomped up the stairs. She listened to the sounds of men loading and unloading, bustling under bright lights, despite the lateness of the hour.

Sulat didn't bother scanning the rigging. She knew *Martinette* was still there and that *Meltythia* wasn't. She didn't much care about the others, though she was a little curious about how Dilys was handling Fermin. But she was too tired to go in search of company tonight.

She lit the candle on the table in her room and pulled off her shirt. The deep and unmistakable bite on her shoulder had begun to scab. It was as though her shoulder were an apple and someone Alois' size had bitten into it before deciding they'd rather have something else.

It was a brand, that was what it came down to. A mark of ownership, such that she'd never had before, even when she lived in bondage at the convent. Of course, it was also a mark of protection, but only because merfolk were territorial. Even the friendly ones.

There has to be a way. She touched one of the toothmarks

and it throbbed.

Anger flared in her. She didn't fear Okala, she knew he wouldn't hurt her, that he'd done it to protect her from the others on the beach, that he was probably the safest merman in the world to be bonded to, but that didn't change the fact that she was now someone's property, something she'd been promised would never happen to her.

Alois began his story with Sulat coming to Parry House to hire him. Johanne listened quietly, sniffling occasionally, until he got to Rhythlin Island. She stiffened at the name.

They must have told her that's where we went down. He kissed her forehead and pressed on.

She shook all through his description of what happened on the island, his Kiss, the breaking of the ship, and waking up to find Sulat talking to a merfolk prince. The frustrations in Vurdia and Okala's acclimatisation to human life provided a moment of levity before he got to the worst part: the Call and his time in the bubble with the Rocky Shore Merfolk.

Johanne sat still while he described how he felt passing Rhythlin a second time, how Sulat and the crew had used him as bait and how Breen had gotten the better of them anyway, how he'd been taunted by the merfolk, terribly dehydrated and drugged, then used as bait by them against Sulat.

It was well past dark when Rustiss poked his head into the room and asked if they wouldn't like at least something cold for supper. The time for a hot meal had passed, and, given the circumstances, been packed away without serving. Alois' stomach growled loudly, and he realised that it had been almost a day since his last meal of raw fish and tainted magical freshwater. He hadn't eaten human food since before the Call, but ship rations can hardly be considered real food. His last fresh meal had been in Vurdia, which of course, didn't serve food fit for a Viehlish-man. So, really, he hadn't eaten properly since he saw Johanne last, at luncheon, the day Sulat recruited him. And they had fought.

He told her that and tears welled in her eyes again. He squeezed her fingers.

'But it's all right now,' he said, drying her eyes. 'I'm alive, and I'm here. I told you I'm hard to kill.'

Johanne sputtered and nodded against his hand.

'You need a bath, though,' she said hoarsely. She stood and went to the servants' quarters to have a word about heating up water, leaving Alois alone on the sofa.

The curtains were open, displaying the glorious view of the sea that they paid so dearly for in this neighbourhood of the island. City lights twinkled below them, only a couple of ships on the water, making their way for the safety of the harbour and a night of rest.

A shiver ran up his spine. It used to be comforting to watch the waves, to imagine the lands beyond, to daydream about sails strained by salty wind and the snapping of rope and creaking of wood.

Now, having been out there, all of those images darkened and soured, choked by the dread of what moved under the waves. Fins and pincers and tentacles and teeth.

He shuddered and pulled the curtains closed. *We should sell this house.*

But Johanne loved it too much, it was a significant piece of social currency to say one lived on the Overlook. And anyway, someone with knowledge needed to watch the Ildecoke Coast.

He opened the curtains just a little, enough to see the streak of moonlight, but not all of that black expanse.

Johanne came back with a tray of cold meat pies and pitcher of cider. Alois moaned at the wholesome Viehlish fare and resisted the urge to shove everything into his face at once. Johanne's forgiving nature only went so far, even in the event of her husband's return from the dead.

She didn't eat, but sat with a hand on her stomach. Alois wanted to apologise for everything she'd gone through. It wasn't his fault, of course; if he'd had the choice, none of it would have happened. But all the information she had was that he had died, and so she'd begun the process in earnest: the grief of losing another husband, the bother of organising *another* funeral without a body, informing all of their friends and her family.

'I'm sorry,' he said at last.

'For what?' She turned shocked eyes on him. 'You didn't do anything. You can't say no to the king. You can't say no to Sulat.' She smiled indulgently. 'You can't control what happens at sea, or what people tell me, especially when you're in Vurdia. Surely, you're not apologising for coming back to me.' She hugged his arm and laid her head on his shoulder.

He laughed. 'No, I'm not sorry for that.'

'Well then, as that's the only choice you've had in this whole affair, you've nothing to apologise for.'

'I should say that I'm sorry you went through all of this.'

'Well, it's over, now.' She kissed his cheek and snuggled closer.

'There's still a lot more to tell you,' he said around a mouthful of pie. 'There's the reason for it all, the politics, the battle--'

'Tomorrow,' Johanne said. 'Rest now. Finish your supper, have your bath, and come to bed. We can face the rest of it together in the morning. I have news for you, too.' She kissed him and stood.

'What news?' *What happened in the two weeks I was gone?*

'Tomorrow.'

Alois' mind reeled. The shock of being back home and eating pie and cider like it was any normal day, like normal life just went on after spending days in a bubble with half-fish people, and then a battle, and international politics to debate later, and now Johanne had news.

But she was right, he was tired. When the bathwater was

ready, he nearly cried with joy. Hot water, soap, fresh clothes. And his bed, with Johanne in it to look forward to later, was more than he could have hoped for, even this morning. He never truly believed that Kellac would give him back, that he'd ever be free of Breen.

Sulat lowered herself into the fresh hot water and moaned as her muscles relaxed. Dirt melted off her skin, clouding the water as she slid down, dunking her whole head under. She winced at the heat on her face, but stayed under for a moment longer, scrubbing her hair and face with her hands. She sat back up, squeezed the water from her hair, and twisted to reach for the soap. She had ordered it specially made, scented like fir and amber, with a touch of sweet vanilla.

She lifted the soap to her hair, and dropped it with a loud *plunk*! on top of Okala's face floating in the water.

'Why are you always in my bathwater?' she hissed.

'It's the only time you're near water.' Okala pursed his lips. 'Maybe if you drank something other than brandy every once in a while--'

'Water's not safe to drink, I told you.'

'I'm not actually in your bath, I just use the surface like a window. I can't see anything. Though I don't understand the modesty, you've seen me naked.'

'It's not the same. What do you want?'

'I wanted to check on you.'

'You can't just *sense* how I'm doing?' She twitched her shoulder at him.

He grimaced. 'I could... but I, I don't really...'

Why? Would that be invasive?

'It's fine.' Guilt nudged her for jabbing him, but she wasn't done being angry about it.

'I need to meet with you. Tomorrow, if you can,' Okala

said. Sulat wanted to keep being petty, but there was no point to it. He knew what she wanted to say. 'I'm not going to Call you, I don't want us to be like that.'

'I'll hopefully have an audience with the king tomorrow, but I can come after.'

Okala nodded. 'Just touch the, you know, you shoulder, and say my name. I'll come.'

'The Call works both ways?' Sulat asked.

'No, not really. But I'll hear you, and I'll come.'

Of course, it doesn't.

Okala grimaced again and vanished.

Alois picked up the brooch sitting on Johanne's dressing table. It depicted a nighttime scene of a scruffy dog howling at the moon. The image had come from a story, one from long ago that illustrated the love between them: he the lowly dog, she the distant moon.

'I don't know what to wear tomorrow,' Johanne said. 'I packed away my chatelaine days ago. I didn't expect to need it here.'

The chatelaine, a brooch from which hung the symbols of the lady of the house, was the mark of a married woman; the mourning brooch marked a widow. Johanne now had two mourning brooches--one for each husband--and three chatelaines-- one for each wedding and one smaller one to suit her new fashions. A woman as well-known as Johanne going about with neither would cause quite a stir.

'I'll just have to spirit you away to the country as soon as I can,' Alois whispered, climbing into bed beside her.

'I never got to say I'm sorry,' Johanne said after a long pause. 'Before you left, we were fighting so much. And it was all so pointless. And when they said you'd died, all I could think of is that that midday, we'd been fighting about you chewing with your mouth open.'

Alois laughed. 'Yeah, it was silly.'

'It's still unacceptable, but I'm glad it wasn't the last thing I said to you before you died.' Johanne's face scrunched in anguish.

'I wouldn't have minded, if it was.' Alois wrapped his arms around her and pulled her close. Her soft cotton night-gown smelled like summer flowers. 'It's normal, and all I've ever wanted was a normal life with you. If chewing is the worst of our problems, we're doing pretty well.'

It isn't, but fertility problems are also normal.

Johanne didn't answer, but pulled his arms tighter around her and closed her eyes.

Sulat climbed out of the tub, wrapped her hair in the luxuriously oversized bath sheet, and pulled her dressing gown over her damp, perfumed body. The crisp night air brought with it the scents of the city, mingling with the sea breeze. She'd had her fill of clean salty air, for a while, and revelled in the smoke and baking, and sweet tree-filtered smells that grounded her on land.

Tansy bustled about downstairs, so Sulat went to say good night and get a glass of the good brandy to dissolve her sleeping powder into. As she stepped foot on the floor, someone knocked at the door. The housemaid opened it and admitted Eaton, also freshly washed, and dressed in clean breeches and crisp white socks.

'Aren't you dapper,' Sulat said, waving him to sit, and pouring a glass for each of them.

'I started looking for work straight away, so this is the first chance I've had to wear my new kit. The wife was so sure the reports were wrong that she stayed up several nights in a row to sew clothes for my return. She's a spiteful thing, but in the best way.'

'You have a type, sir,' Sulat said, clinking her glass against his.

'It's why I like you so much.' Eaton lifted his glass at her. 'To doing the opposite of what people expect, just to make them look foolish.'

'And sometimes to save the world.'

They drank together and Eaton pulled something out of his pocket-- one of his figurines, a man with messy brown hair and a blue jacket.

'My wife trusts what my little dolls tell her, so they work for people other than me.' He slid the doll across the table to Sulat. 'I knew you were alive, Captain. I made a carving of you some time ago, so I knew you'd survived the wreck. That's why I didn't give up. I thought you might like one of His Lordship, in case something like this happens again. I imagine you two get into scrapes often.'

The little figure didn't much resemble Alois in the face, but the minute she picked it up, a wave of relief and guilt and giddy happiness hit her like nothing she had ever felt before.

She put the figure down. *Souls, is that what it's like in his head? That's... a lot.*

'It can take some getting used to,' Eaton said. 'Feeling other people's emotions on top of your own. But it helps a lot. When the person dies, the doll just feels like wood. So, I find them handy to have around, even if just to know everyone is still alive. They're also good for finding common ground during a fight, if that ever comes up.'

'Is that the secret to your marriage?' Sulat asked, pouring another glass.

'One of them.' Eaton held his glass out for a refill.

The two drank together in silence for a while. It was nice to have someone to sit with quietly, who didn't fill the space with noise. Sulat glanced up at him a couple of times.

Was Alois right-- was Eaton the new Alois? Was he enough like her to replace her old partner in her heart?

Eaton was quiet, stoic, dependable, and never made a fuss; but Alois...

She remembered that first night she'd had to trust him, when he'd lowered his guard by going to sleep first and letting her have his gun. All the things they'd been through, all the things he knew about her that no one else did. She trusted Eaton with those stories, but couldn't bear the telling. Alois already knew-- he was there for most of it.

She had almost shot him last year, and he had comforted her about it. That kind of trust and loyalty was hard to build quickly.

No, she liked Eaton, but Alois was irreplaceable.

Still, Eaton had potential. He was an excellent first mate. However, maintaining that professional distance meant that she couldn't get as drunk as she wanted to with him.

He must have had the same idea, because he set the glass down and smoothed his trouser legs, the universal signal that he planned to leave soon.

Sulat corked what was left of the brandy and the two stood.

Eaton looked at her for a moment and even as bad as she was at reading faces, she knew what he was thinking: *after all that had happened, what was there to say?* He nodded stiffly and made his way to the door.

'Eaton,' Sulat called, and her lanky first mate stopped on the doorstep. 'I'll show you mine, if you show me yours.' She tugged the collar of her dressing gown to expose Okala's Kiss.

'Not me, Captain.'

'I saw you carving a mermaid in the tavern.' Sulat adjusted her clothes.

'Not for myself,' Eaton said, stepping closer and lowering his voice. 'Wese. He doesn't move so fast these days, especially on land. And with the rain...' He waved his hand to indicate other factors not mentioned.

'Well, that's not ideal.' Sulat slumped against the doorframe. 'What should we do?'

'He doesn't want to resign or retire. So, I figure we keep an eye on him and if he gets too squirrelly,' Eaton jabbed a thumb as if to suggest throwing the Second Mate overboard.

Sulat laughed and shook Eaton's hand. 'Good night, Eaton.' He waved and set off into the night.

Chapter Twenty-Two
Ambassador

Alois wanted to stay in bed for hours longer, but Johanne never could stand lying around when there was work to do. Though her reason for being in the capital was resolved, she still at least had to discuss the day's menu with the cook. Alois decided that he wanted to be with her more than he wanted to sleep, so he dressed, and they went downstairs together.

He sat at the breakfast table and picked at the buttery rolls and hot coffee while Johanne and the kitchen staff worked out the menu. She came back in and sat herself opposite him, reaching for her silver pitcher of hot chocolate.

'So, the battle,' she said casually.

What a strange marriage we have. How many couples discuss war over breakfast?

His smile faltered as he gathered his thoughts. *How do I tell her everything that happened? Where do I even start-- being thrown at Sulat's feet and watching her reject me, or centuries back with the colonisation of Ildecoke Island?*

He decided on leading with Okala-- how they'd been suspicious of him, how he had made them trust him, the things he told them about merfolk, and all he knew about the Kiss.

'But you're free, now?' Johanne ran a thumb over the cut on Alois' lip. Her hand was soft and warm, and he couldn't resist leaning into it.

'In a way,' he said, slowly. 'From what I understand, the cut will never heal, but also no mermaid can kill me.'

'But you can still die some other way.'

'Oh yes, I'm not immune to murder or misfortune. But, I'm lucky.' He winked and she smiled warily.

'Where is Breen now?'

'Is that jealousy, I hear?'

'Is it unusual to be jealous of other women kissing my husband?'

'She's dead.' A lump rose in his throat, and he hated himself for it. 'She killed the Sandy Shore king, and his daughters killed her.'

'And how do you feel about that?' Johanne asked softly. He squeezed her fingers and smiled.

'It's complicated. I hated her, of course. She was crazy and cruel, and she wanted to eat me. But the Kiss comes with a strange devotion. And really, as Sulat pointed out, she wasn't totally wrong in her mission.'

Johanne jerked back as he had done when Sulat had said it.

'The history of this kingdom is... murky,' he said. 'We've done a lot of good, but we've done a lot of bad, too. What happened to the people who lived here before the Viehlish came in? What do we do to our own people who are different? We kidnapped Sulat's ancestors for the purpose of mistreatment. We can't begrudge people being angry about it, just because we've moved on.'

'The kingdom's history isn't your fault.'

'I know, but how are things going to get better if the people with the power to do something don't feel some sort of empathy or shame about it? How can we say we stand for justice if we ignore the victims?'

'So that's what you're going to do? Fight for merfolk rights, the day after they tried to invade?' Johanne sipped her chocolate delicately.

'I know how it looks, but Kellac's win would have been disastrous for the merfolk colonies, as well. But someone like Okala's sister may be more sensible. So that's the plan: tell the king that there's a threat on his doorstep, but that it can be negotiated to everyone's benefit.'

'You don't think the sister has any surprising demands?'

'I don't think they'll be outrageous, the way Okala talks about her. She may put herself between us and the more radical colonies, and we can't know anything more yet. I'll hammer all of that out with the king's counsellors when the time comes.'

'Oh no, not you,' Johanne said sharply. 'You can't talk. It has to be Sulat.'

Alois choked on his coffee. 'Sulat?' He gasped. 'She'll insult the king to his face.'

'Let her.' Johanne said. 'He's a grown man, he can take a spirited woman's words. You mentioned it yourself, we mistreated her people, she's closer to this than you are. She has the power to make change, same as you, so let her. She knows Okala's people better, she's tied to him, and besides, she's not a loyal subject. She won't bow to authority. If you mean to deal with this head-on, the king needs to hear everything and face the demands. Sulat is unpolished and direct, and that's what's needed here.'

Her argument made sense, but he dreaded what might come out of Sulat's mouth. He usually followed her lead in a fight or most other things, but in negotiations, she let him talk, while she kept an eye on what was going on around them. She was tactical, he was tactful.

Yet, Johanne was right. This particular issue was one of emotion and strategy together. The person to do the talking needed anger and indignation, but also the bluntness and the cold logic to list demands.

If that doesn't describe Sulat...

'You're right. It has to be her.' Alois wiped his mouth and sat back. 'So that's my news. You said you had some, too.'

'Oh, yes.' Johanne took a deep breath and straightened herself with a hand to the stiff front of her dress. She opened her mouth, but just then, someone outside knocked on the door.

She and Alois sat quietly, listening to the visitor speaking with Rustiss, and a moment later, the butler bowed at the entrance of the dining room.

'A messenger for you, my lord,' he said. 'You have been summoned to the palace, at once.'

'Tell me quick,' Alois said to Johanne with an apologetic smile, rising from the table.

'Later.' waved him away.

Alois kissed her forehead. 'I promise I won't die,' he said with a wink.

'Don't joke about that,' she scolded as he left the room.

Sulat tugged on the waist of the dress she'd borrowed from Ashryn. This was the first time she'd had an official audience with the king since the one after the royal wedding last year, which meant she had to wear an actual dress. She'd seen him at the battle, of course, but she had known there would be a fight, and petticoats would have slowed her down. Today, she had to dress well and speak politely, and hopefully that would be enough to avoid future conflict and get her another ship.

Alois would do all of the talking, of course. She couldn't be trusted to use the right words or tone, but she'd find a way to say what she needed to, and let him smooth over her bad manners.

Loud footfalls announced Alois' arrival before she saw him, dressed in a nice suit of fine grey wool and heavy embroidery.

'You look nice,' he said, pointing at the periwinkle pattern on her wide-hipped dress. 'If a little behind the fashion. Florals?'

'It's Ashryn's,' Sulat said, rolling her shoulders around, trying to find a comfortable posture. She had always stood straight, but apparently, decent women were supposed to pull their shoulders back nearly to touching, or be accused of slouching. The only way Sulat could maintain the pose was with the aid of a corset, which irritated her even more. The new fashion that Johanne had designed eschewed the rigid things, but a woman like Ashryn wouldn't be able to afford that, and Sulat didn't have time to order one made.

'Well, it suits you. You ready?' Alois held out a hand to help her into his carriage.

Sulat's skin tingled, but her insides were calm. It was always like that before a fight.

They inched slowly back up the spiralling streets to the tip of the island. Courtiers milled about in the outer chambers of the reception rooms, muttering in frustration.

'You take the lead in there,' Alois said, as they stopped in front of the doors.

Sulat's jaw dropped. 'What?'

'You know the politics better than I do. I was a bargaining piece, they didn't talk to me. You had Okala and the princesses, and all of them. This isn't the time for diplomacy, or making Bertold feel like he's on the right side of this. He needs the truth, fast and hard, and you're the woman for the job.'

Sulat heard his words, but they were more foreign to her than Vurdence. 'You want *me*... to negotiate peace... with the king?'

'Yes.'

'This king.'

'Yes.'

'The one who kicked his crown all around the throne room when the queen was unfaithful.'

'This situation is a little different.'

'He's volatile and I'm blunt.'

'I'll be right there with you, if you need me. You can do this. The merfolk need you, they need someone who is brave enough to tell their story to the right people.'

'Are you appealing to my ego, making me the saviour of the merfolk?'

'No, I'm appealing to the Second Mate and captain in you. These people need an advocate. You can fight for them.'

That's true. Bertold needed to be slapped in the face with reality. He would listen to her before he listened to Kellac or even Marya. Probably even less to Marya, who was not only a mermaid, but a woman, and he might interpret her calmness as weakness.

Sulat rolled her shoulders back and the fabric of the dress eased a bit. She nodded curtly at the doorman, who opened the doors and allowed her in, Alois following close behind her.

King Bertold, Prince Bertold, Prince Meinard, Lord Renir, and a scribe sat lined up in decadent chairs at the far end of the room. Alois and Sulat approached, their footsteps echoing in the empty stone chamber.

'Do you hear them outside?' the king asked, gesturing at the courtiers in the outer chamber. 'They're so angry. They like to be near me, always. But I cleared the room so that we can talk in private. Renir told me the relevant points, but I want to hear the details from you.'

Sulat and Alois recounted their stories. The king and his sons gasped and muttered 'the bastards,' and shook their heads. When they finished, King Bertold unclenched his chubby fingers from the arms of his throne.

'Well, I'm glad we routed them yesterday. The audacity. Oh! You'll like this. Meinard, bring my sword.'

The prince grinned and fetched the sabre the king had worn on the beach the day before.

'And look what we found twisted around it!' The king held up the Day Star, glittering on a silver chain. 'Princess Dahna is very pleased to have it back, I can tell you. Anyway, I've named my sword: The Shrimp Skewer.' The princes chortled along with him. 'What do you think of that? Do you think it'll strike fear into the hearts of those rock-dwelling sav--'

'Don't *crow*,' Sulat sneered. 'Your Highness,' she added, at the looks of outrage and shock. 'These were humans once- citizens- and something terrible was done to them.' Silence followed her words. 'They're angry, they're bitter, and now they've lost the man who gave them hope.

'You can be the king who heals this wound. Step into his place, give them something to make them feel like we can come to some sort of peace. I don't think they'll ever want to be human again, now that they have their own lives, but rubbing it in their faces will only make them angrier, more likely to rise up again, stronger, and better prepared. We need to give them something.'

A hush fell over the throne room. Sulat's stomach fell so fast she thought she'd collapse with it, but she held her nerve, letting out a low breath. She'd said what needed saying, and everyone heard it.

'You.'

All eyes snapped to the king. Alois tensed.

'Your Highness?' Sulat asked.

'We'll give them you. You're sympathetic to them, and you work for me. If I'm to discuss peace, there will need to be intermediaries, especially while their leadership is in transition. You will be my ambassador.'

Alois' eyebrows nearly disappeared behind his mess of curls.

'I'm not...diplomatic...enough.' Sulat glanced at Alois to back her up.

'You know them and they know you. It's enough.' The king waved to a scribe behind him, who scribbled on a piece of paper.

Sulat took a deep breath. 'When do I start?'

'Today, if you like.'

'All right, then.' She stepped her feet apart and rolled her shoulders back.

'First, I want an island of reasonable size and vegetation

for the merfolk who want to transition to land. Second, I want a system of passports set up to begin trade negotiations between friendly colonies and Viehland. Third, I want treaties at least drafted to deal with passing through territory colonised by Open Sea Merfolk. They hate the shipping lanes, and part of their agreement with Kellac involved control of the trade routes between here and the other kingdoms. I believe that setting up a toll-like system will be helpful to them for acclimatising to humans and safer for us, particularly if there is a colony that operates within the Squalls.'

Her words echoed off the marble walls in the silence.

'Anything else?' the king asked, twisting a finger in the long curls of his powdered wig.

'I want a new ship. You owe me one, since mine was lost on a mission for the Crown. I also want compensation for the families of my fallen crewmen.'

The king jumped in his seat as though he'd been poked in the ribs. He waved a hand at his scribe.

'My, you're bold. We'll look into it. Will that be all?'

'That's enough to start,' Sulat said.

'We'll be in touch,' the King said, and Sulat and Alois were dismissed.

'Souls, I love you!' Alois crowed as the door shut. 'They did not expect that.'

'Did you?' Sulat's body still buzzed from her demands.

'Expect it? I was holding my breath! You were clear, confident, all the chambers loaded. You appealed to his self-interest. There was history, humanity. You didn't pause for breath, you didn't falter, it was just--' He punched his hand three times. 'They didn't know what hit them.

'This is a momentous occasion. This is your legacy. They can either agree with your terms, which, for a revolution, were pretty gentle, or they can risk outright war.' He sighed dramatically. 'Masterful. Let me buy you a drink, to celebrate.'

'I have brandy at home.'

'But I want to spend money. Do you want me to find you a

man? A woman? Either, both. What do you want?'

'I want a nap.'

'You're hopeless.' He punched her arm. 'All right, let's talk to Okala, and go home. You can sleep, and I'll drink to the success of your career in politics.'

Sulat's stomach squirmed. *My Legacy: politics. We're all going to die.*

At the dockside tavern, Sulat pulled her tight neckline aside and touched the circle of cold spots on her shoulder.

We're ready to meet with you, she thought loudly, unsure how all of this worked. A rush of warmth spread over her body, which she took to be a response.

She and Alois headed to the sandy cove. The sea had washed away most of the blood and evidence of the fight, but a few traces still remained in the sand, for those who knew what they were looking at.

'How are you feeling?' Alois asked, nudging her with his shoulder.

A tingle rose up Sulat's spine and she knew that Okala was nearby. She didn't dread it, nor did she feel docile or compliant. She was sharp as ever, ready to meet a friend and discuss plans for the future.

'Ready,' she said.

A round dark head poked out of the surf, followed by the tan shoulders and torso of a young human man. Okala stepped out of the ocean, kicking water out of his trousers, and hobbling up the beach on bare feet, holding something in his hand

Sulat and Alois gaped at him.

'Did you transform again?' Sulat asked.

Okala shook his head and ran a hand through soft, shiny black hair. 'This is the potion. Much as I love humans, and you two in particular, I can't face that again for a very long time.'

'At least you've got clothes on, this time.' Alois grinned. 'And you're not blue.'

'Adeto took my advice and tweaked it, a bit. Though he and I both think that Breen's spell was likely another king-maker, so we're going to see if there's anything going on in me.'

'Will you still get your Breaching?' Sulat asked.

'It'd be a bit anticlimactic at this point, don't you think? "Here it is, the human world. Go look around for an afternoon, but don't be seen. We don't want them to know about us".'

That was Sulat's cue. 'On that topic, I'm here on official business. The king made me an ambassador. I'll work with your people to find a peace that will satisfy everyone.'

'There have also been some changes made in our colony,' Okala said. 'Marya is in talks with other colonies and she's going to have Neri start training fighters, though still no army, that I know of. And I've been made an ambassador, too.' He beamed. 'Because I love you all so much and I've actually spent time up here. Finally, I have a function, I'm *useful*.' He chuckled.

'And this is for you.' He handed Sulat what he'd brought with him, a brass hand mirror. 'It's so that you can call me when you need to. I have one like it so that I don't have to, you know...'

'Yeah.' Sulat's skin itched, and she fought down the rising anger.

'Oh, and this is very, very secret. Only four of us will know about it after I tell you. If anyone else, including Marya, found out, it could be the destruction of my people.'

Alois and Sulat stepped closer, closing a tight circle with Okala.

'Ytaso is secretly working on a way to modify the Kiss, or even a way to remove it entirely.'

Sulat's heart leapt and Alois leaned forward.

'But we have to go about it carefully,' Okala said. 'It's really the only weapon we have that can't be bested by something you have. You saw, even a great sea witch was killed by a dagger.'

'So why would Ytaso want a way to remove it?' Sulat asked.

Okala lowered his head. 'Because I asked her to. I don't really understand how it works, or how she'll be able to change it, so don't ask me any particulars. But I do know that she's looking into it.'

'And what about Kyri?' Alois asked.

Okala crumpled in on himself. 'Kyri is...well, she's being looked after. It's generally agreed that she's young and made a stupid mistake-- albeit a very big one that I certainly would not have been treated so gently for-- but she's not being punished, as such. Marya wants to get to the bottom of why she did it, and how we can prevent such things happening in the future. I think that's how we all feel about everything that happened.' He waved a hand at the beach.

'Us, too,' Sulat said. 'So, we'll be in touch more as things move along.'

They hugged, said their goodbyes, and watched the prince walk back into the sea.

'Drink?' Alois offered Sulat his arm and they headed back to town.

Chapter Twenty-Three
Skipping Jill

A knock came at Sulat's front door, and Tansy answered it, admitting a black clad messenger with a smart white wig and shiny buckled shoes.

'What does Renir want from me?' Sulat asked. She had just gotten back from drinking with Alois and was hoping for an early night.

'I wouldn't know, Captain,' the messenger, hardly over fifteen years old, said politely.

The title stung. Without a ship, with only a handful of crew left, was she still a captain? The boy probably didn't know what else to call her. She wasn't a lady like Johanne, she wasn't married, so 'madam' wasn't appropriate, and 'miss' probably felt wrong for a woman in knee breeches and a long coat.

I still have my Lobster, though.

Rain pattered against the glass carriage windows as they bounced through the uneven city streets, passing places street signs for Coral Street and Fin Alley that hinted at the island's original inhabitants, nestled between Hospitality Row and Grey-hill Lane

A chill ran up Sulat's spine. *Politics.*

She had always wanted to be respected and listened to, but always as a matter of human decency, the way all people should value and respect each other, regardless of sex or colour. She'd never had aspirations of government office. The idea of holding so much power felt alien, like being handed a baby and being told to nurture it.

I'm a thief. I'm meant to be invisible.

Her stomach twisted as the carriage passed the ornate palace gates and slid smoothly up the paved driveway. The messenger offered a hand to help her out, but she hopped past him.

'Is he in his office?'

'To the best of my knowledge, Captain.' The boy bowed as Sulat swept past him.

The palace was eerily quiet as she passed by the familiar rooms along the well-worn path. Beneath the mural she'd passed half a dozen times, she stopped.

It took up a whole wall, and depicted a human standing on an island, over several people in the water.

She shook her head at it. King Bertold and his family were new to the Viehlish throne. They'd come in just before the Ettin Wars, after the last of the pro-slavery Viehlish kings had died. Which meant that the previous royal family had most likely commissioned this piece of art.

She sneered. *Always someone standing over someone else.*

Bertold and his lot weren't perfect, but they were better than this. At least they were open to talking.

She squared her shoulders and pressed on to Renir's office under the palace.

'Come in, please, Captain.' Renir opened his door and Sulat doffed her hat as she passed.

'I don't know what you think I can do for you. I don't have a ship.'

'That's just it.' Renir shut the door behind them and beckoned her to the huge table in the centre of the room. Ship blueprints littered the table and Sulat's hands itched to look at them. 'You need a new ship, if we're to keep calling you Captain. Given that you did, in fact, do more than was asked of you, the king has seen fit to give you a bigger ship than last time. I believe *Meltythia* was an Ildecoke Courser... how would you feel about a galleon, this time?'

Sulat shook her head. 'Galleons are slow. Prefer my Courser.'

'Not very defensible,' Renir said delicately.

'When anchored and under magical attack from the water, no,' Sulat agreed. 'Usually, the best defence is getting far away from danger.'

Renir put his head down and smiled. 'I concede that. I thought you might say so, and I set--' he slid a plan from under the stack of merchantmen and set it on top, '--this aside for you.'

Skipping Jill, an Ildecoke Courser, the same size as *Meltythia*. In fact, everything was the same, except that she had been reclaimed from a pirate, rather than the navy. Sulat pretended not to notice.

'Who's Jill? Not the captain's daughter, I hope...'

'I believe, in this case, "jill" refers to a female hare. A reference to her speed, perhaps.'

Even better.

'You can always change it. It doesn't strike the fear that *Meltythia* did, but perhaps it will hold better luck.' Renir smirked.

'Meltythia is just luck, any kind of luck.' *In a way, she was lucky. Not all the crew was lost, and she steered us right at Kellac.* 'But I always liked hares.' *Alois says I'm like them: small, fast, always ready to fight, and I don't do well in captivity.*

'I hear the males box each other for mates. I wonder if jills do, too.'

'This one will. I'll take her.' Sulat held out her hand and Renir shook it.

'She's in drydock right now, getting fitted. You can take her out as soon as next month. Though, as it's already autumn, I imagine you won't want to before shipping season begins again.'

'We'll see.' Sulat stuffed her hat back over her fluffy hair and threw a hasty salute as she left.

Alois bade goodbye to Sulat at the tavern and made his way back up the hill, through the winding streets and wide avenues to the fashionable side of town. The chunk of rock that jutted out over the sea gave the Overlook its name and high price point. The cream of Viehlish society had houses here, but seldom actually visited.

The original plan was to buy a modest house somewhere in the city for the Court Season that summer, but when Alois heard that a house on the Overlook was available, he put himself into significant debt to both Sulat and Sir George-- Johanne's uncle who still hadn't warmed to him-- to buy it for Johanne. Despite everything that had happened in those weeks, Johanne still beamed with pride whenever she mentioned her fashionable house.

When Alois stepped back into the house, the smell of chocolate washed over him. Johanne was still awake.

He found her upstairs in the drawing room, steaming silver chocolate pot on the table, reading a book under the huge windows overlooking the sea. He sat hastily beside her to keep from looking at the water. Okala was controlling the situation, and he had to trust him.

'So, your news,' he said, pulling her to him.

She set her cup and book down and blurted, 'I'm pregnant.'

Alois choked. 'Are you sure?'

Johanne nodded. 'I thought I was feeling tired and ill because of all the fighting, but after you left, it didn't get better, so I called the doctor. There is no doubt.' A wide grin lit up her face.

Alois pulled her into a tight hug. Emotion bubbled up and surrounded him.

If I'd died in that bubble, she'd be going through this alone. She'd have been pregnant at another husband's funeral.

She gave a little gasp and pulled away, wiping her cheeks.

'So you see why I'm here. I needed answers.'

Alois held her face as her hand found her middle again. 'I'm not going anywhere for a long time.' He hoped he wouldn't have to walk back his words. 'I'm going home with you, and I'm going to stay. And if I have to leave, remember, I'm hard to kill.'

He smiled, but she shook her head.

'You're not invincible, Alois. You need to be careful.'

'I know. But I'm tough and I'm lucky. That has to count for something.'

Johanne pursed her lips like she wanted to scold him for his flippancy, but instead laid her head on his shoulder and snuggled closer. Alois wrapped his arms around her and laid his cheek on top of her head.

'I promise I'll be careful,' he said, already dreading what new scheme Renir would find to make him break his oath.

Sulat walked on a cloud down to the docks. Wese and Eaton sat at a table outside the tavern, smoking and drinking. They raised their glasses in salute as she passed and she detoured to tell them her mission. They scrambled from their seats to accompany her to *Skipping Jill*'s berth.

Wese whistled. 'She's a beauty, Cap'n.' He gazed at her slender masts, graceful bow, and white sails billowing in the breeze.

Perfect. Sulat's heart swelled at the figurehead: a hare with her ears angled back toward the hull, her muzzle a wedge into the wind, and one paw raised to punch.

'Will you repaint her?' Eaton asked.

Sulat ran her eye over the neat brown paint job and the light blue accents on deck. 'No. She's perfect.' She suddenly remembered what she'd seen in Renir's office. 'Oh! I haven't told you! *Meltythia* had been refurbished from the navy, but *Jill* here--' she paused for effect, '--belonged to a pirate.'

Grins spread across both mates' faces as they turned their gazes back to the ship.

'I wonder what she's got hiding in those long ears,' Wese muttered.

Acknowledgements

Firstly, as always, thanks to my family and friends for indulging my endless anecdotes, ramblings, and mermaid playlists while this thing was coming together. Also for the literally hundreds of pieces of mermaid- and ocean-related merch. My room looks like a theme park, now, and I love it.

Secondly, to my beta team, particularly my mom, Becky, and my mentor, Kate Whitaker- thanks for keeping me grounded, ladies.

Thirdly, to the Finfolk Pod Squad, Society of Fat Mermaids, and various crafting groups on Facebook, for their boundless support, enthusiasm, and guidance. I don't know why it took me this long to find out that mermaids are real, and how easy it is to become one.

As always, to my best friend and editor, Breanna Clark, who had to do double-duty this time, as editor and critiquer; and to my illustrator, Ana King, who outdid herself with all the damn multiple-figure and scene drawings. I'll keep it simpler, next time, I promise!

And last, but not least, a special shout-out to merman Wesley John Croft and photographer Mike Croft for the amazing cover photo. Find them at www.instagram.com/jurassicmerman. I couldn't have asked for a better Prince Okala.